Web
of
Scandals 2

From Around the Way

LATOYA JOHNSON

authorHOUSE®

AuthorHouse™
1663 Liberty Drive
Bloomington, IN 47403
www.authorhouse.com
Phone: 1 (800) 839-8640

Published by AuthorHouse   08/07/2017

ISBN: 978-1-5462-0361-2 (sc)
ISBN: 978-1-5462-0360-5 (e)

Print information available on the last page.

Any people depicted in stock imagery provided by Thinkstock are models, and such images are being used for illustrative purposes only. Certain stock imagery © Thinkstock.

This book is printed on acid-free paper.

Prologue

I went too far with this. I had a job to do, and I couldn't even do it. I was so stupid when I fell in love with him. Now we were both going to die. I paced back and forth in the motel room, holding onto my 22. Caliber. I was trained by them, so I knew they would find me soon. They were professionals, and did their job unlike myself.

A small knock was at the door. I paused slightly debating to go to it. It could've been a trap, but then again I was expecting him. What if he turned on me and tried to kill me first? But he wouldn't. He was the one who trained me and trained me well. He was also my ex-lover, and I knew he cared for me. That was one of the reasons I called him last week to meet for dinner. I was in trouble and I knew he would help.

I walked to the door and looked through the peep hole. Maceo stood there staring right at me. He knew I was looking through the peep hole.

"Open the door Ashley." His thick accent was sounding more American.

"Are you alone?" I asked.

"You called me. I'm here for you, so open the door. There was no need for you to get all paranoid."

I closed my eyes and counted to five. I then opened the door, and Maceo rushed in. I pointed the gun at him, while he locked the door behind himself.

"Put that away." He looked at me as if I was pitiful. "Why the hell you keep on insisting my father is after you? If he ever wanted you, he'd find you."

"I know they're after me." I paced around the room. "Three years they left me alone. I thought I was safe. I'm so sorry I brought you into this."

"I quit ten years ago. My father knows I'm done with this shit, then you call me outta the blue and pull me back in. My wife thinks I'm cheating on her. Someone seen us having dinner and told her. They even told her about that kiss." He sighs. "I shouldn't have come Ashley."

"I'm sorry about that. I didn't mean to kiss you. I just missed you. Did you get my gift I stuffed in your pocket?"

"What gift?"

"I had went to the bathroom and took off my thong, and when I kissed you I stuffed them in your pocket."

"Dammit Ashley! If my wife finds that, she'll really think I'm cheating."

"But you're not, I was just depressed and lonely and you know how I feel when I get that way."

"Where's Jermaine?" He changed the subject.

"He's home. I told him I was in Florida, and he thinks I'm visiting my so-called parents. I have to go back and get him. I don't want him to get hurt. I love him. I really do."

Maceo sat on the bed and put his head down. I watched as he pulled his phone out and just looked at it. It must've been her; the one and only Melanie. He ignored the text, and I was happy. This was all about me. He came to my rescue today.

He was sexy, and I was in love with him back in college. I was an 'around the way girl from the hood', so he was different from all the boys I use to deal with. He wasn't from the hood, but he was straight from Russia. He hardly knew English and I somewhat taught him the American language. I liked Maceo and thought he was different. Or that's what I thought. He wasn't your average college boy, but I loved every bit of him. He introduced me to his father and their family business. I was all for it, since I grew up around violence and danger. My first hit was my abusive stepfather who beat my mother black and blue every day. That was personal, and the feeling I got afterward felt good. From there, Maceo's father seen that I had a talent and had Maceo train me. When I became an assassin, Maceo and I drifted apart and that was fine. I loved him, but I had fell in love with murder more. Then murder was no longer my first love. I found real love that I never knew existed in me. Jermaine wasn't his real name and he didn't think I knew that. Of course I knew. I was the one who was soupose to kill him. I fell in love in the process of my job. Even after I knew he was HIV positive, I still loved him. He was a good man and I didn't want to kill him. That's when Jermaine and I ran off to another city and tried to live a normal life. I knew one day the Russians would find me but I didn't care. I was living in the moment and that moment was being in love with Jermaine.

"I need you to drive me back so we can get Jermaine, then take us to the airport, please."

He looked up at me. "No Ashley. You got me in trouble the last time I met with you. My wife thinks I was out there cheating on her. I couldn't tell her the truth because I promised her ten years ago that I quit this job. I sell houses and properties now, I have a wife, children and I even have friends. I live a normal life. My father let me go, and I don't want to be caught up in all this."

"Your father won't kill you. If you help me, then I will feel safe. Please Maceo. I will pay you. I'll do anything."

He stood from the bed, and pulled out his phone. "My wife has an important meeting tonight. She's going to really kick my ass."

"Tell her you're helping an old friend with an emergency."

He sighed and shook his head. "That's a three hour drive to your house. I really can't believe I'm about to do this. You need some help….. With your crazy ass."

I jumped up. "Yessss! I love you so much! Thank you."

He looked mad, but he headed to the door, and I followed with my purse.

"Where's your car?" He asked me.

I took the bus here. "They probably put a tracker on my car."

"Please quit with that shit! You're acting like a crazy woman. I'm pretty sure it's not my father's people who are after you."

"Who else would be following me? Someone is after me and those damn Russians are my only enemies. Sorry."

He looked as if he wanted to say something. He then shook his head and headed to his car. "Let's go!"

We were in Maceo's car and driving off in no time. I felt much better and was finally able to relax. I pulled out my phone and dialed Jermaine to let him know we were on our way. Soon as the call went through, it went straight to voicemail. After the third time I called, I began to panic.

"Maceo, he's not answering." I called again. "What if they got him?"

"They don't!" He yelled at me. "Just leave a message. Tell him your on your way home and you love him. He's probably busy or maybe the phone is dead."

"Uugghhh. I swear I'm going to cry."

I called back and it went to voicemail again so I decided to leave a message.

"Jermaine, I have so much to tell you, but no time to explain. Be ready. I have a friend that will help us get away. There are people after you and me and they are going to kill us. If for some reason, I don't make it there, I have a safe in the basement behind the furnace. 13-27-44. It has files in it, and lots of information that will explain to you who I really am. I love you so much baby, and I'll see you seen. Please don't be mad."

I looked over at Maceo shaking his head and I notice the smirk on his face.

"What?" I asked him.

"I'm only doing this to calm your nerves. You're being really paranoid Ashley. I am not soupose to tell you anything and in my contract I wasn't soupose to ever see you again. My father promised me years ago that he'd leave you alone."

"He said that?"

"Yes!"

"Then how come you never told me."

"I'm not soupose to tell you." He almost yelled irritated. "I'm only meeting with you to calm you down, but you just went too far when you blew your cover with your husband. I can't believe you just did that."

"Why the hell you let me?"

"You have a lot of explaining to do now."

"Then who's been following me?"

"Probably no one. You caused a lot of commotion blaming my people for a lot of shit. I could now get into some trouble for telling you that my father called off your hit. I violated my contract by meeting with you last week, and again today."

"So, he did have a hit on me?"

"Yeah, and your moving! You're too close to my home anyway. I'm glad I'm taking you and Jermaine to the airport. Me, seeing you again can cause trouble with my family."

Bam!

My head went all the way forward and quickly jerked back. Maceo almost went off the road. I looked back and a big truck was coming at us again.

"Shit Maceo! Who the fuck is that?" I panicked.

"I don't fucking know but they trying to kill us. What did you do?"

"Nothing! I don't know who these people are. They have to be your father's."

Bam!

The truck hit us again and this time, it pushed Maceo's Benz off the road. We went flying down a hill and I think the car flipped a few times. When everything was finally still, I was hanging from my seat belt and Maceo wasn't moving.

"Maceo! Maceo, you okay! Please say something." I began to cry.

"We got to get the hell outta here." He finally started to move.

I tried getting the seat belt off but I was stuck. I started grabbing at it hard, and pulling but it wouldn't budge. Maceo finally got himself free and escaped out the car.

"I'm coming Ashley."

Just as I was about to say okay, Maceo was kicked to the ground. I stayed silent as I watched two men stick a syringe in him and drag him away. I cried and panicked as I tried taking my seat belt off again.

"Ashley!" A man poked his head in the window.

"Who are you? Who sent you?" My lips trembled with fear.

"I was hoping you weren't dead." He smiled at me. "My boss wanted you very much alive, and that man was not Malcom Jamieson. What are you doing Ashley?"

"Who are you?"

"Roger." He bluntly said. "I work for a very good man name Markus. He will take great care of you, I promise."

"Who the hell is Markus?"

"Roger!" I heard the other man yelling his name.

"What?"

"We have a big problem! That man you just put out, that's Victor Ankundinov son!"

The guy Roger quickly looked back and went over to his friend. I don't know what they started arguing about, but Maceo was right. These people weren't sent by the Russians, but by some guy name Markus. Next thing I knew, Roger came back, and did me the same way he just done Maceo. My eyes immediately felt heavy, and then the world was black.

Chapter One

Twenty years ago
Melanie's Story

I sat on the front porch waiting on everyone to get ready for church. I was pouting and missing my big sister. She moved out last week leaving me depressed in this small country town. Mom was so strict on me, but since Debbie left with a baby and another on the way, mom's beyond crazy now. Every five minutes she's on me about school, boys and more boys. I have six brothers and three of them are older and overprotective. So mom, plus three older brothers makes my life miserable. Living in our small three bedroom house was crazy by itself. Dad was extremely cool and laid back. It was my churchgoing mom that I wanted to run away from. She even had me wearing long skirts and dresses all the time. She act as if it was a sin for girls to wear pants.

"Hey Mel?"

My friend Rebecca from next door snapped me from out of my thoughts. I stood up from the porch and walked down on the sidewalk near her. She wasn't my best friend, but she was one of the few white girls that was nice to me.

"Hi Becca, what you doing up so early?" I asked her.

"Well, I seen you outside sitting on your porch. I was already up bored as heck." She turned to look at her house. "You want to come inside to see my new CD's. I just got Pearl Jam, Nirvana, Slint….ooohhh and I even got Dr Dre and Little Kim."

"You are so spoiled!" I whined. "You know I can't come over. I have to go to church."

"Wow! You guys go to church too much! You go like three

1

times a week."

I rolled my eyes. "Tell me about it."

Just then we heard the screen door open to my house. I turned around to see my mom standing in the door. She was dressed for church with rollers still in her hair.

"Get back in here before you get yourself dirty."

"Yes ma'am." I looked back at Rebecca. "I'll come over after church."

"Mel!" My mom yelled my name.

"If I don't come by, you know why."

"Okay, well see you later." Rebecca then waved to my mom. "Good Morning Mrs. Lewis."

"Hello Rebecca, you have a nice day."

"I will, thanks."

Rebecca stood there for a second while she watched me walk into the house behind my mother.

I couldn't take sitting in the house watching TV with my rowdy brothers, so I called my sister. We talked for almost an hour before she had to go. Of course she made me feel better. I was definitely moving to the city with her when I turn eighteen.

I let out a big sigh as I fought my way out of the living room. My younger brother David plays too much and kept throwing the sofa pillows at me. I had to punch him hard in the shoulder and run out before his crybaby self-yelled for mama. I entered the kitchen and sat at the table, watching my mama cook dinner.

"You need some help mama?"

She looked around, finding me something to do. "Sure…uh…you can come over here and chop up these green peppers."

I got up and walked over to the sink and began washing my hands. I then grabbed a knife, and rinsed it off. I walked it over to the table along with the green peppers and a bowl, and I began cutting them up.

"So what's Debbie and my grandchild been up to? I heard you on the phone with her. Is that belly poking out yet?"

I slightly laughed. "No mama, she still skinny. She said her breast were really big though."

I could see my mom smile at the thought of her grandchildren and missing Debbie, but then she must've realized she was smiling and she looked over at me with a mean look on her face. "I know this better be her last baby. Her fast tail just poppin' babies out one after another."

"Lisa is four mama. You act like the babies are a few months apart."

"Mel you better listen to me, and listen to me good….."

"Ma….." I tried interrupting.

"Don't you interrupt me chile! Now Debbie's only nineteen and managed to get pregnant again by that same no good ol' Bubbles."

"Bubba!"

"Whatever they call him. Now, I'm kinda glad she was smart enough to move four hours away to get away from that no good alcoholic."

"I'm not Debbie! I would never date anyone like him."

My mom shot me this look. "Gurrl! You better not even think about boys. Leave them knuckleheads alone. They just want to get what's in them panties."

"Uuugggghh ma! I'm not going to be like Debbie."

"I know you won't, because I won't let you."

I sighed and shook my head as mama went on and on about them no good boys. I was tired of hearing about this every day. I was always being punished for Debbie's mistakes.

After I finished cutting up them green peppers, I was not about to offer helping with anything else. I wanted to get far away from mama fast. I quickly washed my hands and turned to my mother.

"I'm finished mama." I stood there for a second afraid to ask the next question. "Can I please go to Shavon's house? I promise I'll be home around dinner time."

Mama put her cooking spoon down, and looked at me with her hand rested on her thick hip. I knew that look she was giving me, and she didn't believe that I was going to Shavon's house. That was something Debbie use to do. Instead of going to her girlfriend's house, she'd make a detour to Bubba's. I was nothing like Debbie, and I was going straight to Shavon's house. I always do! I just wish she believe that I wasn't sneaky like my sister.

"Two hours." She finally answered. "That's all you have. Not a second late."

I kissed my mama on the cheek before running out the kitchen.

"Mel!" She yelled out.

I stopped dead in my tracks and slowly faced my mother. "Ma'am?"

"Take them pants off. You know better!"

"But you said that I was allowed to play in pants."

"Play? Gurl, you almost sixteen years old. Those days are over with you. You're a young lady and I say you wear them dresses all the time now."

"Ma! None of my friends have to wear dresses or skirts. I'm tired of people asking me why I don't wear pants."

"Who cares what your friends say. Im yo Mama!"

"But ma?"

"Stay here then!"

"Okay!" I pouted. "Sorry, I'm going to change right now."

"Gone then!"

I swear I wanted to move. Mama thinks it's a curse for me to wear pants.

After slipping on my knee length jean skirt, I quickly left the house before mama thought about telling me to stay home. I wish my father wasn't always out gambling and drinking with his friends. He needs to stay home sometimes so he can put mama in her place. Instead, she plays mommy and daddy, and that's starting to get on my nerves.

I headed toward my best friend Shavon house. Her mother was a single parent who worked two jobs. She was never home, leaving Shavon and her older brother Anthony practically raising themselves. Of course mama don't know about her night job or I would never be allowed over here. Shavon only lived two blocks away from us, so I was there in no time. She was sitting on her front porch with another friend of ours name Shelia McDonald. Anthony was also on the porch talking with his friend Ronald James, aka Ronnie. Ronnie had it goin' on and I sort of had a crush on him. Who didn't? He was so popular in school, eighteen and a senior. Ronnie was good in everything he did, especially boxing. He was extremely handsome and every girl I knew wanted him. Lucky Sandra Jacobson! That was his girlfriend. She was tall, skinny with big ol' titties. Light-skinned chick with that good hair. I knew he was never looking my way. I mean, I was far from ugly. I was cute, had a nice shape, probably better than Sandra. I was dark-skinned complexion with chinky eyes and cute full lips. I just heard around the way that Ronnie was into light-skinned girls.

"Mel!" Shavon yelled out. "I'm so happy to see you!"

She stood up and ran off the porch, greeting me with a big hug.

"Hey guys." I greeted everyone.

"Hey Mel." Ronnie stopped everything to look up and smile at me. I blushed.

"Hi Ronnie."

I just became jittery all over. My nerves went crazy when he stood up and walked off the porch to meet me. He was so fine with them deep dimples. Shavon left our side and walked back up the porch. She just had to leave me alone with him.

"So what you been up to?" He asked. "I haven't seen you in a while."

"Oh, I been just….hangin' with my brothers."

"Your brother Jerome was playin' ball with me yesterday at Monroe Park. I didn't see you there."

I continued to blush, happy he was checking for me. "I was probably hanging out with my other brother Mikey."

Ronnie slightly laughed. "You must've been invisible, cause Mikey and Calvin was playing too."

"Wow!" I sighed. "I'm a bad liar, huh?"

"Yeah, a terrible one. But it's okay, your here now."

I stood there feeling so embarrassed. I didn't want Ronnie to know that I'm hardly ever allowed to go anywhere. He'd probably quit talking to me.

"You staying awhile?" He asked me.

"Yeah, what you guys doing?"

Ronnie looked back at Anthony. "We were bout to play some video games, but Anthony talking about watching some movie. Wanna join us?"

"At the theaters?"

"Nah, in the house."

"Oh," I looked back at Shavon. "Hey girl, you watching a movie?"

"Yelp. You staying?"

I looked back at Ronnie who was smiling at me showing them sexy dimples again.

"Yea." I sang out.

I walked up on the porch with Ronnie behind me. My instincts told me to look back, and when I did his eyes were on my booty. Our eyes then locked with each other. He was caught red handed, but I didn't care.

"Just admiring the view." He smiled.

He gives me butterflies. Soon as we all entered the house, Anthony and Ronnie plops down on the sofa. Shelia followed Shavon to the kitchen. I didn't want to be in that living room with two boys. Especially good looking Ronnie, so I trailed into the kitchen as well.

Shavon turned on the stove and held the tin of popcorn over the burner. Soon after, it began to pop.

"My mother is putting in overtime tonight, so DeAndre is on his way over." Shavon seemed happy about that. They weren't dating, just messed around a few times.

"So, you guys still kicking it?"

"Yelp, and I'm leaving you two; taking my ass to the bedroom."

Shavon and Shelia began to laugh as if that comment was some funny joke. I just smiled, cause I really didn't think her going to the bedroom was funny at all. I knew what they were going to do, but I wasn't like that so I didn't care.

"Maybe I can finally get a little bit of yo' brother." Shelia said as she popped her butt.

"Anthony don't want yo' flat chested ass." Shelia commented. "You my girl and everything, but you ain't got no meat on that body of yours."

"Whatever, I can have him if I want."

"Maybe, if you suck his dick."

Now I was dying laughing. Shelia quickly shot me a look like she wanted to kill me.

"Both ya'll go to hell!"

"You know Shavon hit that on point." I said still laughing. "Anthony likes tities girl."

Shavon gave me a high five while Shelia rolled her eyes and sucked her buck teeth at us.

"It's okay Shelia baby, me and Mel will let you borrow some titties. We do have plenty of them." Shelia laughed hard at her own joke, and I joined her.

"Oh shut up Shavon!" Shelia then looked at me. "You shut up too, Virgin Mary!"

"Oooooh Shelia got you there Mel!"

I somewhat felt embarrassed. I swear I was the only girl at my school who was still a virgin. "I'm….I'm okay with that. I haven't found me a boyfriend yet."

Shavon grinned at me. "I know Ronnie wants you baaaddd!"

"He does not!" I rolled my eyes. "He has a girlfriend anyway."

"So! She not here."

"I'm not messing with that boy, so stop!"

"You know you want to."

"I do not." I turned my head away from Shavon and Shelia. "Forget about Ronnie, please."

"I see somebody has a crush." Shelia teased.

I ignored them and tried changing the subject. Truth is, they wasn't lying. I did want Ronnie. I never felt this way for no boy. I just wanted to steal him away from 'Miss Prissy', but I'm not that type of girl. Besides, Ronnie would only want to by my friend, nothing more.

The popcorn was ready and Shavon poured it into a big bowl. Shelia and I grabbed a few cans of coke, and we followed Shavon into the living room.

The movie was hardly watched. I had no idea what scary movie they had playing. DeAndre did come over, and Shavon had immediately took him upstairs to her room. Shelia sat close to Anthony trying her hardest to get his attention. He might've been the only one into the movie. As for me, I sat real close to Ronnie and we talked the entire time blocking everyone else out. He was so funny and he seemed caring. I could tell he really loved boxing cause he talked about that a little too much, but I was there to listen. I really liked him, and when I had to go home, I wasn't ready. Ronnie begged me to stay, but I knew if I was a minute late, mama would not let me out the house again. I promised Ronnie that I be back over Shavon's house tomorrow evening at the same time. It was a date.

Chapter Two

For the next month, Shavon's house was where I was always hanging out at. Soon as her mom left for work, Ronnie and I was always there. We became close friends. He was still with his girlfriend, and I didn't mind because Ronnie was just a friend. Ronnie was my crush, but he never seem to be attracted to me. He loved my company and conversation and I enjoyed his. Although, I liked him a lot I never minded that he hasn't made a move on me. Sometimes, I would think his eyes were telling a different type of story. He'd look me over with lust, but then he'd catch himself and stop. Ronnie was holding back with me and I just think he did that because he respected me. I was not like them other girls who practically threw themselves at the boys. I sometimes wanted to towards Ronnie but was afraid. I didn't want him to turn me down and that would crush my soul. I would just dream of that kiss I was praying he'd give me one day.

It was a Friday evening and mama went to a church convention, and those usually lasted all night. They'd first have service and then do an all-night prayer session. I told mama that I had real bad cramps, so she didn't make me go. I told my mom little stupid lies, but that was the first time I told her a big lie that could get me grounded for life. Tonight would be the first night I'd get to stay at Shavon's until early morning. I was excited about my little stay. With me staying all night, I had a feeling me and Ronnie's relationship could get stronger. Of course, Ronnie didn't know I was staying past ten.

Mama left a little before seven that evening. I then left at eight because that's when daddy left for the night. Daddy was pretty much an alcoholic, and when he started, no telling when he came home. I just knew it wasn't going to be tonight.

As usual, Shavon, her boy-toy DeAndre, Anthony and Ronnie were chillen on the porch playing dice. Shavon screams my name and runs off the porch to give me a hug. I loved my best friend like a sister. We became even closer since my crush on Ronnie. Shavon puts her arm around me and walks me up the steps, where the three guys played their dice game. They were all into the game and no one acknowledged me. Not even Ronnie, and I was looking good too. I wore the shortest and tightest skirt I owned, which was probably two to three years old. I then wore a red tank top that showed off my belly. Of course I didn't own anything like this. I borrowed it from Shavon last week when I was trying on her clothes. My tits looked so good in it, and I knew I had to have it. I was glad my brothers weren't home to see me leave, and the two younger ones were too busy watching TV. Anthony's eyes looked up first when the dice rolled by my feet. I swear he did a double take. He stood up in front of me smiling real hard.

"Well, well, well…look at Mel." He scanned me. "I never knew how much body you was packing girl. Where all this come from? Damn!"

That comment caught Ronnie's attention, and he quickly stood up next to Anthony. His smile widened as well.

"Damn Mel!" Ronnie seem to push Anthony over. "You be looking sexier and sexier as each day pass by. What you tryna do to a brutha?"

Ronnie seem to move closer to me, getting up into my personal space. I watched as his eyes checked me out. He was so fine.

"You sure you not tryna do nothing?" Ronnie questioned. "I'm kinda likin' this feeling I have right now."

I blushed. "Well…I…"

"Hey, no hanky panky on my porch!" Anthony interrupted.

I looked at Shavon. "Yeah, we need to talk Mel."

Shavon pulled me inside her house, and practically dragged me to her bedroom. She starts the conversation off about Ronnie constantly talking about me. I knew he may have wanted me, but Shavon was making it seem as if he was in love with me. Don't get me wrong, hearing that Ronnie talks about me was music to my ears. I wanted him just as bad as he wanted me. Reality was, Ronnie had a girlfriend and I didn't feel right messing with another girl's boyfriend. I really wish he'd dump Miss Prissy and be mines. Then I'd have a big problem, because I wasn't even allowed to date.

Ronnie and I would be forced to sneak around. Sooner or later, he'd be tired of sneaking around and leave me anyway.

There was a small knock at Shavon's door, and she yelled come in. My heart skipped a beat when Ronnie's head peeped through.

"Hey Shavon, Anthony walked to Amanda's house and Andre waiten' on you downstairs."

"Ok."

Shavon looked at me and winked, then glanced in her mirror checking herself over. She then slid past Ronnie letting him in. She was out of our sight. Ronnie grinned at me as he closed the door.

"Do you mind?" He asked.

"What?"

"If we hang out for a while?"

"Oh, sure."

I sat on Shavon's bed and he walked over sitting next to me. The way he made me feel was lovely. I sat there speechless with my hands messing around with my itty bitty skirt. My thighs tightened and my coochie tingled.

"Why you so nervous girl?" He asked me. "You act like we ain't friends."

"I'm not nervous, just bored."

Ronnie laughs. "Bored? Girl you crazy. You want to play a game or something?"

"What kind of game?"

Ronnie looked around as if he was looking for a game. "Uhhhh…. let's see…"

"Truth or dare!" I surprised myself.

"Oh wow! You getting a little bold."

Ronnie turned towards me and I did the same. He smiled so hard showing dimples and I just realized how cute his gap was.

"Go ahead." He said. "You first."

"Ok. Truth or dare?"

"Truth."

"Are you a good boy?"

Ronnie sucked his teeth. "C'mon Mel! Give me something else. Make my black ass blush."

"Okay."

"Don't be shy!"

"Okay." I hesitated. "Are you a virgin?"

"Hell no! Are you?"

"Hey…you didn't say truth or dare."

Ronnie licked his lips. "Alright, truth or dare?"

"Dare!"

"Damn you're brave." He began rubbing his hands together. "I dare you to take yo' shirt off."

"Ronnie!"

"You choose dare, not me."

I hesitated. "Do I really have to?"

"If you don't, you have to uh…kiss me."

"Now you making up some crazy rules."

"So you want to quit?"

"I'm no quitter!"

I slowly lifted up my tank top and pulled it over top my head. Thank God mama bought me a new bra yesterday. Ronnie's eyes were glued to my perky 34 DD, and yes I had them DD's. I was always proud of my assets, especially since his stuck up girlfriend had gigantic tits that sagged on her little body.

"Are those real Mel?" He asked.

"Boy, you know they are. My mama always bought me the best bras, so they don't sag."

"Well, that's a really nice bra. I bet something else is nice too?"

I giggled. "Ronnie, it's your turn."

"Okay, ask me."

"Truth or dare?"

"Truth."

"Uh, you need to pick dare."

"Nah, I want truth."

"Fine!" I hesitated as I thought about the next question. "Do you go down on girls?"

"Nope!"

"You're lying."

"No I'm not." He slightly grinned and I knew he was.

"There was a rumor last year about how you went down on Allison Jones."

"That bitch be lying."

"We're friends Ronnie, you can tell me."

"Nah Mel!" He seem to get mad. "I don't do that nasty shit."

I had no idea why so many boys did it and then lied about it. Allison went into details and I knew it was true, but I was going to drop it... for now.

"Okay, whatever you say." I rolled my eyes.

"Truth or dare?" He was back in the game.

I crossed my arms over my chest and looked Ronnie right in the eyes. I knew what this boy wanted, and I was going to be fast and give it to him.

I smiled. "Dare."

"Aww shit, it's getting good."

Ronnie grabbed my arms and removed them from in front of my breast.

"I dare you to take your bra off.

I just knew that was next. It was exactly what I wanted, but didn't want to seem like a hoe and throw it out there. I was about to have fun with this game, so I gave Ronnie a little seductive smile. Next thing you know, I was slowly unfastening my bra strap from the back. I watched as his eyes stayed glued to my bra until it fell, freeing two plump chocolate honey dews.

"You should be a stripper!" Ronnie smiled at my breast.

"Boy! Anyway, my turn to ask you. Ready?"

He wasn't even listening. His eyes would not leave my tits, and I actually loved every bit of this. I had tricks up my sleeves though.

"I dare you to suck my nipples." I blurted out.

"Huh?"

That snapped Ronnie out of his trance, and his eyes were now looking into mine.

"You dare me?" He asked.

"I double dare you!"

I sat there on the bed poking my chest out towards him, urging him to do it. Of course, no boy has ever done this to me before but I was ready. Ronnie's eyes were back on my honeydews. He slowly moved in closer, and his hand massaged my right one. He then gently began rubbing his forefinger and thumb around my nipple. I closed my eyes and slowly began to lay back. Ronnie's fingers never left my nipples. Next, he massaged them both with his hands. He was getting real comfortable. I then felt a warm sensation on my right nipple. I opened my eyes and seen Ronnie sucking on my right nipple as if he was a baby sucking on a bottle. He then began to go back and forth on each nipple, making sure not to get one jealous. This was such a good feeling, and I never wanted him to stop. I'd let him suck my nipples all night. Ronnie then began to part my thighs open, and his hands slowly crept up to my very moist love nest. Soon as his fingers slipped in my panties, I jumped.

"What?" He looked up at me.

I just stared back at him shaking my head. I was scared, speechless, and I felt dumb for letting him go this far. I started it, and I was afraid to let him finish.

"Are you on your period or something?" He asked.

"No! I...uh....did I ever tell you that I was a virgin?"

Ronnie sat up. "Oh."

I sat up and pulled my shirt over my exposed breast.

"It just frightened me a little." I then let out a small sigh. "Do you want to have sex?"

"For real?" He was excited.

"Why not."

"Damn Mel, I like you."

Ronnie quickly jumped up and began to undress himself. Before I knew it, his clothes were completely off, and his thang stared right at me. It was pretty and although I never seen a real live one, his look big. I knew I shouldn't be doing this, but I liked Ronnie and I wanted him to like me back.

"Take all your clothes off." He demanded.

"Okay."

When I was completely naked, I lay back on the bed, and let Ronnie climb on top of me. Next thing I knew, he was forcing his tongue inside my mouth. It was a crazy feeling at first, but after a short while, our rhythm matched and the kiss began to make me tingle. I just knew I was doing it right. He then gently tried forcing himself in, and after a couple of attempts he gave up and did the impossible. Ronnie kissed all the way down to my stomach and made it to my southern paradise. He parted my thighs more and began licking me slowly. He then looks up and sees me smiling. That felt so damn good.

"Don't tell anybody I did this." He said as he went back to licking my pounani.

He came back up after a long while and I just knew he enjoyed every bit of my taste. Ronnie tried to enter my flower a second time. He was a bit gentle but consistent and would not give up. Every time it almost goes in, I beg him to stop. After the third time, I finally let him do it and it hurt like hell. First he began moving around real slow, then he started to hump me like a jack rabbit. It didn't last long, and when he pulled out, his stuff squirted all over my stomach. I was pissed, but I kept quiet. Surprisingly, he apologized and found a t-shirt of Shavon's. He began to wipe every bit of it off of me.

"How did it feel?" He asked me.

"It was okay."

"The more we do it, the better it'll get."

I smiled. "We? What makes you think I will do it to you again?" I joked.

"I know I put it on you, but this your first time. Your second time, you will beg me not to stop."

Ronnie was right. A year and a half has passed, and Ronnie and I were still kicking it. Although he left for college, he was always back on the weekends sexing me. Sex was what we did best and it was great. I was almost 18 and life has really changed for me. Mama was still strict as ever. I talked her into giving me a midnight curfew, and she went along with it. I'll be eighteen in a couple of months and my mother still treats me like I'm a kid. I was out doing a little more with my friends but I still had limits. Ronnie and I would get together every so often when he was here and go on dates and have sex. We were basically friends with benefits, no feelings attached. I never made him my boyfriend because I didn't want to drag him into my boring life. Especially since I know he was doing it big in college with the girls. I didn't want mama to know I was with any boy, so I told him we could only be friends. He liked me a lot and even broke up with Miss Prissy, and I liked him more. I started to get all kinds of attention from other boys and I knew Ronnie hated that. There were times, he'd put his arm around me in public and try to claim me, but I always had to put him in his place.

On my eighteenth birthday, I was surprised with the news of my life. Of course, you have unprotected sex for almost two years, you might get pregnant. That's exactly what happened and I was more scared than anything. First thing I did was call Debbie. I didn't want mama to think I fell in my sisters footsteps. I wouldn't hear the end of it. After I graduated, I moved to the city with my sister and got an abortion. I never told Ronnie, or any of my friends back at home why I was leaving. They all think I was going off to college like most high school seniors, but I was going off to get an abortion.

After the abortion, I stayed and got a job at some local restaurant. I had to pay Debbie's boyfriend back for the abortion. I didn't mind, cause I was loving the city life. It has only been two weeks since I been here and I been at my job for a week. It was cool, cause I was making my own money. I hated the bus rides to and from work, but that's what I had to do until I got myself a car.

It was 10:30 when I got to Debbie's place and she was getting dressed to go out.

"Ooooh girl, you cute." I told her.

"Thank you. You coming?"

"Are you serious?"

"Yeah, the club I go to don't check ID's. You look grown as hell, so you can come."

"Really?"

"Gurl, get yo' ass in the shower so we can go."

I smiled as I ran to the back. I was so excited cause I never been to a real club before. I searched through Debbie's closet looking for something sexier than what she had on. After I took a shower, it took me a good hour to get ready. By then, Debbie had one of her boyfriend's sister come over to babysit the two kids.

We went to some club called "Kasha", and soon as I walked in behind my sister I felt live and quickly loosened up. I Knew I was cute in this short skin tight mini skirt and heels. I swear all the attention was on me as I sashayed in behind my sister. She seem to know a lot of people, so every few minutes she was stopping to talk and introduce me. I wasn't trying to say hi to people, I was trying to get to that bar. No questions asked, they was going to let me drink. When we finally got up to the bar, and I put my order in, I was feeling like a grown ass woman.

"So what you think?" Debbie yelled to me over the loud music.

"Do you go out all the time like this?" I asked bopping my head.

"I try to get out every once in a while. I wanted to make you feel good. I know you haven't done anything but work, so I thought you needed this."

"Oh yeah! I'm loving it!"

"Well, you ain't seen nothing yet. Just wait till tomorrow. We going to the Southside!"

"Damn Debbie! We going out tomorrow too?"

"Gurl yeah! Southside is where it's at. Everybody be over that way."

"Cool."

We finally got our drinks and I immediately began sipping on my drink like it was Kool-Aid. At first I didn't like the dark liquor, but sipped the whole thing anyway and wanted more. I felt a little different after I half way drank the second one.

"How you ladies doing tonight?"

Debbie and I both turned around to see this tall light-skinned guy with a small afro. He was sort of cute with a mouth full of gold teeth. Debbie had told me about all the dudes here with gold teeth and gold chains. This one was fine and I think he was trying to flirt with me.

"Yo', can I get them digits?" He asked.

"Me?" I asked.

"Oh yeah, yous a cute lil' chocolate drop."

"Oh, uh….you can buy me another drink."

"And how bout yo' pretty ass friend right here?"

I looked over at Debbie and she shrugged her shoulders. She was too busy grinding in her chair to "Freak me" by Silk.

"Sure, she want one too."

After we received our drinks, Mr. Light-Skinned man squeezed his way in between me and my sister and he started to kick some game. I was getting drunk and irritated by his arrogant attitude. I end up excusing myself to the bathroom, and of course Debbie was right behind me. We didn't even go to the bathroom, instead we went on the dancefloor.

"You'll run into plenty of them kind!" Debbie yelled out.

"Uggghhh...what a turn off!" I yelled back as I danced along with the song.

"Fuck these men around here, I know a perfect match for you."

"Oh, for real?"

"My boyfriend has a cousin that be getting money. You will like him. He fine!"

"How old is he?"

"Maybe nineteen, or twenty."

"Well, where he be hanging out at? I want to be where all the fine boys at. I hope he not lame like these wannabes at the club."

"First of all...correct yo' self-little girl." Debbie rolled her neck. "You're about to deal with a man. He may be young like yourself but he a grown ass man. He handles his!"

"What's his name?"

"Tip."

"Tip?"

"Leroy, but he likes to be called Tip."

Tip was the name I was calling that night. It happened so fast, and I couldn't believe I had given myself to this stranger. I knew I was drunk, but that was no excuse. As soon as I seen him, my heart melted and I knew I had to have him. I even forgot about the fact that I had an abortion two weeks earlier, but I wasn't bleeding so I did it. He had this sexy thuggish sex appeal and I was instantly hooked to this man. We all had went back to my sister house and dranked a little more, but then Tip wanted to take me for a ride. We talked and chilled and I watched him smoke about two blunts. Next thing I know, we was at some stanky motel room, and Tip was doing me like I've never been done before. I was easy, and at that moment, Tip made me fall in love and I wanted more of him.

Chapter Three

I fell in love and never looked back towards my home town. I found me an apartment, and Tip moved in with me. Life seemed so wonderful because I had Tip. We had sex nearly two, three, or sometimes four times a day. I was addicted to that man. He bought me gifts, name brand clothes, and laid out my two bedroom apartment. Tip was getting money, and it wasn't the legal way. I was young and naive and didn't care. He was treating me like a queen. That treatment didn't last long though. Six months into our relationship I found fault in him. He became abusive and crazy, and I should've left then, but I didn't. I stayed and became his punching bag. It's like, I knew he didn't give a fuck about me. I mean, he didn't give a fuck about no one. Tip was the devil and I let him in my heart. When I was twenty, I got pregnant. Abortion for this child was no option. I couldn't abort another baby, I already felt bad for the first one. I was for sure the abuse would stop when I told Tip I was pregnant. It only got worse, and I was still hanging in there hoping and praying it would stop. Tip was never there for me. Every time he beat me, I would call the police. He seem to be always in jail, for either me, stealing, or fighting. The more Tip drank and get high, he'd seem to get worse.

My belly was finally poking out. I was around six months pregnant, and my belly was perfectly round and cute. Mama finally got over me being pregnant and she was sending me baby clothes in the mail. I dare not to tell her about Tip abusing me. I gave her the biggest lie of all that Tip worked at the restaurant with me. I had quit the restaurant when I got pregnant and fully depended on Tip's illegal money. I had painted this big lie for mama and she fell for it. Debbie knew Tip was in the streets and she knew he abuses me. She's angry about the situation but quit talking about it because I won't leave him. She tries to stay out our business unless she sees a big ass bruise on me. She will then go off on Tip and then he'll promise not to do it again, but he always do. Debbie tells me all the time to leave, and since I won't we always argue. Therefore, our relationship was starting to become sour. I made a few other friends, and one in particular was ShaQuitta. Quitta was one of Tip's older sisters who I truly adored. I was chillen at her house bored out of my mind. She had five bad ass kids that I usually babysat for while she turned her tricks. I never knocked ShaQuitta for being out there like that. When Tip was in jail, Quitta was the one giving me money, so I was grateful for her.

She sat there with a beer in one hand and a joint in the other, telling me about her recent trick and how he had lots of money and would spoil her to death. I didn't personally care, instead I was mad about her smoking in the same room as the kids. I kept looking back at four year old Jay-Jay, making sure he didn't smack his two year old sister Te-te in the face again. Just as I expected, he did it again, and of course Quitta curses at Te-te for crying. I had enough and I jumped up and walked to the corner where poor little Te-te went hiding to.

"You always spoiling her little bad butt." Quitta yelled to me.

"You didn't just see Jay-Jay smack the shit outta her?"

"He what?"

"Yes Quitta! Jay-Jay was over here killing my poor Te-Te."

I popped Jay-Jay in the head, and grabbed Te-Te into my arms.

"See how you like it." I scolded Jay-Jay. "Little bad ass."

I sat back in the chair and began rocking Te-Te. Whom all of a sudden stopped crying.

"Your baby gonna be a spoiled brat!" Quitta told me.

I smirked at her. "Good. I'm gonna love her like no other, and protect her from little bad asses like Jay-Jay. Nobody gonna hurt my baby."

"What about Tip?"

I looked at her from the side and rolled my eyes. "Tip won't touch my baby."

"I didn't say that shit. Tip may be whopping yo' ass, but my brother loves kids."

"You did say that!" I said with attitude. "So what are you saying then?"

"You gonna let Tip keep fucking you up. Yo' baby gonna see that shit.

That will hurt her Mel! What you gonna do when he hit you in front of your daughter?"

I sighed. "Leave!"

"When? You always say that."

"Just forget it. Let me deal with Tip. You just deal with yo' new pimp daddy and finding out who all these kids daddy is."

"You can say what the hell you want about who my kids baby daddy is, but at least they don't see what the fuck I do and who the hell beating they mama black and blue. You need to think that shit over Mel."

I looked down at Te-Te who was fast asleep. I didn't want her to see the tear that had escaped my eye. ShaQuitta was right, but I don't play her talking to me like I'm some little ass kid.

I stood up with Te-Te in my arms. "Fuck Tip! He aint gonna do shit to me no more! I'm through with him."

I walked out the room, taking Te-Te to her bedroom which she shared with her other two sisters. Bianca was six and Danielle was six months old. I love all ShaQuitta's kids, but each and every one of them some bad asses. I knew it was out of attention, and I vowed to be there for my child at all times.

After tucking Te-Te in and kissing the other two girls who were fast asleep I went back into the kitchen where ShaQuitta was grabbing another beer.

"I'm gone!" I told her.

"You still gonna babysit for me tomorrow night?"

"Yes Quitta, I'll be here."

"Ok gurl, and be careful walking home. Melvin out of jail and he crazier than ever."

"I'm not worried about that ol' crack head."

"You better be, he'll rape pregnant women too. If you want, I'll call Omar to walk you home."

"Thanks, but I'm good. I only live four houses down."

"Okay, and don't be late tomorrow."

"I'm never late!"

I turned to walk out. I rolled my eyes at Jay-Jay who was now sitting on the sofa watching TV. I then walked his way and gave him a little tickle and a kiss on the cheek. The other little boy CJ was fast asleep on the other sofa sucking on his thumb. I quietly kissed him, and tiptoed out.

I shut the door behind myself and sighed. I prayed that Tip was still out doing shit he had no business doing. I had told him earlier in the day that I was going to be at his sister's house. Knowing Tip, he'd still question me about my whereabouts. Especially if he was out drinking and getting high. He need to take his ass to jail. That was the only time I could ever get me some peace.

Soon as I was about ten feet away from my duplex, my other nightmare appeared out of nowhere. Melvin Johnson the sex predator, we called him. He was a very crazy man and often we wondered what he put in his crack. He raped women and bragged about doing it. Before he got hooked on crack, they all say Melvin was a great athlete and all the girls wanted him. Now they all run the opposite way. I was ready to run, but his perverted ass was practically in front of my house. He was standing there grabbing his dirty, infested crotch area. I heard he had every disease known possible, even AIDS. I believed it all, because Melvin looked hideous.

"You finna have a baby?" He asked me.

"Yea." I mumbled in a nervous tone.

"You still look good. Uh….damn, I forgot yo' damn name."

I slowly backed away from him, trying to get back to Quitta's house. I was not about to volunteer my name to this crazy man. Now I wish that I let her neighbor Omar walk me home.

"Where you going girl?" He notice I took a few steps back. "I ain't talk to you yet."

"I gotta go."

I turned to walk away, and Melvin caught up to me and grabbed me. He was strong for a crack head, and it was hard trying to fight him off. He then tried kissing me in my mouth. I screamed out loud as I tried mushing his face away from my way. I was hoping someone would hear me, and come to my rescue. I was ready to kick his nuts off when I heard the screen door open. Melvin and I looked at the same time and it was Tip with a gun in his hand. This was the first time I was actually glad to see Tip. He ran off the porch towards Melvin, and Melvin took off running. I didn't even see which way he went.

"Next time, Imma kill yo' ass!" Tip yelled to Melvin.

21

Tip then looked over at me, and I looked away.

"You see what kind of shit happens when you come home all late! Damn Mel, you got me in the fuckin' house worried about you."

I sucked my teeth and rolled my eyes. "You knew I was down the street at yo' sister's house."

"Like ten fucking hours ago! I know you wasn't over there this whole time."

"Yes I was Tip, damn." I tried walking away. "Just let me go to sleep. I'm tired."

I walked up on our porch and into the house, while Tip walked behind me cursing me out and calling me every name in the book. Soon as we got inside, he pushed me onto the sofa.

"Now tell me where the fuck you been?" He yelled out to me.

I quickly scrambled up off the sofa and ran out of the living room. He still had that gun in his hand and no telling if his drunk ass had bullets in there, I locked the bedroom door behind myself and sat on my bed terrified. I had to listen to him banging on the door nonstop and he even threatened to shoot the door down. His crazy ass even tried because I heard the gun click. Tears ran down my face as I sat up against the headboard and prayed he go away. When I heard him walk away I finally exhaled and my heart began to beat at a regular pace. I got off the bed and walked over to the window hoping to see him walking out of here. I opened the blind, and seen that his car was still there. I was mad he didn't leave. Dammit! Now I was going to have to stay up all night, and wait till he passes out. I was going to have to sneak over to my sister's house. I stood close to that window, biting my nails, hoping to see him get into his car. BOOM! Gunshots hit the door and I quickly got on the floor. Tip then busts the rest of the door open, and I rolled my ass under the bed. He seen me roll under the bed, and he went to grab ahold of my hair dragging me out. He then lifted me up from the floor, and pushed me back on the bed. I watched as he set his gun on the dresser, and then walk back over to me. He stood at the foot of the bed enjoying the fact that I was scared as fuck of him. He practically watched every bead of sweat form on my forehead.

"Why can't you just do what the fuck I say?" He was surprisingly calm, but I stayed silent. I was scared he hit me for answering.

"You out there fucking someone else, and with my baby in yo' belly? Huh? Who the fuck is he?"

"Please Tip." I begged. "Believe me, call Quitta and ask her. I promise I was there all day."

"Why you keep lying to me?"

Tip got into the bed and on top of me and began to put his hands around my neck. I was never going to win this battle.

"Let me check my pussy and see if someone else been in it."

"Please!" I cried. "I didn't do anything."

"Then let me check!"

He forcefully pulled at my pants with one hand while he still held me down with the other. I grabbed his arm trying to fight him off, and he slapped me in the face. I slapped him back, and he then punched me dead in my lip. Tip never cared that I was pregnant. He'd still fight me and beat me like I was a man. I always knew what to expect, but I always had the reflex to fight him back. I was stupid for even trying, he'd only whop my ass worse.

I knew what was next. It was a basic routine. We'd get into a fight, he'd beat me, and then it seem to make him horny so he'd rape me. That's exactly what he started to do next. Although I fight and scream, and the people next door act like they can never hear me; Tip always manages to break me down.

I was lifeless, and crying as he finally exploded inside of me. He then kisses me on my lips and gets up off me. He didn't even care as I continued sobbing like I was dying. He grabbed his gun and walked out of the room.

"Fucking bastard!" I said underneath my breath.

Two hours later, while Tip was laid out on the sofa passed out drunk, I called the police. I wanted him the hell out of my house. Soon as they came and arrested him, Tip was begging me to drop the charges. He promised he marry me and be a better man. He make me feel so guilty and say the baby won't have a daddy if I send him to jail. But, the guilt went away when I felt the big lip I had. I smiled on the inside as they hauled his ass to jail. I hate him. I hope they find that gun and give him a few years.

Chapter Four

Three days had went by and Tip was still in jail. Fuck him! I wasn't even going to visit his trifling ass. I just want him to stay there and rot. I had so much stress built up and I swear I needed to talk to someone. I just wanted a friend to be by my side at this moment. Well....not really any of my friends. I had this one friend name Tia who would straight cuss me out and dog me to death. She wouldn't even let me express my feelings. She'd just judge me and call me names for letting him abuse me, but that was one real ass friend because she'd tell me to my face.

That's just how she was, but I didn't need any of that right now. I wanted someone there for me, and to tell me it will be okay. My mother was miles away, and although I wouldn't tell her about the abuse, I wanted to just cry on her shoulder. Believe it or not, Tip's mom was real good to me. Sometimes I felt she loved me more than her son. She was nothing like Tip. She was sweet, kind, and well respected in the neighborhood. They called her Queen. I never knew why until one of her nieces told me. They said she was a drug dealer and the Queen Pen of it all. I didn't believe any of that. She was too sweet for that. Not sweet Miss Queen. She took care of her grown kids, and their kids. She cooked big ol' Sunday meals, so I knew her niece had to be lying.

I usually don't go to Queen's house. There was always so many people over there and I hated the crowd. The only reason I was coming over here besides having someone to talk to was, money. Tip's been gone, and I needed money for my electric bill. She didn't know Tip was locked up, nor did she know he was abusive to me. A girl could take so much, and I was ready to squeal to his mother.

I knocked on the front door and her seventeen year old son Jerrod answered.

"Whass up Mel?" He scrunched up his face. "Who fucked you up?"

I touched my face not realizing that I still had a big bruise and a busted up lip.

"She didn't fuck me up. I fucked her up. She just got me a few times."

"Oh, I see."

Who knows if Jerrod knew his brother was a woman beater. As far as I knew, ShaQuitta was the only one that knew and that was because I told her. Knowing her, she probably told the whole family. You know what they say; never trust a bitch. Especially a thieving, fuck a dude for money type of bitch.

Soon as I stepped inside the house, Tip's three year old niece Tanya ran up to me. I loved all his nieces and nephews. They all called me Auntie Mel, and that made me feel good. I bent down and gave her a hug, then I touched her knotted up hair.

"Girl, where's yo' mama?"

Tanya shrugged her shoulders.

"Where's grandma?"

"At the stoe."

"Oh." I stood up and looked around. "Go get a comb and grease so I can braid your hair."

"Otay!"

Tanya happily ran upstairs and I stood there watching about six other kids under eight run around, three teenagers doing practically nothing, and two grown ass men playing cards at the dinette table. Every last one of them lived in Queen's house. I had no idea why I even bothered to come over here. I just knew this is what it was going to be like. In a way, I liked it thinking of my big family that I missed. I missed mama, daddy, and all my crazy brothers. All I really had was my sister, but she was too busy living her life with the new boyfriend of the month. I tried not to bother Debbie, cause she always had an attitude when I came to her with my problems. So here I was trying to feel at home with Tip's ghetto ass family.

Someone knocked on the door and I watched as fifteen year old Keisha got off the sofa and ran into the kitchen. She came back out with a small clear baggy in her hand that had something white inside. She opened the door with the chain still on it, so I couldn't tell who was behind it. Next thing I know, she was closing the door and walking back to the kitchen with money in her hand. When she came back out, she plopped on the couch as if everything was alright. It seemed as if I was the only one noticing what she was doing. It was none of my business, so I didn't press on. I walked over to the same sofa Keisha was sitting on and sat next to her, and stared at the soap operas.

"Oh, hey Mel." She greeted as if this was her first time noticing me.

"Hey gurl."

Keisha never took her eyes off the television, and my eyes roamed over towards Janet who was laid out on the other couch snoring her ass off. I don't know how she can sleep and Keisha can watch TV with these loud kids screaming and running around. Finally Tanya came downstairs with a comb and some blue magic grease. She sat between my legs and I began working on her bird nest. As I sat there for the next hour, I notice Keisha got up about five or six more times and repeated the same operation she did earlier. After the last time, she came back with the baggy and threw it on my lap.

"What's this?" I finally looked at the small crack rocks.

"I gotta go meet my boyfriend, so if anyone come; you give them one of these. Make sure they give you fifty dollars first. Queen only sells fifty dolla bags. Got it!"

"Okay."

"I'll let Queen know you took half my shift and she will pay you $100."

"A hundred?"

"Yeah, I'll be back later tonight. There's more in the blue cookie jar in the kitchen. Put the money in the red and blue jar right next to it."

I shook my head, letting her know I got it. Keisha quickly left out. I looked down at the bag, and frowned up my face. Now I knew the rumor was true about Queen. She was a drug dealer and actually had her kids selling the stuff for her. Tip never talked about what his mama did, and I never bothered to ask. Tip must've learned everything he knew from her, except the robbing part, or even the beating on a woman part. I'm sure Queen wouldn't take that shit.

I was scared shitless when somebody knocked on that door. I looked around and everyone seem to not move an inch. I did notice Miles look my way. He must've knew I had the baggy cause he pointed to the door. I slowly rose up and headed to the front door. I cracked it open the same way

I seen Keisha do. There stood a young woman who looked around my age. She didn't look like a fiend at all. Her short curly hair looked moisturized, and she wore a cute orange tank top with short daisy dukes, and her gold sandals were even cute. I thought maybe she was here for Miles or Jerrod, and I was about to take the chain off the door. That was until I noticed a small twitch, and her scratch at her arms. Then she opened her hand and I see a crumbled up fifty dollar bill. I asked no questions then. I just snatched the fifty and threw the baggie in her hand. She looked at it, nodded at me, and then ran off the porch.

"Damn." I mumbled to myself.

Soon as I closed the door, I turned around. Miles was hovering over me.

"That was Jessica." Miles said. "She's a fresh one, but in a few more weeks she won't be as hot as she is now."

"Oh."

I walked away from Miles, hoping he won't talk anymore about it. I was pretty scared and wanted no part in any of this, but after a few more hours I actually got the hang of it, and didn't mind. I even got into the stupid talk shows that was coming on back to back. When Queen finally came home, she caught me in action and said nothing about it. Before I went home that night, she gave me a couple hundred and said when I needed any money I can get it from her by helping out around the house. I knew exactly what she meant. That whole week, I found myself over there every day.

Chapter Five

Tip got out of jail that next weekend. He came over to my apartment with a bouquet of flowers and he even bought the baby a bassinet. Why was I such a sucker for him? I even let him take me shopping and he spoiled me and my unborn baby very well. When we got home, we made love and watched movies all night. This was the same routine Tip did when he got out of jail. That was only because he was sober and in his mind he was going to quit it all. Then the next week would come, and Tip be back drinking and getting high again. It never failed.

I was now eight and a half months pregnant and I was huge! Although I was all belly, my ankles were fat and I wobbled every step I took. I just got a call from my one of my best friends Denise. Denise was really down, and the coolest friend ever, except she was always in people's business. That's why her and Tia couldn't stand each other. Denise talked shit about people behind their backs and was fake as ever while Tia told you the truth and never bit her tongue. It just got on my nerves with the both of them.

Tip was in the living room with his cousin Pete smoking weed and drinking as usual. I was frying chicken when Denise called.

"What's up girl?" I said into the phone.

"What you doing?"

"Frying some chicken, southern style." I slightly giggled.

"Oooohhh I should be over there. What else you cooking?"

"French fries. I'm not cooking Sunday dinner, so calm down. Just cooking a little something for Tip and Pete."

"Humph!" I could hear her smack her lips. "Speaking of yo' baby daddy, you never guess what I heard."

"What?"

"Korina's cousin Taisha is pregnant by Tip."

"What?" I almost dropped the cordless phone.

"Word! And the bitch about seven months too. Ya'll babies going to be born at the same time."

"Please De, tell me you lying."

"I'll take you to her now. Let's confirm this shit."

"Ok, come in thirty minutes."

After I hung up the phone, I poked my head in the living room. Tip and Pete instantly looked up from their card game. Tip took a long drag of his blunt, then turned his attention back to me.

"Where the food at baby? We hungry."

"It's almost done." I smiled. "I was just wondering if any of you needed another beer."

"Hell yeah girl! Bring that shit!"

I walked away smiling cause I knew Tip. If he was drunk and full off some food, then he was done for the night. After he eats, it'll take a good twenty to thirty minutes and he'd be stone cold sleep. I planned on filling both their plates up and get the hell outta here so I can beat that pregnant bitch ass.

Tip was happy after I set his plate down on the coffee table. Knowing Pete, he'd get full and fall asleep too.

"You want anything else?"

Tip started biting into the chicken. "Nah….I'm hungry and this shit is good baby."

"Thank you baby!" I said in my cheery voice.

I slowly backed away until I was back in the kitchen. I waited about ten more minutes then I grabbed my house key and snuck out the back door. Soon as I walked out to the front, Denise's raggedy pinto looking car pulls up. I quickly jumped in and she checks me out.

"Damn your ass looking like you ready to pop."

"I'm almost nine months, how else should I look?"

"I'm just saying Mel, you still look good though."

"All you had to say was, I look good. You can't make a pregnant girl like me feel bad."

"You cute; shut yo' sensitive ass up. Anyway, you could've changed your clothes, smelling like old chicken grease."

"Just go! I'm ready to smack this hoe!"

Denise had me hyped to kick Taisha's ass. We were both pregnant, and one of us was not going to survive. It definitely was not going to be her.

A five minute ride took forever, but when De pulled up to a duplex apartment I jumped out immediately. There were six people on the porch drinking and smoking. In the midst of it all, a light-skinned, nappy head pregnant girl sat there looking fat and ugly. Tip could've cheated on me with some gorgeous model chick. This fool done went straight to the hood and grabbed the first hoe with a big ass. I bet that's all she had. De couldn't keep up with me. I was very pregnant, mad and ready to fight. All eyes were on me as I wobbled up. As I suspected, the light-skinned girl stood up and mean mugged me. Yeah, she knew who I was, and I wasn't bullshitting.

"You Taisha?" I sassed her.

She walked down the stairs to me, and she stood there belly to belly.

"Whass up?" She rolled her neck.

"You pregnant by my baby daddy?"

"Who yo' baby daddy?"

"Don't play dumb bitch! You know who I am. Everyone knows Tip is my man."

Taisha laughs. "Well, I guess yo' man got me pregnant too."

"That's what I thought."

Before she could react, I grabbed her by the neck, and put her in a choke hold. Wrong move, cause the bitch punched me in my stomach, and I let her go. De then punched Taisha in the face, and a couple of girls jumped off the porch to double team De. While I was in excruciating pain, I gathered all my strength and kicked her my hardest in her private area. She fell down, and one of the guys pushed me backwards causing me to fall on my ass.

"Get the fuck outta here!" He yelled to me, but then looked back to Taisha too. "Both ya'll bitches pregnant, fighting over some fool who don't care shit about neither of you."

I got up and grabbed De, helping her up. "Whatever! I'm a be back to kick yo' ass some more too!"

"Try!" Taisha yelled out. "I bettchu Tip will be licking my pussy tonight."

I almost charged her again, but the pain in my stomach wouldn't let

30

me. I gotta hold of De who had went back to fighting them two girls. She actually had them this time. I hated to break it up. Especially since, no one else cared. We both got into De's hoopty and she pulled off.

"Damn girl!" I was breathing hard. "Take it easy on these corners. I'm hurting."

"Do you need to go to the hospital?" She got worried.

"Yeah, I think so."

De wasn't playing around, she sped up and drove me straight to the hospital. They quickly took me in, checked me out, and I was thankful that my baby girl was okay. She done survived more shit with Tip whooping my ass every other day anyway. Here I was fighting over a man that has not a bit of respect for me. I want to hate and leave him, but the shit only makes me want to kill Taisha.

Doctors kept me overnight for observation. I called Tip a thousand times at our apartment, his mama house, his friends, and of course I paged his ass. I was mad that he was nowhere to be found. When they released me, Tia came and got me to take me home. Of course, she was yelling and throwing speeches at me for putting myself in this situation. I lied about De bringing me over there. I didn't want her to be mad at De, and cuss her out.

"You call me or De if you need anything." Tia told me as she opened the passenger side door.

"Thanks for everything Tia."

"You know I got you girl. I always do. Oh, and I will get that bitch for you when she drop this load. I won't touch her now, but I gottchu girl."

"You know I don't need any help whooping a bitch ass." I laughed.

"I know, but she almost hurt my little god daughter. She gotta deal with me now."

I smiled as Tia hugged me. "You need me to walk you in?"

"You've done enough, I got this."

I walked a couple steps, and when I got on the porch, I turned to watch Tia pull away. I sighed as I turned back around and pull my key out to open the door. I hope Tip was really gone. I just wanted to rest and forget about his ass.

I opened up the door, and I nearly fainted when I stepped into my living room.

"What the fuck!" I yelled out.

Tip pushed the girl off his dick. She scattered trying to find her clothes and put them on. I held my belly and ran into the kitchen. I grabbed my thick iron skillet that mama gave me and ran back to the living room. The girl was almost out the front door when I threw it at her. It missed her head but got her in the back, and she fell forward. I wobbled over to her, hoping to jack her ass up, but her scary ass screamed as she hauled ass out my door. I picked up the skillet, and went for Tip. I chased him around the house screaming all types of names at him. Finally he stopped and turned to grab my hand with the skillet, and he also grabbed the other. The skillet fell out of my hand as he pinned me up against the wall.

"Calm down Mel! Chill out before you mess around and give birth to my shortie too early."

That comment brought heavy tears to my eyes. "It's bad enough you didn't come see me at the hospital, but instead you were here disrespecting me in my own house. Let me go! I am so through with you. I almost lost our daughter over you."

"Mel, please. Come on now. Let me tell you the honest truth. I couldn't get that bitch out of here. I don't know why she came over here acting all sexual and shit. I didn't even know you were in the hospital. I was looking everywhere for you. I was crying baby."

Tears continued falling down my face. "You are such a liar Tip. Just get out. I am fed up with your bullshit."

"Fuck that!" He yelled. "I'm not leaving. I pay yo' rent and all these damn bills. What the hell will you do without me?"

"Survive!"

"Bullshit! I aint going nowhere."

"Get out!" I yelled at the top of my lungs. "I hate you. You no real man anyway. I can do better and find my baby a real father."

"Bitch!"

Tip practically slapped the taste out of my mouth. I fell to the floor holding onto my bloody lip. Instead of fighting him back this time, I stayed on that floor. Tip stood over me talking all kinds of shit.

"If I ever catch you with another man, yo ass is dead, and that's a promise."

I put my head down, and laid on the floor trying to ease some stress. Tip walked away and when I heard the shower running I did the routine. I called the police.

Chapter Six

ia had just dropped me off from my doctor's appointment. I swore I was dying from pain. I been having cramps all day and I thought I was going to lose my baby. Doctor just told me to stay on bedrest for the rest of my month, and I was going to do just that. Tip had to do thirty days in jail, and I miss that man like crazy. I was in peace though, and life was less stressful.

Soon as I walked into my apartment, I dropped my keys and purse on the coffee table and I plopped down on the sofa. I swear I was just going to fall asleep right here. I pulled my entire body up, and got real comfortable on the sofa. These swollen ankles weren't going anywhere. I was exhausted, and all I wanted was to rest. Soon as I picked up the remote to flip the TV on, someone started to bang on my door. I swear I wanted to cry.

"Now who the hell could this be?" I cried out to myself.

It took me awhile to get off the sofa but I finally got to the door and pulled back the curtain. I shook my head when I see Shaquitta. Whenever she came by she only wanted one thing, and that was a babysitter. I hesitated for a second, but opened the door. She practically barged in.

"What's going on Quitta?" I dryly asked.

"You really have to do me this one big favor." She pleaded.

"I can't Quitta. I'm not feeling well. Doctor put me on bedrest."

"C'mon Mel! Trevor in town and he wants to see me tonight. You know Trevor hooks me up. He's going to give me two grand, and I really need that. I will give you five hundred Mel. I promise."

I sighed. I needed that five hundred. Whenever Quitta say she going to give me money, she always do. Damn, I'll be set for a while if she gave me that money. Tip in jail and I have no money to pay my bills. On the other side, her kids bad as hell and all I wanted to do was sleep. They was going to get on my nerves and probably send me in labor early. I know what the doctor said, and I really should listen.

"As bad as I need that money, my baby's at risk. I need to rest Quitta."

"Girl, you can rest at my house. Just relax in my recliner. I'll even order the kids a pizza and you won't have to get up and cook nothing."

"Damn you Quitta! You don't have anyone else?"

"NO! Please, I just gave the girls their bath, so they set for the day."

I looked back at my purse, then back at Quitta.

"Fine, let me grab a soda out the fridge."

ShaQuitta hugged me and ran to my kitchen. "I'll get it for you."

I grabbed my purse and opened the front door. Just as I did that, I heard a big explosion.

"Damn!" I yelled. "What the hell was that?"

I slowly wobbled off my porch and started to see a crowd of people screaming and yelling towards a house. Someone's house was on fire.

"Here girl!" Quitta gave me my soda. "What the hell?"

Quitta walked further out and at the same time we both noticed the same thing. Everything in the world seem to stop. Quitta knees buckled and she bout fell trying to run.

"My babies! All my babies are in there!"

I was not too far behind her trying to keep up. Her house was totally up in smokes and I knew there were no survivors.

Later we found out that her furnace blew up. All five of her kids were trapped inside and died. What was sad, little Jay-Jay was at the door with his baby sister as if they were trying to get out. All I could think about was the fact that I could've been there with them kids and also died. It haunts me. I love her kids, and was around them as much as Quitta was. ShaQuitta was no good after that day. No one would ever see her out, and she stayed locked up in Queen's house for a month straight. Then suddenly Quitta comes out and her mind began to deteriorate and she was lost. Queen couldn't take her anymore. She was already taking care of a village. It was like, she was taking care of a disabled child. She would try to get her help but nothing worked. Sooner or later, we all noticed a change in Quitta. She was talking to us and for a minute, we all thought she was back to her old self. For a few weeks she was. Then I finally knew why Quitta was back out there, she was hooked on crack and it was bad.

She was hooked immediately, and I really felt sorry for her. I was still there for her. Every time I see her out, I give her a hug and encourage her. It was no use, and was always talking upon deaf ears. I know life was really hard for Quitta but that girl will never be the same.

Chapter Seven

Months had went by and of course, I had my baby girl. Her name was NaTisha Monae. She was beautiful and she was the love of my life. No matter how much joy NaTisha brought me, she definitely never changed Tip. I swear he was only getting worse. He'd hit me for the stupidest reason, and I got to the point where I quit fighting. I just let him hit me and yell at me as if I was some child. I knew I was stupid. I should've been stronger since there was a baby now, but it only seemed as if I was weaker. I'd blame myself for everything and even found myself apologizing after Tip done whopped my ass.

NaTisha was eight months old and I had just laid her in her crib and closed her bedroom door behind myself. Tip was always sitting around on my sofa drinking and cursing me out about money lately. Today, he lost a couple grand gambling and now he was ready to take that out on me. He act like I lost it for him. I really didn't care this time. I was fed up with Tip and wanted him out my house today. Last weekend, I was at the grocery store and met this guy name Rasheed. All I could think about was his fine ass and wishing he was my man. I bet he wouldn't beat and rape me every night. Today I was feeling brave to pick a fight with Tip so he could take his raggedy ass over to one of his other bitches house. Hopefully, he go on to Taisha house and take some shit out on her. Taisha had a baby girl too, and soon as she got out the hospital I whooped her ass again. I told her every time I see her, I owe her an ass whooping and I haven't seen the bitch since.

I returned into the living room with Tip rambling at his mouth saying he ain't giving me shit this week, and I better get a damn job. I was tired of him. Why do I stay?

"I really don't care Tip!" I stood in the doorway yelling his way. "I didn't tell you to gamble away so much money. You act like that was all you had. Suck it up and go fucking rob another drug dealer!"

"Keep talking shit, smart ass! I put yo' ass out there and make you sell pussy for me."

I pursed my lips up. "I wish you would."

Tip stood up. "What you say?"

I stood there eye to eye, daring his ass to come after me. This was the only way I could get Tip to leave a day or two. Did I want to risk getting a bruise on my face or body just so I could go out with Rasheed? Maybe he's nice.

"Fuck you Tip!" I yelled.

BAM! Wrong choice of words, cause Tip punched me in my mouth and I could feel the swelling grow at that very minute. I just knew my night was over.

"What Mel? What yo' ass gotta say right now?"

Tip would hit me from time to time and do brutal things like rape me, but that punch in the mouth did not feel right. How can a man that says he loves you to death do something so terrible? That's not love. I cried out loud and then ran to my baby girl's room closing the door. I walked to the corner of her room by the crib and sat there. I tried my hardest to hold in the cry that wanted to come out some more. I grabbed a nearby stuffed bear and put it to my mouth to hold in the little cry that tried escaping. My cry suddenly stopped when I heard the front door slam. I swear that was music to my ears. I got up and opened the door, slowly walking out the room. I searched every room, double checking that Tip was really gone. I then looked out the window and was happy his car was gone. I was so relieved, as I sat down on the sofa. I looked down on the coffee table and seen five, hundred dollar bills. Oh, so his ass want to leave me money. I shouldn't take it. I then stared at the blank TV, and my mind began to wonder. I move away from home, listen to my sister and let her hook me up with this psycho lunatic. Debbie never keeps a man but she always finds the good ones. I'm twenty-one, and I'm stuck with an abusive-drug dealing-stickup kid-alcoholic. I should have stayed at home with mama and had my baby by Ronnie, who I knew would've been there for me. Don't get me wrong, NaTisha is my heart and I love her dearly, I just wish I choose a better father for her. I wish I would've went to college, instead I'm on welfare. I hate my life. My eyes started up again on the tears, as I looked around the living room. When my eyes hit my purse, I thought of Rasheed. It was the same purse I had when I was at the store, and he gave me his number. I got up and grabbed it, and also grabbed my cordless phone. I sat back down and began to search through my purse for the piece of paper with his number on it, which I had slipped in my food stamp book. That was one thing Tip would not touch. He would not be caught dead in the store with food stamps. But will sho' eat the food I buy with them. Punk ass.

I took a deep breath and slowly dialed the number Rasheed gave me. It frightened me when a woman answered the phone. I debated for a second to hang up cause that could have easily been his girlfriend, but after hearing her say hello for the second time, I finally answered her.

"Ummm....is Rasheed there?"

"Hold on!" She said with an attitude. Then I heard her yell for Rasheed.

I listened for a minute, as I heard rumbling noises, and when Rasheed said hello, I could hear the other line hang up.

"Rasheed?" I said into the phone.

"Yeah?"

His deep baritone voice sent jolts rushing to my wet paradise. Damn, that voice had me.

"Hey Rasheed, its Melanie from the grocery store?" I said unsure he would remember.

"Yeah, fine ass Melanie. I remember you. You wore red and black sundress. It was too sexy for a grocery store."

I slightly frowned remembering the fight I got into with Tip about me trying to look cute to go get groceries. He can kiss my ass.

"Yelp, that was me."

"About time you called me. I thought I was going to have to run around town to find you. So, what's been going on?"

"Just working." I lied.

"Oh word? Where you work at?"

"Oh, uh…I work at a doctor's office."

"Damn! What, you a nurse?"

I was mad, but that's what came out. I was thinking of the doctor appointment I took my baby to earlier and seen the young black nurse. I was wishing I was her. "No, I'm just the receptionist."

"Shit, that's cool. You got it going on."

"Not really." I didn't want him to get his hopes up. "I'm just the receptionist."

"Well, you're a step ahead of most of these chicks around the way. They all on welfare, not doing shit with they lives, or tryna find the next fool to take care of them. Damn Melanie, I like you already."

I laughed a little, but I was so screwed. One little lie that slipped out is now blown to be some big news. Shit, I was one of them around the way chicks he was just talking about. Why Rasheed gotta discriminate on us? Even though I was telling a bold face lie, I love the attention he was giving me.

We talked for the next hour, getting to know each other and I was loving his conversation. All I could do, was giggle and act like a little school girl with a crush. I was having so much fun with this conversation, and it really showed. You would think I knew this man for a long time. As I continued to laugh and giggle at everything he said, the unthinkable happened. I didn't hear the keys jingle, the door opening, or the floor creaking. I just seen him standing in the doorway with a dozen of roses.

"Who you talking to?" Tip asked me.

I didn't even say bye. I just hung up the phone and stood up. "Ummm, that was Tia."

"If I didn't know any better, I'd think you were talking to a man. So, who the fuck was that?"

"Tia, I swear!"

Tip threw them roses at my face, and the thorns cut me.

"You talking to some man in my house?"

"Your house?" I snapped back. "This my house! You can step right now, and don't you ever come back. I should've called the police on your worthless ass when you gave me this busted lip."

Tip grabbed me by the neck and nearly picked me up off my feet. I started grabbing at his face trying to scratch his eyeballs out, but he quickly turned me around in a bear hug. Next thing he did, was drag my ass in the bedroom. I yelled at the top of my lungs trying to stop him from what he was about to do. He didn't care, he never cared.

While he continued to force me on my bed, I began to fight him. That was something I had stopped doing awhile back. I was seriously through with this man and didn't want him touching me. He spit in my face, and slapped me around a few times. The more I fought back, hits and punches were harder, and I could no longer take it anymore. I was ready to give up, until I heard NaTisha cry out. The fuel kicked in, and I fought him some more. I wanted him to get tired, but he never did. I was the one who was getting weaker by the minute.

"I felt bad earlier and try to buy yo' ass flowers, and a ring." He pulled a box out of his pocket and showed me a diamond ring. "I was going to ask you to marry me. All them other bitches mean shit to me, and you the woman I want. Why you gotta always go and fuck up our relationship. We could have it real good Mel! I love you to death, and I will never let you go."

Tip grabbed my left hand and forced the diamond ring on my ring finger. I just lay there crying my eyes out. I didn't want this anymore. I was tired of this hurtful love.

"Make love to me baby."

I lay on the bed with his 180 pound body on top of me. I could feel parts of my body burning, and my entire back was sore from being slammed on the bed. How the hell was he expecting me to make love to him. Selfish bastard!

"This my pussy, right baby?"

"Yea." I cried.

"And you're my bitch!"

"Yea." I continued to cry.

Then like always Tip had his way with my painful aching body, which lasted a couple minutes. Thank God! He usually will fall asleep next to me, but tonight he gets up and goes straight to the closet, pulling out a duffle bag. I almost shit my pants when he pulls out a gun and walked back over to me. Tip put the gun to my head and I swear my entire life flashed before my eyes. I see my mother, my sister, my father, my brothers, and my baby girl. I sobbed like a baby and closed my eyes waiting for him to finally put me to rest. Tip didn't even say a word as he pulled the gun away from my head and walked away leaving the bedroom. He came back with NaTisha sucking on her pacifier and he handed her to me. I was relieved as I cradled her into my arms. He walked back out the room and I could hear the shower turn on. Five minutes later, he was back in the room with a towel wrapped around his waist. He put on some drawers and then crashed in the bed beside me. I lay there until I hear his snores. Soon after, I jumped up with my baby and hurriedly grabbed some clothes. I went to Natisha's room to put my clothes on and grabbed her diaper bag and blanket. I packed a few things and then grabbed my purse. Natisha and I left the house and went to a neighbor's house. She let me use her phone to call the police, and I stayed there until the police pulled up in front of the house. I thanked my neighbor and met them on my porch. I escorted them into the house and to the destination to where Tip was still asleep. It was hard getting him up like always, but when he finally did he wore a mean scowl on his face. He knew the deal. He's been through it way too many times. He should be tired of this. I knew the police were. As they walked him out, I turned my head holding onto a crying NaTisha. With that, they took my baby daddy away and this time I was seriously done!

Chapter Eight

Three weeks went by since Tip was put in jail. I knew he was out because he came by banging on my door, and threatening me to open it. Unlike other times, I actually had the locks changed. I was seriously done and not taking that man back. Life has actually been peaceful for me and I loved it. My bruises were completely healed and my mind was back in control. The only thing that I hated was that I was broke. All I had was $13 in cash and $156 in food stamps. NaTisha and I will not go hungry, that's for sure. I was tired of sitting around in the house, so I called De to take me and Natisha to the grocery store. Maybe I'll cook a big dinner and invite my sister, the kids, and maybe even a couple of my home girls over.

After waiting damn near an hour for Denise, her slow ass finally came. I got into her hoopty after buckling my baby car seat in the back. Soon as I looked over at Denise, I did a fake scream. Her ass looked like hell and that wasn't her. Denise was fly, always have been. She was one of them mixed chicks that had that good hair, and pretty eyes. She wore her hair short and always slicked it down mimicking the halle berry style. Today, it was a short frizzy mess, and her light skin was red. I knew she was mad.

"What's wrong with you, coming out the house like that?" I asked her.

"Fucking trashy bitches!" She yelled out, but then looked back at NaTisha. "Sorry baby Tish, auntie mad as hell. Anyway, Imma kill Candy."

I just shook my head at Denise. Candy was her first cousin who she hated and loved. We all had them type of cousins, and Denise had the nerve to be close to hers. Candy always running her mouth and telling De's business, then they fall out but gonna be at the club together this weekend.

"Did you guys fight?" I asked her.

"Yeah, and I whooped her fat ass. All she did was scratch me under my eye. I gave her ass a fat lip. Damn I hate her. She actually told Daniel that I been seeing Benji. Can you believe that shit?"

"That's messed up De."

"I really didn't know she was with Benji. I honestly didn't mean to mess with him, but it was just once."

I knew my friend too well, so I gave her a smirk and sucked my teeth. "Yeah right De! Did you forget that I was there when Candy told everyone the guy she was seeing had a monster dick and a long tongue? I assume that guy was Benji."

"Nah Mel, do I look scandalous to you?"

"Hell yeah!" I busted out laughing. "I love you, but I know you better than you know yourself. Tell me the real. You're my best friend. You love good sex, and we all know that Benji is it!"

"Damn Mel!" De busts out laughing. "Okay bitch damn! I knew Candy and Benji was kicking it, and it was more than once."

"Candy should've slapped yo' ass, instead of you slapping her up."

"She don't know we had sex. She just assumes it because she seen me in Benji's car. I wish she would step to me, scary ass."

"So, let me get this straight…..you just whopped her ass because you messing with Benji? De, you got a man, and you always fighting chicks around town over Daniel, especially Quitta."

"Girl please, Daniel don't want that washed up crack whore. Anyway….I don't really care, he aint going nowhere."

I just laughed at my scandalous friend. She knew she was dead wrong for acting like that.

"Yo' baby daddy was over that way watching me whoop Candy's ass." She added.

I stopped laughing and rolled my eyes. "His stupid ass better stay over that way too."

"He was on the corner making money. Girl, you better tell him to bring you some. He need to take care of Tish."

"Hell nah! Tip always think he can get back with me with gifts and money. Fuck him! I rather be broke!"

"Girl, take his money! You don't have to give him none. He Tish daddy. He needs to take care of his responsibility."

Denise really don't know how bad Tip can get with me. She knew he would hit me here and there, but she didn't know how bad it really was. It was bad, and I refuse to go backwards. I will stay broke. I'll even pawn that ring he got me before he went to jail.

"De! You know how Tip is, and I'm not going through that again. I already took all his stuff to Queen's house, so I don't have to see him. If he wants NaTisha, he will see her through Queen."

"I guess. He staying with Taisha anyway."

"Fuck her too! Better her than me!"

Denise didn't mention no more about Tip nor Taisha. Secretly, I was jealous that he was with Taisha. I do still love him, but I will never let him get comfortable with me again. My only wish is, to get close enough to that bitch so I can whoop her ass real good. Both of us have baby girls, same age. He was my man before he was hers. I just want to beat her ass. She think she the shit, when she was nothing but a busted down hoe.

It took us no time to get to the grocery store. Soon as we walked in, I handed the baby to De and grabbed myself a cart.

"So what am I cooking tonight?" I asked De.

"You know you gotta make some macaroni and cheese, cause you the only one that make it good."

I pursed my lips up. "I'm so tired of making the same ol' foods."

"But I love your macaroni and cheese. You even make it better than my own mother."

I let out a big sigh. "Fine, I'll make it. What else?"

"I don't care, as long as we got macaroni and cheese."

We went through a couple more aisles throwing more stuff in the cart. I was just thinking of things to cook along the way.

"So, who else you invite?" De asked.

"Tia, my sister and ShaQuitta."

"ShaQuitta? Tip sister Quitta?"

"Yelp."

"Have you seen her lately?"

"Yes, I think she doing better."

"You think?"

"Well...not really but she needs me. She needs help."

"That worn out pussy bitch is a crack head!" Denise reminded me.

"Her kids died! All five of them. Imagine how you would feel, besides she wants off that shit. She wants to live a regular life."

"I doubt she ever gets one."

I would've ran my best friend over with this cart, if my baby wasn't in her arms. She never liked Quitta to begin with, but damn.....does she even have a heart? She don't care that Quitta's been suffering the loss of her children and struggling with this addiction. I felt that I was the only one in the world who cared about Quitta. Queen finally gave up and kicked her out the house. She said Quitta's addiction was uncontrollable and she couldn't take it any longer. She now lived with a friend who was also on crack. I felt sorry for her.

Denise and I was finally at the checkout line and the cashier gave me the total of $102.49. I whipped out my book of food stamps, and right when I ripped out the stamps I heard a deep voice call my name. De and I both looked behind us to see that fine ass Rasheed.

"Damn." I heard De mumble. "You know him?"

"Yes." I mumbled back.

"Always in the grocery store looking sexy." Rasheed looked me up and down. "I was worried about you. What happened that night?"

"Uh.....we got disconnected somehow. I'm sorry, it's just..."

"Excuse me ma'am." The cashier interrupted. "I said $102.49. Are you going to give me the food stamps or what?"

"Chill out lady, damn!" I sassed her.

Ghetto chick busted me out. I handed De the book and she counted it out to pay. I was so embarrassed that Rasheed seen me with food stamps. He thought I was a working girl, and now he probably won't talk to me anymore. Lucky for me, I don't think he noticed because at that moment another guy who looked similar walked up next to him. He was equally handsome, and smiled at me forgetting his friend was there.

"You going to introduce me to your beautiful friends." The other guy smiled.

"This the girl Melanie I was telling you about. Melanie this is my brother Rakeem."

I extended my hand to his brother. "Hello Rakeem, this is my friend Denise, and my daughter NaTisha."

Denise quickly moved on up to shake Rakeem's hand. No offense, but he didn't seem interested in her. She should never came to the store looking a hot mess. No matter how bad of a day I'm having, I always leave the house looking my best.

We all walked outside, and the brother's helped put the groceries in the car. Of course, I was embarrassed by Denise hoopty, but then again, she had a car. I didn't. I notice Denise try to make her moves on Rakeem and I held onto Natisha ready to put her in the car seat.

"Your daughter is very beautiful, just like her mother." Rasheed complimented.

"Thank you."

"So, when are you ready for me to take you on a date?" He asked.

"Soon."

"Soon?"

"She's having a get together tonight. I invited your brother." De just came out of nowhere interrupting us. I looked over and notice Rakeem behind De, and he winked at me. I blushed, but looked away.

"A get together?" Rasheed asked.

"Well, just a few friends."

"Can I be one of your friends?"

"Say yes, so the brother will come." De interrupted again. We all look back at Rakeem who started to walk away.

"It was nice meeting you Melanie." Rakeem said as he continued walking away. "Hope to see you again."

"You too, I yelled out."

Denise act like she had a little attitude. "What's wrong with your brother?"

Rasheed laughed. "He cool, just use to more boojee women if you know what I mean."

I smirked as I looked past Rasheed and seen Rakeem turn back and smile at me. Boojee women my ass. He wanted me.

"I'll just call you in an hour to give you my address." I told him.

"Okay, I'll be waiting."

Rasheed licked his sexy suck able lips and every inside part of my body tingled. I smiled on the outside, and tried not to show how flattered I really was. He was much taller than Tip, and more built. Maybe even more handsome. For a split second, I fantasized about his body on top of mines. Hot, sweaty, and him moving down my body kissing every inch. Tip was rough and hardly showed me foreplay. He drank so much that sex with him was always wham bam! Tip was too young to be going through bad sex already.

"Alright then Melanie, I'll be waiting for that call."

"Okay."

I watched Rasheed walk away, and De walked over to me watching the same man.

"Fuck Tip!" De whispered to me. "Where'd you meet his fine ass?"

"Here, awhile back."

"You shoulda left Tip the day you met him. As for his stuck-up brother, fuck him too. But if he do ask about me, let him know it's on."

I settled NaTisha in the car seat and we were off. Of course the subject all the way home were them fine ass brothers. Then Denise slick ass talked me into having more than a get together. Now it was a party.

I had to drop Tisha off at Queen's house, and tell my sister it was now a grown folk's party. Of course, she all of a sudden couldn't come. She hated my "ghetto ass" friends. She claim it was too late to find a babysitter at the last minute, but I knew better. I was mad, but oh well. All I could do was invite more of my ghetto fabulous friends.

Chapter Nine

I haven't felt this good since, way before Tip. I was actually wearing a mini skirt, hair was done up and make-up was flawless. I finally felt pretty. Me and four of my girls were in the living room dancing to the newest line shuffle dance. I was just learning it since I haven't been out in the club in a while so I was cracking them up at my skills. There was a knock at the door, and I ran over to open it. He was so damn fine that I just wanted to throw myself at him.

"Melanie live here?" He looked past me trying to look around.

I was blushing inside out. "Boy get in here and stop playing."

He gave me a hug and I hugged him back, inhaling his sexy smelling cologne. He act as if he didn't want to let me go. Finally he pulled away, looking me up and down.

"Mmmm, what the hell took you so long?" He licked his lips. All I could think of was LL Cool J. Damn.

"You got me now." I seductively told him.

I could tell he was slightly high, but it's all good. I was use to Tip being high 24/7. I just hope Rasheed didn't go crazy when he got high. I moved aside to let him in, and that's when I notice the small bear he held in his hand.

"Oh, this for the baby." He handed me the little pink bear.

"Aww, thanks Rasheed. She's at her grandmother's house for the night."

Rasheed just nodded his head, and walked further into the living room. He greeted all my friends, and of course De had to give him hell about his brother not being with him. He then walked back over to me bopping his head to the beat of the music playing.

"So, is this a party now?" He smirked.

"Something like that."

"So, I can call a few of my friends over?"

"Please do, before my crazy friends steal you from me."

"Never that sweetness."

I blushed.

"Let me call them right quick. You got somewhere quiet where I can use the phone."

"Yeah, you can go in my bedroom."

I pointed my bedroom out and Rasheed walked away to call his friends. Just as Rasheed disappeared, Quitta walked into my house. She looked a hot mess as she had her arms in the air and singing along with the song. All my friends stopped dancing and De hurriedly ran by my side.

"So now this hoe finally want to show up?" Denise said it loud enough for Quitta to hear her.

"Fuck you De!" Quitta snapped her fingers in the air still acting as if she was jamming.

"Get yo' ugly crack ass out my friend's house, before I beat you out."

Quitta stopped dancing and stepped up to De. "I must look better than you, your man got me pregnant!"

"Bitch!"

De instantly slapped Quitta across her face. I quickly got in between them trying to process what she just said.

"You don't know who that baby daddy was!" De spat.

"Daniel! Yo man! Why the hell you think I named her Danielle?

"Let me go Mel." De yelled to me, but I wasn't moving.

"Stop it!" I yelled to both of them. "Both of you in here disrespecting me by fighting in my house." I turned to De. "And don't speak about any of Quitta's children, God rest them babies soul."

"I never said shit about them Mel. It was just a rumor back then that her baby was Daniel's. I never would think Daniel would cheat on me with a bitch like Quitta. I just wanted to know if it was true."

"Who cares if it's true!" Quitta suddenly cried out. "She's gone! All my kids are gone."

Just that quick, Quitta breaks down and falls to the floor. I finally let De go and kneeled down to Quitta trying to console her. She pulled away from me and stood back up. She quickly wiped her tears away with the back of her hand. She didn't want us to see her break down.

"I can't stay Mel!" She backed up to the door. "I got shit to do. Maybe I'll come by tomorrow and we can watch a movie or something."

"Quitta, please don't." I knew what she was about to do. De just pissed her off, so now she was ready to run and get high. "You can stay here with me Quitta. I'll help you."

"Nah, I'm okay. I'm just going down the street to that bar."

"C'mon Quitta." I almost wanted to cry. "Stay with me."

I didn't want her to leave. I knew she was about to go suck on that glass pipe.

"Just let her go Mel." De added. "She has to want the help."

Quitta turned to look De straight in the eyes. She looked as if she wanted to say something back. Instead a tear slipped out. She quickly turned around and left out my door.

"She only gonna get worse." De shook her head.

I sighed and walked out the living room. I opened my bedroom door, and I actually forgot that Rasheed was in my bedroom. He was sitting on my bed, rolling up a blunt.

"What are you doing?" I asked him, as I closed the door behind myself.

"I'm sorry, I should've asked. I'm just going to roll it. I wasn't going to smoke in here. I was going to smoke outside and wait for my boys."

"It's ok. Can I smoke with you?" I surprised myself.

"Word?" He smiled. "You smoke?"

"I did a few times with my baby's father."

I sat on the bed next to Rasheed and watched as he lit it up.

"So....where is he?"

"Who?" I asked, knowing he meant Tip.

"Yo' dude." He took a long pull of the blunt.

"We not together."

"That's good."

"Why is that good?"

"I'm tryna make you my girl now." He said as he took another pull and passed it over to me.

I brought it up to my lips and inhaled it. I didn't mean to pull on it that hard, but I was trying to bypass that last statement he made. *He wants me to be his girl?* I began to choke and Rasheed took the blunt from me.

"I thought you smoked it with the ex." He patted my back.

"Like twice."

"Let yo' new man show you how."

"My new man?" I looked at him eye to eye.

Rasheed leaned over and gave me the most succulent, sexiest kiss I have ever encountered. Tip didn't like to kiss, so I always thought if I kissed another man I wouldn't know how. Our chemistry was like magic and I felt every tingling sensation in my body.

"Damn." He said when we pulled away from each other. "I never had a woman kiss me the way you do. Got my dick hard fast."

I giggled. "You just kissed me good, that's all."

"I'm going to fall in love with you."

Rasheed took another hit of his blunt, but this time he was teaching me. Sexy was written all over his face. I could tell he was horny, and the more I smoked I felt the same. We haven't even had our first date yet and already Rasheed had my panties off. I probably hit that blunt about four times, and I was already high. I never experienced this feeling with Tip. It wasn't meant for Tip to ever get this side of me. I was beyond horny and ready to do whatever. Rasheed kissed me all over, and the lower he got, the more excited I was. Tip wouldn't dare go down on me. He thought it was so nasty, but he expected me to always go down on him. The feeling was so unreal when I felt Rasheed's tongue flickering on my clit. Ronnie use to do me but he was nowhere as good as this. This shit felt so good that I thought I peed in Rasheed's mouth. When I tried to pull away, he grabbed me by the ass and pulled me in closer to him. He was feasting on me and I absolutely enjoyed every bit of it. I even felt guilty for grinding all on his face. I swear I was smothering him. Rasheed didn't stop until there was a knock on the bedroom door. I was finally able to let it all out and just lay there. There was no way that I could get up and answer that door. I watched as Rasheed fixed his hardness in his pants, then look over at me.

"You sexy as fuck baby." He grinned. "Pussy taste good too."

All I could do is giggle. Rasheed went to open the door just enough to poke his head out. I could still hear the music playing, and I didn't feel bad about leaving my girls. Rasheed closed the door then turned to me.

"Damn baby, I hate to leave you. I really gotta roll. Something I need to handle."

"It's okay." I smiled and held my arms out.

He walked back over to the bed and pulled me into his arms. He began kissing on my neck, and I threw my head back enjoying it all.

"You know you my girl, right?" He said.

"Yelp."

"This mine right here." He rubbed his hand between my thighs and slipped his finger inside. He played around a minute, and I moaned out. "This mine, right?"

"It's all yours."

Rasheed kissed me one more time, and stood up smelling his finger. "I love the way you smell."

"Stop it." I flirted to him.

"You and yo' girls go out and have fun. I might not see you till tomorrow."

I watched as Rasheed dug in his pocket and pulled a wad of money wrapped in a rubber band. He then peeled off 5 $20 bills, and he gave it to me.

"Drinks on me tonight."

I was speechless as Rasheed left my room. I just lay there thinking that this man was too good to be true. Just as I stood to take a shower, De rushes in with Tia behind her.

"I knew yo' nasty ass was in here doing it!" She teased.

"Damn nosey asses!" I tried covering up my naked body. "This my house and I'm naked."

"You were loud and we heard you." De continued.

I rolled my eyes and smiled at the same time. I haven't felt this good in a long time, I couldn't even be mad.

"It's still early, you guys want to take this party to the club?"

Both of my friends looked at each other, then back at me. In the real world, I don't go out. I haven't since the beginning of Tip and I relationship. Tip was my reason for me staying my ass at home. I need to have fun, so tonight was the night.

"What?" I put my hand on my naked hip. "Quit looking at my naked ass and say something. I know ya'll want to roll."

"Hell yeah!" De exclaimed. "Let me run home and change."

"Bring me back something tight and sexy." I told her.

"Nah, I will." Tia interrupted. "I have the perfect hoochie dress for you."

"Thank you girl."

They both left out my room, leaving me to jump in the shower.

Chapter Ten

Every song that came on, I was on the dance floor shaking my ass. This is what happens when your controlling ex keeps you on lock down. Dancing never felt so great. My entire body, mind and soul felt free. I had all my girls with me, and we were all having fun. The $100 Rasheed gave me been gone on round 2, and now we were on round 4. This fat guy who looks identical to the rapper Big Pun was now buying all of our drinks. He sho' thought he was getting into one of our panties tonight, and I was definitely bout to sneak away before he thought it was me.

De, another friend QuanTina and I were waiting in line to get to the ladies room. We left our other two friends Lala and Tia with the Big Pun guy. Hopefully they keep him interested so our drinks can keep coming.

"So, who dude think he going home with tonight?" De asked us.

"Lala." I spoke. "He been all up in her face most of the time."

"Nah, I think he wants you Mel."

"Well he can't have me. I may be taken."

"By who?" Quantina asked. "That guy that was at yo' place?"

"Maybe." I blushed.

"Girl whatever." De slightly pushed me. "You still single. Look at all these fine ass men around you. Stay single for a while."

"I don't get you De. First you want me to stay with Tip for his money, then I meet Rasheed and you say fuck Tip get with Rasheed for his money. Now I need to stay single. Make up your damn mind. Besides, you not single. You still stuck on Daniel so shut up!"

"I don't like being single." Quantina interrupted. "Why am I still the only one who can't get a boyfriend."

"Cause you jealous and mean." De told her the real.

"No I'm not!"

"And picky." I added. "You always try to go for the tall, light-skinned men with good hair. I notice."

"I do not!"

"Humph….Leon, Chad, freckle face….what's his name?"

"AJ!" De started to laugh really hard. "Yo' Mel, you are so right."

"And all those dudes were players Tina, and nan of them liked you. You know they only wanted one thang." I added.

"Whatever you two." Quantina rolled her eyes and flipped her braids back. "I'm fly and you know it."

"You may be fly, but your attitude is not! That's one of the reason's your always single."

"Both ya'll bitches jealous! Tonight, I will pull me a dude black as midnight. I'll prove you two wrong."

"We'll see." De sucked her teeth.

"Damn shorty got a phat ass!" A voice yelled out.

We all turned around to see some dude with dreads and he was looking directly at me. I give it to him; he was fine and I didn't mind him looking. I gave him a flirtatious smile until I seen who walked up beside him. My whole insides just wanted to jump out. My night was over.

"That's me right there, yo." He said.

"Nah man, I seen shorty first." Dread head spoke back.

"Serious Keith, that's my baby mama."

They finally got close enough to us and I was now steaming mad. Not because I hated Tip, but it was because I loved him. Seeing him, only confused me, and for a second my insides settled and wanted to melt. I tried not to show any emotion. I only wanted him to look at my face and see hatred for him. Both he and his dude looked me up and down. Tip licked his lips in a sexy way that I haven't seen in a while, as he finally made his way to my face. Was I looking that good that I had this man mesmerized?

"Fuck you got on?" Tip yelled at me.

"Don't start with me Tip."

He then brought on a smile. "I like it. You sexy as fuck Mel."

"Really?" I was melting even more.

"I let a pretty thang like you slip away. Damn baby I miss you."

I could feel De pinching at my side. Yeah, she had to bring me back to reality. Why am I so soft over him?

"Well, I don't miss you." I rolled my eyes.

"She sho don't!" De added. "She got a man!"

I looked at De and almost wanted to slap her big ass mouth right then. She knew how Tip was, and he was a very jealous person. I just knew he would clobber me upside the head right then and there. Instead, he shocked me and took a step forward and pulled my body close to his. He leaned down and sucked my lips up as if no one was in the room. I joined in and actually threw my arms around him. Tip kissed me like this in the beginning and that was it. That was his way of reeling me in. His kiss was what made me fall in love in the first place. As I continued kissing him, I felt like I was in my own world. I could hear my friends and even other bystander's cheering us on. Finally, Tip pulled away and looked me in the eye while licking his lips again. I thought I just got high because that kiss was the shit.

"Damn." Tip mumbles.

Tip grabs my hand and pulls me away from my girls. They began yelling out shit that I couldn't understand but Tip's friend Keith assured them that I be okay. I was speechless as I let Tip drag me out the club. He continued to hold my hand as we walked around outside, and I knew I'd regret coming with him.

"Where are we going?" I asked him.

He didn't say a word back, but began to walk back behind the club to the back. Next thing I know, we in between two buildings and Tip was all over me. I was shocked as I looked around my surroundings hoping no one as watching, but what he did next really shock me. Tip got down low, and threw my leg over his shoulder. He fingered my panties to the side, and I felt a lick. The lick turned into sucks and the sucking and licking became more intense, and my eyes were being rolled to the back of my head. He did things I've never known him to do. I grinded in circles all over his face and to my surprise he was loving every bit of it. Why he all of a sudden wants to put it on me? What's gotten into him? Just as I squirted all in his mouth, he slurped the remaining's of my sweetness and stood up. He turned me around, had my hands against the wall, and he entered me hard and rough. Unlike other times, this was enjoyable, and I could feel myself getting turned on more and more with each thrust. I was so wet, I could hear my juices splashing. It was a good quick minute, and I was actually disappointed when he came. I wanted more. We were both out of breath and Tip actually kissed me all over my neck. It was the exact same spot Rasheed was kissing on a few hours earlier. Damn, Rasheed!

"You know I miss you." Tip continued to kiss my neck.

I pulled away, and started adjusting my clothes back. Although I still love this man, I knew it was a bad idea to let him sex me in the alley.

"I'm really with someone else Tip." I confessed.

"So, you can't love him. We just broke up not too long ago. I miss the hell out of you. I'm comparing every woman to you, but she not you. I go to my mom house to see our baby, and I shouldn't have to do that. Natisha needs me at the house. That lame better not ever touch her neither."

"You're not drinking?" I asked out of the blue. I knew it was something different about him.

"No, I'm trying to quit for you baby. Can I come home?"

I began walking away. "I'm proud of you, but no! I did enjoy our little session though."

"You'll be back!" He yelled out.

I kept walking, hoping that Tip didn't chase me and whop my ass. I was too afraid to look back, but when I did he was just standing there watching me. Wow! All I can wonder is, what's gotten into him? He was nice, sexy, and he ate my pussy. None of that was like my baby daddy.

Chapter Eleven

Four months later

*L*ife has never felt so good. It's only been four months since Rasheed and I started our relationship and I let him move in. He was paying my bills anyway so why not? Rasheed was nothing like Tip. Rasheed love to take me out around his friends. He always bought home gifts for me and Natisha, and to my knowledg he doesn't cheat on me. He was a good man, and I was really starting to fall for him. I didn't have a woman beater for a boyfriend anymore. Rasheed was really sweet and caring, so I don't know why I was still sleeping with Tip.

That night in the alley was only the beginning of me letting Tip back in. I don't know why I was still head over heels for that guy, but I was. Every time I had sex with Tip I would tell him it was the last time and that I was really feeling Rasheed. Tip would then get all aggressive and go crazy as if he was going to hurt me, but wouldn't. It was actually better this way. Now that we sneak around, Tip was better to me. He would rock my world better than I could imagine. Tip was crazy and I fell right back in love with his crazy ass.

It was a Friday night and Rasheed decided to stay in and lay up with me and watch a movie. Rasheed was all about getting money and he stayed in the streets. He and Rakeem were really getting money out there. They daddy was pretty big in the streets until he was murdered. Now it seem as if they get a little more money than before, but something wasn't right with Rakeem. He's been pretty angry ever since the death of his father and I often hear them talk about a half-brother they had who was taking over their father's business. I don't know much about the situation, but Rasheed seems happy about it. Rakeem's the one that's been moody lately. I guess he don't like this other brother, but that wasn't my problem so I didn't care.

Tonight was special to me, because I was finally getting alone time with my man. Natisha usually went to Queen's house on the weekend since I was always out or laid up under Tip somewhere. Tonight, I had to forget about Tip and focus on the relationship I was trying to build with Rasheed. He was every woman's dream and I didn't want to mess this up. I was so for this night that I left my cellphone deep inside my purse and snuggled up on the sofa with Rasheed. Ten minutes into the movie, we had all of our clothes off and started to make love right there. I was putting my all into it until I heard some sound coming from the front door.

"Wait baby..." I pushed on Rasheed. "Do you hear that?"

Rasheed wasn't hearing that, as he continued to grind slow. For a second he looked up at the door.

"Probably the wind." He said.

He then stated humping on me faster, but I was so focused on the door. All of a sudden, it flew open. My worst nightmare stood at the door. Why was Tip at my house?

"Who the fuck you is, walking up into my house." Rasheed jumped up.

He quickly went under the sofa and pulled out his gun. I didn't know he had a gun under the sofa and I didn't like that one bit. Natisha was walking around and could easily access that gun. Oh, we was going to definitely talk about no guns in my house.

I was finally dressed, and I quickly walked in between Tip and naked ass Rasheed. I threw Rasheed his jogging pants, and pushed Tip back toward the door.

"What are you doing here?" I asked through clenched teeth.

Tip wouldn't budge. I never brought him back to my house since Rasheed moved in. He just stood there in amazement at all my new furniture. I watched as he took in the whole scene. Finally he snapped out of it and looked at me. He then looked over at Rasheed who finally had pants on, but was still pointing the gun.

"You know this fool, Mel?" Rasheed asked me.

I looked back at Rasheed. "I'm sorry baby. This is Natisha's daddy. I haven't heard from him in a while and he didn't know I had a boyfriend. He must've just got out of jail." I lied.

"I'm sorry." Tip went along with it. "I just uh….thought I visit my little girl. No disrespect."

"At 11'o'clock at night?"

"Yelp."

"Well, give my girl back the key. This not yo' place no more. You can't just walk up in MY house!"

Tip gave Rasheed a devilish grin and I knew he was up to something. I knew what was on Tip's mind. Tip hustled and sold dope once in a while, but that wasn't his thing. He was more into robbing other drug dealers. I could see wheels turning in his head at this very moment. He had that thought, and Rasheed was it.

Tip handed me the key that I never knew he had. I changed them locks long ago. Slick ass. "I'm sorry. I'll just go see my baby at my mama's house. I just thought maybe my baby's mother wanted my company."

"Nah bro, she got me. I'm that man in her life."

I looked back at Rasheed. "Let me handle this."

I pushed Tip outside and away from my house.

"What the hell you pull a stunt like that for?" I slightly yelled.

"I been fucking calling yo ass all night. But I see you was busy with ol' boy, all up in my pussy."

"Ol' boy is my man. You can't use keys that I never knew you had. Where the hell you get it from, last time I kicked you out I changed the locks."

"Well, I copied your key." Tip pulled me into him. "And I was worried about my baby. You didn't answer your phone, so I thought that punk hurt you."

Hurt me? He got some nerve. I quickly pulled away from him and looked back. Sure enough, Rasheed was looking out the window.

"Look Tip, I gotta go."

"Tomorrow?" He begged. "Can we hook up?"

"I'll call you."

"Okay, and I see yo' boy bought you some new furniture."

"Yes."

"He keep his shit at the house?"

"I swear Tip, you better not. Rasheed is my boyfriend, and he's crazy."

"I'm crazier."

Tip then turned to leave, and at that point I wanted to cry. Bad thoughts of Tip doing what he does best ran through my mind. I love Tip dearly, but there was no way I was letting him rob my boyfriend.

I finally found the courage to drag my ass back into my house to face Rasheed. Soon as I opened the door, there stood Rasheed with a duffle bag packed to capacity with clothes.

"You still fucking him?" Rasheed yelled at me.

"No, and what are you doing?"

"What the fuck it look like?" He was mad. "Why he still got a key to your place?"

"He never gave it back. I'm not sleeping with him Rasheed."

"You got my ass out there looking like a fool! I'm tired of fucking with ghetto ass bitches. I shoulda left you when I found out you had no job."

"What?!" I snapped my neck.

"You heard me!"

"Well, fuck you then Rasheed! I'm the best bitch you'd ever have."

"You ain't all that. I've had better." He said as he grabbed his bag and walked out the door.

I ran to the door but he closed it in my face. I was mad as hell and wanted to kill Rasheed. I thought he really liked me. I thought we actually had a future together. Maybe we did, and I messed it all up. I opened up the door, letting all my anger out. I knew my neighbors thought my drama ended with Tip, but they just don't know. Tip's punk ass started this all.

Chapter Twelve

"Come on Mel, I know you got it. Look at your apartment. You really upgraded and got a man with money. You gotta have a twenty around here somewhere."

I was tired of Quitta begging me for money. I shook my head at her and was about to tell her to get her ass out. Soon as I opened my mouth to speak Natisha began crying from her crib. I looked from Quitta and then to the bedroom where my baby's cry was getting louder. I grabbed my purse from off the table and out of Quitta's eye sight and I left to go into my baby's room. Last time I left Quitta in my living room alone, she took my whole damn wallet. With Rasheed gone, I was back to being broke and only had $27 to my name. I didn't even have any food stamps. Tip would come by every so often and throw me a couple dollars to pay my bills, but not much. It's only been a week since Rasheed left, but it felt like a month. I was actually shocked that he didn't come back yet. His clothes, and personal things were still here so I knew he'd run out of clothes soon and come back. I was even surprised that he didn't take all the furniture he bought me back. That was hope for me that he was just mad, and he come back home.

I picked up Natisha out her crib and kissed her tears away.

"You want to see Auntie Quitta?" I kissed her again. "Her been a bad auntie but she still love you."

"Mel! Yo' Mel!" I heard Rasheed's voice calling me name.

He continued calling my name like crazy. I held onto Natisha and rushed out of her room and into the living room. Rasheed had Quitta by her throat, and I quickly put Natisha and my purse in her playpen I then ran over to help Quitta. I knew he didn't like her, but damn.

"No Rasheed!" I shouted. "What are you doing to Quitta?"

"I walk in, and she trying to pull the fucking TV out the wall."

Rasheed let Quitta go and she ran and hid behind me.

"Get him Mel!" Quitta ranted on. "That fool tried to kill me."

I turned around to face Quitta. "Get out!"

"What?"

"Get the hell out Quitta."

"Oh," She began with an attitude. "You just going to choose his bitch ass over me? Well fuck you Mel! I don't need you anyway."

"Get the hell out." Rasheed boomed. "And don't bring your ass over this way no more!"

Shaquitta walked over to the door, and mooned us on her way out. I kinda felt bad for kicking her out. I had so much love for her and knew she needed help. Then I thought about who was standing before me. Rasheed was looking so delicious, and in an instant I sighed a bit of relief. I was so happy to see that my man came back home. I missed him so much. I swear, if Rasheed took me back I was done with Tip.

"What are you doing here?" I tried not to smile but I knew it was coming out.

"I miss the hell outta you, what you think."

That smiled couldn't hide for long, cause soon as them words slipped out of his mouth I was grinning. I bit my bottom lip trying to keep the smile from forming.

"Well, I missed you too."

Rasheed went over to the end table and got the gift bag he must've brought in with him. He handed it over to me. "This is for you. You gone put this on after I spend some quality time with Tisha."

Rasheed kissed me on the lips, and then walked over to the playpen and picked up Natisha. I smiled as I watched him talk baby talk, and play with her as if he was her real daddy. I was happy that Rasheed was back, but mad that Tip didn't act the way Rasheed did. This past week, Tip would come by, sex me up, give me money and kiss Natisha on the cheek. He never played with her, maybe picked her up once or twice but nothing more. So why was I even messing around with his bum ass? Was I really that crazy in love over him?

A couple hours later, I took a nice long hot bath with Rasheed's favorite scent on me, lavender vanilla. When I got out, I rubbed my body with an eatable tasty oil that was also in the gift he got me. I did my hair and make-up and then slipped on the sexy negligee that he bought for me. He was putting Natisha to bed, and I could finally hear him leaving her room. I stood in my sexy red heels that I hardly ever wore. Rasheed opened the door and he stood there with his mouth wide open holding a bottle of champagne and two wine glasses. I love when he drools over me.

"My girl is so damn sexy." Rasheed walked in further.

I smiled ear to ear loving the compliments and awaiting to make love to him. He licked his lips as he kicked the door closed. He couldn't keep his eyes off of me as he set the glasses on the dresser and poured us both a full glass. He then walked over to me holding them both in his hand and handed me mine as he kissed me on my neck. All the while his neatly trimmed goatee tickling me sending a tingling sensation to my love spot. He then nibbled on my ear.

"You my girl." His whisper was sexy but stern. "And I better not ever hear you messing around on me Mel. I got too much love for you and I swear I'll kill you and the fool you messing with."

I wasn't angry. In a strange way I was turned on that he just threatened me. I don't know why, but it did and I began to love this man more. That night felt so good and after making love multiple times until the sun came up, we finally fell asleep until Natisha woke. Then his fine ass got up to feed and change her diaper.

A month has went by since Rasheed and I got back together. We were doing so well, and nothing or no one was causing us problems. Rasheed bought me my first car which was a BMW, and that only made females hate me more. Rasheed said he was going to buy me a house out in the country, and I couldn't wait. I was more than happy to leave this little ghetto ass neighborhood for good.

After telling Tip that I was really done with him, he actually listened and quit coming around. Deadbeat asshole! I was glad he left, and life was good. I haven't seen his face since I told him and that was three weeks ago. Rasheed has really been making big money lately with his brother. It wasn't Rakeem, but the other brother that I never met. I stayed out of his business so I never asked. I just felt if he wanted me to meet that brother then he will introduce me one day. Besides, if he was as fine as Rakeem was, I hate for him to come around. Rakeem was a good man. He came around every so often, and when he did he was pretty respectful towards me. He also played with Natisha and babysat a couple times while Rasheed and I went out. These brothers were fine and very good men, so I knew this third one had to be just like them.

It was a Saturday afternoon and I had just pulled up front of De's apartment building to pick her up. We both had a hair appointment, compliments of my man of course. He was always treating my friends and my sister when they were with me. De was going to be mad when I told her my new plans. I didn't want to go to my appointment, and had to tell De our new plans. De walked out looking fly as usual. She sashayed over to my new ride, and got in looking in the backseat. I knew she was looking to greet Natisha.

"She at Queen house." I told De.

"Oh, I thought she was rolling with us. I bought my little god baby. some shoes."

De pulled out a pair of small Jordan's and I rolled my eyes.

"Gurl, didn't I tell you to get my baby some walking shoes." I yelled at her.

"Hell nah, my baby gonna be fly like her god mommy."

"You know what I said about sneakers hurting her feet. I want my baby to walk right. Anyway, I dropped her off because I have a problem De."

De turned all the way in the seat, facing me. Of course, my gossiping friend wants to know the bad that's going on in my life. I know she was jealous because I have Rasheed and Rakeem still don't want her cute ass. I knew how she felt about my relationship. Although Rasheed treats her good, and always show her the upmost respect she was secretly jealous of us. I just notice things in her and my other so-called friends lately. They all been trying to hang out with me to get free stuff. Other times, they all two-faced and tells me what each other say about me. Just like a couple days ago, Tia told me that De said I been acting stuck-up and think I'm too good because I'm rolling a BMW. I really wanted to check her on that cause her ass sitting all in my BMW thinking she about to get her hair done for free. I really wanted to check her, but I had a problem and actually needed her. Tia was always busy working at the hospital so she never had time for me. She was probably my only true friend, and I needed her more than I needed De. De was just going to have to do for today.

"What's going on?" Denise asked.

"I'm pregnant!" I blurted out. "Natisha still in diapers and I'm pregnant."

"So! Yo' new baby daddy got money so it's all good."

"I'm like five or six weeks. That's around the time that Rasheed left me. I think its Tip's baby."

"No Mel! Dammit girl, not again!"

"I mean it's 50/50."

"So, what you going to do?"

"I don't know." I suddenly started to cry. "I thought about getting an abortion, but then that thought left quick. I'm not ever going through that again. I can't kill my baby. Even if it is Tip's."

"Gurl please, I had three abortions. Fourteen, sixteen and eighteen. It wasn't really a baby yet."

"Yes, my baby is a baby!"

"Then stay yo' ass on welfare! You never going to come up if you keep having babies."

I rolled my eyes at De and pulled off heading to wherever because I damn sure wasn't taking her to the salon with me. Sometimes I wonder why I keep running back into the arms of my so-called negative friends. No matter how much she got on my nerves, I always had a soft spot for her.

As I took a turn on Riverside St, I spotted Shaquitta coming out of a corner store, and stand next to a group of young guys. She looked bad, but not as bad as she use to look. Something was a little different about Quitta but I wasn't sure what. I really hate seeing her out on the streets like this.

"Oh hell nah!" De yelled out with an attitude. "You better not whip this ride over there to that bitch!"

"She not your friend De, she's mine! Let me handle her and you keep your mouth shut."

"Whatever!"

Soon as I pulled up to the corner, everything stopped. All eyes were on us and dudes were really checking in the car, for real. Quitta was even checking all in the car until she finally realized it was me. She sucked her teeth at De and then ran over to the driver side.

"MEL!" She screamed out. "Whass up Mel! This you?"

"Yes Quitta. Rasheed bought it for me."

Just the mention of Rasheed brought a somber look over Quitta's face. Last time I had seen her was at my house when Rasheed caught her trying to steal my TV.

"You still mad about the TV?" She asked. "I was only playing around. I wasn't really going to take that TV."

"What?" De rose up in her seat looking towards Quitta. "That bitch tried to steal your TV?"

I turned to De and placed my hand on her leg. "Calm down. She didn't steal my TV."

"But she tried. That hoe a crackhead, and you still be letting her around your ass."

"Leave her alone De, she only sick."

"I'm tired of you giving her excuses. She know what she be doing."

"I'm not ever abandoning Quitta!" I yelled. "If you don't like it, you can go."

De snapped her head at me as if she couldn't believe what I just said. Shaquitta was there before any of my friends, and helped me when I didn't have anything. I don't like her doing the shit she do, but I will not turn my back on her. I will be there when she's ready to get off the drugs. I turned back to Quitta, and she was rolling her eyes and smirking at De. Poor Quitta, her beauty was ruined. She was a gorgeous woman, with the baddest body ever. She had it all. Now she was skinny, pale and her eyeballs seem to stick out of her face. My friend Quitta wasn't pretty anymore, and to top it off she smelled bad.

"What you doing out here Quitta?" I asked her.

"Nothing. I'm just chillen with my friends."

I looked over at the group of young thugs. "Them your friends?"

"Yeah gurl! You know I don't roll with females like that except you. Hey, and I also just ran into an old friend from high school. He in the store and you gotta meet him Mel. He is one helluva man. He got his own business."

"That's good Quitta, maybe one day I will."

"He gonna help me get clean. I know he will. You always tried, and I knew you meant well. One day we gonna be best friends again. That way you don't have to hang out with them stuck up bitches!"

"Get yo' ugly ass away from Mel's car." De blurted out.

"You the only ugly bitch I see."

De jumped out the car and Shaquitta ran around to meet her. I swear I was just going to kick both of their asses if they put a scratch on my car. I quickly put my car in park and jumped out to break it up. Them stupid punks were doing nothing but cheering them on, and I couldn't break it up alone. Quitta was actually stronger than I thought and was throwing blows at De like crazy. She bout knocked me out as I tried pulling them apart. Then we all hear a deep baritone voice calling Quitta's name. It was as if she heard the Lord and stopped everything. I looked toward the entrance of the store and seen the most handsome dude ever. He had the pretty boy look. Light-skinned, green eyes and good hair that we all wished we had. He wore a nice, expensive suit, and looked important. Who the hell was he?

He walked over to us and took a long swig of his bottle water before gracing his eyes upon each of us. His eyes landed back on me for a while and he actually smiled.

"You know you too pretty to fight." He spoke.

"I wasn't. They are my friends and I was trying to break them up. Them assholes back there wouldn't help me."

"Oh, I see." The man then looks at Quitta and gave her a serious look. "Go to my car."

Quitta looks at me. "Sorry Mel, maybe next time we can talk."

"That's cool Quitta, and be safe girl."

She walked off and rolled her eyes at De as she passed her way.

"C'mon De." I then looked at the man. "Thank you sir."

"Bryson. What's your name?"

"Melanie."

The guy looks at my car then back at me. "Is this your car Melanie?"

"Yes."

"Nice."

"Thanks."

I walked away from Bryson and back to my driver side door. De got into the car first as I stood there looking at him look at me.

"Hope to see you again Melanie." He said.

I smiled. "Have a good day."

I closed the door and pulled off.

"He wanted you Mel!" De exclaimed. "Who the hell was he? How Quitta know him. He probably her drug dealer."

"No, he no street dude. He seems conservative and so damn good-looking. He dressed too expensive and talked like he went to college. He somebody!"

"How Quitta know him? Was that the friend she was talking about?"

"I don't know De, but you and Quitta better quit this petty shit over a man that neither of you are with. I'm so tired of you two."

"It ain't even like that! I just hate that bitch! I don't know why I stoop to her level. She a damn crackhead anyway."

I sighed regretting that I ever picked her butt up. "Anyway, both of you stupid idiots fighting could've made me lose my baby."

"Oh yeah, just that quick I forgot you were pregnant. So what you gonna do?"

"Tell Rasheed."

"But what if the baby not his?"

"I'm not really going to worry about that now. I was just talking shit. I think it's his."

"Think? You just said it was a 50/50 chance."

"Well forget what I said. I'm pretty sure this baby is Rasheed's."

"And what if it's Tip's?"

"Damn girl, you act like you want my baby to have Tip as the daddy. Just leave me alone about this shit. It's my business and I shouldn't have told you nothing. Don't worry about who my baby daddy is."

"Humph, I know what you trying to do. You gonna pin that baby on Rasheed regardless."

I glanced over at De, and seen that scandalous look on her face. I wanted to slap the shit out of her.

"No bitch! I'm not you." I huffed. "You know what? I'm tired so I'm just going to drop you off back at the house. I'm going home."

"Are you serious? Right now? What, you mad about me whopping your crack headed friends ass or you mad that you don't know who your baby father is?"

Immediately I hit the brakes. I didn't care that we were a twenty minute walking distance from her crib. She'll survive.

"Get out!"

She happily opened up the door. "Whatever! You been acting stank anyway since you meet Rasheed, tryna act like yo' ass didn't come from the ghetto."

"I didn't."

"Gold diggin'ass bitch! Nobody want to fuck with you anyway."

"Bitch get the stepping with your ragedy ass. Fake ass friend!"

De slammed the door and yelled back at me. "I am the only friend you'd ever had. All those other bitches are fake to you."

"Whatever! That's why you let a crackhead whop yo' ass."

I sped away before I could hear what she had to say. I had the last words, even if her ghetto ass was still in the road cursing me out. I swear I was dropping every last one of my so-called friends.

Chapter Thirteen

Seven months later

I stood in the doorway watching Rasheed and Rakeem put together the baby's crib. They didn't notice me watching them until Natisha yelled out daddy. She ran from behind my legs and towards Rasheed. He quickly kneeled down with open arms and began to smoother her with kisses. She giggled and laughed out loud making me smile. I love how Rasheed treats my baby as if she was his own. Better father than Tip would ever be. Tip doesn't see her that often, and when he does I honestly think it's only to see me. I never pay him any mind, and that makes him angry cause I was falling out of love with him. That fool thought I be stupid forever, but he had another thing coming. I was so over him.

Rasheed stands up with Natisha in his arms and he walks over to me. He kisses me and then rubs my belly. From the side, I could see Rakeem look over in envy. Rakeem will never admit it, but I think he secretly loves me. He watches me when he thinks I don't know, and he goes far and beyond to please me and Natisha. When we both made eye contact he slightly looks away as if he was still screwing in that same screw.

"Hey baby, I didn't know you guys were here. We was trying to get the crib up before you got back." Rasheed said to me.

I looked over at Rakeem and the crib that looked as if it was actually finish. "I love it! Her room is going to be gorgeous."

I heard Rasheed's phone go off, and few seconds later Rakeem's went off too. Rasheed set Natisha down and pulled out his phone. At the same time they looked at their text and both brother's cursed out loud.

"What happened?" I asked.

"We gotta roll." Rasheed said with anger in his voice. "Mel, lock all doors and windows. You and Natisha stay upstairs and don't open the door for anybody. I'm serious!"

I looked over at Rakeem for confirmation.

"We'll be back Mel." He was the patient one. "Promise."

They both ran off and after I locked the doors behind them, and I went back up to the baby room with Natisha and sat in the rocking chair. I sat there for a moment watching Natisha play with her doll, and then out of nowhere I began to cry. Every time something went down, Rasheed rushes out and I'm always worried he wouldn't come back home. I hate the life we lived. It was dangerous and unhealthy for Natisha and my unborn child. I lived an abusive life with Tip and although Rasheed didn't abuse me, life was dangerous. The scary part about it all was, I think I liked it.

"Mel!"

I woke up to hearing Rasheed's roaring voice yelling, and it was angry. I looked over at the digit clock which read 3:58 am. I sat up in our dark bedroom and suddenly the bedroom door burst open and Rasheed stood there. He was mad and I could tell he let a tear fall out.

"You fuckin' played me!" He yelled. "Yo' boy robbed me! Over $100,000. He says you was in on it too."

I jumped up out the bed. "Are you serious?"

Rasheed walks up to my face and grabbed my neck. "DEAD serious!"

Rakeem came out of nowhere and pulled Rasheed away from me. I began to cough like crazy, trying to catch my breath.

"Rasheed, I would never do that. Tip's a liar. He would lie to you just to get me to run back to him. I swear I didn't know shit!"

"There is no fucking Tip to run to. His bitch ass robs me and then goes around town and brags about it. Stupid fool got himself killed and I got my money back. So what you gotta say now thieving ass bitch!"

I started to cry hard. "I love you Rasheed. I didn't know Tip was going to rob you. I'm pregnant with your baby. Why would I do that to you?"

"Maybe it's not my baby. A couple months ago, your best friend told me that baby wasn't mines. I thought she was just lying so she could fuck me."

"You slept with De?" I knew that's who he was talking about. "You let her talk shit about me and trick you?"

"This not about me Mel! Did you set me up?"

"NO!" I cried.

We could hear sirens in the far distant. All of us look towards the window.

"Let's go bro!" Rakeem pulled on Rasheed. "You wasting your time over some damn rumors. You know Mel wouldn't do no shit like that. Let's go!"

Rasheed stared at me hard with kill in his eyes.

"Tip's really dead! What did you do Rasheed? We have a baby on the way. You messed up our future together over lies and rumors!" I was now angry at him. "What did you do?"

"You did this!" He yelled out before him and Rakeem left.

He really thinks I set him up and that hurts so bad that he didn't trust my word. I ran to the window just in time to see the police pull up. The house was surrounded and I knew Rasheed wouldn't get out of this. I couldn't believe what I was witnessing. Did Rasheed really kill Tip? I felt like this was all a bad dream and I was hoping to wake up. Unbeknownst my knowledge, my nightmare was just beginning.

Chapter Fourteen

So much stress and anger filled my soul. Tip was an asshole but I would never want to see him dead. His family was a mess but they never blamed or hated me for what happen to him. On top of that stress was Rasheed. He was now in prison. Rasheed had walked right into a 24 hour diner and walked up to the table Tip sat at and approached him about the robbery. When Tip got cocky and started talking shit about how he did it and fuck him, Rasheed didn't hesitate to pull out his gun and shoot Tip in the head right there in the restaurant in front of many witnesses. Rakeem didn't know that's what his brother was going to do. Rasheed never flipped out like that. Rakeem says the plan was to wait in the car and follow him when he left the restaurant. Instead Rasheed got hyped and ran in. Rakeem stayed in the car thinking Rasheed was just being bold wanting to show his face to Tip. When he heard the screams, and seconds later his brother running out they had to leave right away. That's when they came to the house and Rasheed had the nerve to blame me. That hurt, and I'm sorry to say that I held hate in my heart for him not trusting me. I love him, but I'll never forgive him.

I had my daughter at thirty-five weeks and she was cute as ever. Although, she looked just like Rasheed, I still had them do a paternity test and sure enough she was his. He refused my visits up until today. That was only because he received the test results and my daughter was his. He wanted me to bring his baby girl and now that she was three months, I was going to take her to see him. Rasheed was found guilty last week and his sentencing was tomorrow. I'd let him hold his child until he goes to the big house.

I sat in the visiting area waiting for Rasheed to come out. Natisha was with Queen so I only had Rasheeda whom of course I named after her father. Rakeem was the only contact that Rasheed had to get to me. He told Rasheed everything that's been going on with the birth of his baby and would send him pictures. I wasn't too surprised when Rakeem asked if he can send his brother some pictures of Natisha also. Rasheed did love her as his own.

Since I had a newborn, Rasheed had a special visit. We were in a room alone with the guards who stood by the door. Soon as Rasheed entered, I stood holding the baby. I haven't seen him except in the courtrooms and I was never this close to him. I was pretty nervous. He looked rough, but still handsome as ever. That paradise between my thighs was tingling like crazy and ready to explode. I do miss Rasheed, but I had to hate him. He blamed me for setting him up, and I don't think I can ever forgive him for that. He got all emotional and weak, then he had to go and kill my baby father in front of the world. Now both of my girls will grow up without a father. He smiled the entire time as he walked my way. He wasn't smiling at me because he never set eyes on my face. His eyes stayed on the bundle of joy in my arms. He immediately held his arms out to take the baby.

"They said I can hold her." He told me as he took her out my arms.

I really wanted to say 'no', but decided to be civil with his ass. He finally has her in his arms, and he sat down smelling her face and gleaming with pride.

"Wow, she looks like my mom." He spoke.

I smiled.

"I like the name Rasheeda."

I smiled again with a slight shrug of the shoulders.

He finally looked up at me after five minutes of staring and cuddling our daughrter.

"I fucked up!" He spoke out.

I agreed with a nod of my head.

"I got real high that night Mel. After finding out dude took my money I was bold and did shit I never did before. I got high as hell and thought I was superman. I found dude at that diner, then I headed home ready to dead you. If Rakeem didn't get me out that house, I probably would've. Then I started believing you were against me. Home girl was coming to see me and putting shit in my head. I really fucked up my life Mel."

"And our relationship. We had a good thing going. Were you fucking De behind my back?"

"It was only once. She had me believing you and Tip were together."

"Wow! This beautiful baby girl will grow up without a father now."

"I plead guilty, and they saying I can get up to fifteen years. Maybe less, I had some crazy shit in my system. I wasn't myself. My baby will have a father. You will make sure that she knows who I am."

I rolled my eyes. "You fucked up, not me!" I looked over to the door to make sure the guards didn't hear me, and then I whispered to Rasheed. "And when I see De, I will beat that bitch ass. You were soupose to trust me, not her!"

"I know that babe. I was broken, please forgive me. I'm sorry I doubted you."

"Do you still think I set you up?"

"Nah, De was messing with my head."

"Tell that bitch to stop visiting you, and take her off your list."

"She won't be on my list when I leave. So does this mean your back in?"

I was not strong. "Boy, I never left you. You left me! Tip's family won't like it though. I'm so close with Queen."

"Trust me, she'll be okay. If she has a problem, then my brother would cut her off."

I looked over at the door to see if the guard was paying us any mind. He still had his head turned. I then leaned in and whispered. "Your brother is her connect? Rakeem?"

"No, the one you never met, anyway how is Natisha?" He changed the subject.

"She's getting big."

"When I leave here I need you to come see me." He then looked back at the door. The guard still wasn't paying us no attention. "I owe someone money. I trust you and I need you to handle that."

"What about Rasheed. Haven't he been handling your business?"

He sighs. "I been lying to him about who I was getting my shit from. He can't know about this? You're the only one I trust right now."

"And you should."

He smiled. "Damn I miss your touch. I wish I could make love to you right now."

"I know."

"We'll talk more about my problem when you come visit me upstate."

"Alright."

The forty-five minute visit went fast and we had to depart. The guard was actually cool with us kissing all nasty, and that definitely rocked my world. His kiss could make me cum and I was going to miss that.

Rasheed was actually sentenced to eight years, which surprised the both of us. Queen was there and she was angry at his sentencing. I still haven't told her I was supporting Rasheed. I figure she would understand since she deals with this mysterious brother I knew nothing about. It just makes me wonder, but I wasn't going to ask any questions.

Rasheed owed this guy name Bones $30,000, and he instructed me where to find this money and give it to him. Along the way of my instructions on getting this money, I got caught up. Rasheed had given all his money to his brother to hold onto. He told Rakeem to give me $30,000 to put in the kids bank account. In actuality it was supposed to go to Bones; Rakeem wasn't pose to know that part. I was a terrible liar and end up telling him the truth but told him to please not tell Rasheed I told him. When I gave Rakeem the information that Rasheed gave me, he was angry. Actually angrier than I thought. Whoever this connect was, Rakeem was pissed about it. Surprisingly, he said he'd keep it a secret but he was taking me there.

"You good?" He asked me.

"I'm okay."

We sat outside a real estate agency that was in the upper class neighborhood. Rakeem had explained to me that this guy Bones was actually a real estate agent.

"So, how do a real estate agent become a drug dealer?" I asked him.

"Bones father was a true king pin. He was master of the drug trade and owned these streets. He had other sons, but Bones was the smartest. He went to college and when he graduated his father told him not to touch drugs and stay focused on his career. He even bought him this building and that's how Bones started up. After his father died, he took over his business, taking everything from his brothers."

"Should I be going in there alone?" I began to worry.

"Bones wouldn't hurt a fly. He soft, and I'd whoop his ass if he ever thought about harming you. His money gives him power and he hides behind his weak ass security."

"Why did Rasheed keep him a secret from you?" I wondered.

"Don't worry about it. Just pay that man so we don't have to see him again."

I was curious and I knew there was something serious to this whole story. Rasheed lied to his brother about who he was getting the drugs from, and that has to be something. Why don't Rakeem like this guy Bones?

"Did he do something to you?" I pressed on.

Rakeem sighed. "No, it's between me and Bones."

I frowned my face and squinted my eyes at him. "So, it's like that?"

"Girl, get yo' butt out my car and into that building."

"One day you'll tell me, you know."

"Maybe I will, maybe I won't."

I got out of Rakeem's car with the briefcase in my hand. Rakeem stared at me from head to toe with lust in his eyes. I knew he always had a thing for me, but kept it at a respectable rate. Now, it was as if he didn't care that he was drooling in my face.

"Damn Mel, I'm really just noticing how sexy you are. You trying to seduce homeboy in there or what?"

I wore a fitting sexy two piece pant suit. It hugged my curves and hid my baby fat in my belly. Under the suit all I wore was a satin red push up bra that held my perfect double D's. The red heels just added more sexiness.

"No," I smiled at him. "I just wanted to feel pretty today. I did just have a baby not too long ago."

He smirked at me and licked his lips the same way Rasheed did. "Damn, you look sexy as hell. Don't tell Rasheed I said that. He use to get mad when I told him how beautiful you are."

"You told him that I was beautiful?"

"All the time."

I sighed as I stared into the eyes of Rasheed's older brother. They resembled a lot in many ways. Rakeem was more built and a few inches taller. For a second I drifted off and daydreamed about Rakeem and I naked in a shower. I had to quickly shake that thought and close the door.

"Just tell the secretary you have an appointment with Mr. O'neil. Bones should be expecting you. I'm pretty sure Rasheed gave him a call."

"You'll be right here?"

"Yes, I be right here watching everything from the outside."

"Okay." I was about to walk away.

"Oh, and Mel?"

I stopped and turned back around. "Yes?"

"Maybe we can get a bite to eat later. I mean, I'm starving and I wanted some seafood. You like seafood, right?"

"Not really, but I'm sure they have steak."

"I'm sure they do."

I walked off switching my voluptuous hips, trying to keep Rakeem's eyes on them. I slightly turned around and almost tripped when I see that Rakeem was out of the car and now gawking me. I wanted to say Dayum!! Instead, I smiled and tried to keep walking. Was I crushing on Rasheed's brother? Maybe it was just the fact that I been pretty horny lately. Whatever it was, I had to get my brain to stop. I could not and would not get involved with Rasheed's brother.

I walked into the office and there was an older black woman sitting at the desk. She looked up at me and smiled.

"How may I help you?" She asked.

"I have an appointment with Mr. O'Neil."

"I'll let him know you're here. Go ahead and have a seat."

I sat down on the black leather sofa and looked around the office. It was extremely nice and you could tell the owner had money. The office was a very nice size. Mr. O'Neil or Bones, whoever he is had nice elegant, but simple taste. There were only pictures and small art sculptures on the coffee tables, and many more pictures of the properties he probably was selling hanging along the walls. I then looked back at the woman who got off the phone.

"His assistant will be out to get you." She spoke to me.

"Thank you."

Seconds later the door opened and I stood without seeing who it was. When I did, all the blood rushed to my head and I was ready to faint. This woman looked just like my friend, but I knew it wasn't her. Besides my friend being a crackhead, this woman was very sophisticated. Quitta was far from that. She was the ghetto princess of it!

"Mel?" My name rolled off her tongue.

"Oh Lord! It is you Quitta! I haven't seen you in over a year. I even asked Queen about you. We were worried that you were dead."

"Alive and very well." She smiled a nice one. "You and my boss supported me. He saved me."

"Mr. O'Neil is your boss?"

"Yes, he helped me get clean, and gave me this job. I'm like his errand girl. I do simple things like get his coffee and dry cleaning. I don't mind doing it. I even have my own apartment, and he pays me $300 a week. Not much but I live rent free in one of his buildings."

I walked up to her and threw my arms around her. It was a long minute before we both let go of each other.

"I missed you too Mel! I'm always speaking of you to Bones. I told him you never gave up on me, even when I didn't act right. He calls you dimples. He thinks you're the most beautiful thang ever. Wait until he finds out that you're his two o' clock appointment."

"How does Bones know what I look like?"

"You met him, remember? It was my last day in the hood. The day at the corner store where De and I were fighting."

"No, I don't remember. I only met some fine ass man with some pretty eyes. I forgot his name, but I know it wasn't Bones."

Shaquitta giggled, and led me down the hall. I held tight onto the briefcase while looking around.

"We should do dinner sometime." Quitta said as she held onto me. "I miss you. We have lots to catch up."

"I know, it's so amazing how you look girl, and sound. You acting all proper and shit."

"Bones don't like street talk from a woman. He's a very good man and he's helped me in so many ways."

"Wow, I really can't believe this. You heard what happen, right?"

"I been way on this side of town the whole time. I actually just got out of rehab two months ago. Bones keeps me out that neighborhood. He says I'm not strong enough to go back. Just tell my mom, and all them, that I'm okay."

We stopped at the huge closed door and I looked Quitta in her happy eyes. She was most definitely a different person.

"You know nothing?" I asked her.

"Why? Did something happen?"

"Let me get this meeting over and then we'll talk."

Quitta nodded her head and opened the door. I walked in and stood there, staring straight ahead at a very familiar face. He instantly stood and walked towards me.

"Rasheed's girl is dimples?" He questioned with a perfect smile.

I looked back at Quitta.

"I leave now." She spoke. "This is between you two."

I nodded my head and she walked out closing the door behind herself. Bones took the brief case out my hand and then extended his hand to the chair for me to sit. I watched as he walked the briefcase over to a closet with a combination on it. After putting it away he walked back and sat in his chair.

"How are you Dimples?" He asked.

"Your uh…."

"Bryson, but they call me Bones."

"Yeah."

"You look good?"

"Thank you. So do you."

"Thanks." He was grinning and it was sexy. "Confused….you have any questions. I know you're confused and I'm confused. Rasheed never talked about you to me."

"Can I speak freely in here?"

"Yes you may."

"Your Rasheed's connect and somehow you cleaned my friend Shaquitta up. How are you a drug dealer with a real estate business?"

"I didn't choose that life for me. I choose this life." He said waving his arms around the office. "My father has always sold dope. I grew up seeing it, and my mother died from it. I didn't like that life, and I vowed to be better. I graduated from high school, then college, and my father had my own business waiting for me. It was bought with drug money, but I took it. I wish I could've told him no, but I took every gift he bought me. I never even liked the man. He fed my mother the same poison he sold. Shame on me for taking this shit, huh?" He leans back and laughs.

"So, why do this?"

"Every day I tell myself I'm quitting, but every day that I want to quit, I'm closer to my goal. I've done bad shit in my life dimples. I've done people that love me wrong, and I need to make it better. Quitta and I went to high school together. We were friends but not that close. Years later I heard what happen to her kids. Imagine the shock when I ran into her. She was actually outside of one of my father's shops, high and acting crazy. I didn't like her looking like that because I knew her in high school. She was sweet and innocent, and her oldest child was by one of my good friends. He passed on so I felt I needed to help her. That wasn't her. I took Quitta in, and been helping her ever since. I keep her on this side of town, and as far as I know Quitta just thinks I'm a real estate agent. I'll tell her about my other life when she's ready."

"If this isn't you, just give it up!"

"Oh, don't let my story fool you baby girl, they don't call me Bones for nothing. I can do this shit better than my father, I just want better for my future. I'm a boss fo' real!"

Bryson stands and walks in front of his desk. He leans against the desk and looks down at me.

"I trust that it's all there. If not, Rasheed would not like what comes his way."

"It's there."

I stood up to leave and Bones grab my hand and pulls me into him.

"I told you too much about myself. What can I get in return?"

"Oh, uhh…what do you mean?"

"I want to take you out Dimples."

I slightly laughed. "Please call me Mel. I only have one dimple anyway."

"Okay Mel, what do you say? Can I take the beautiful Mel out this weekend?"

"I uh….you know I'm taken."

"Rasheed?"

"Yes."

"No strings attached Dimples, I mean Mel. Somebody needs to show you a good time. He obviously can't. Don't you want to have fun?"

I was blushing and although I need to say no, I did want to have a good time. "Okay, okay. I will."

Bones takes a card off his desk and hands it over to me. I looked down at it which read Bryson O'neil. I looked up at him and nodded my head."

"Okay Mr. O'neil. I will call you."

"You better."

Chapter Fifteen

His touch felt so right as he guided his hands along my back and down to my butt. I moaned as I felt his lips kiss every place his hands been. It felt as if he was worshipping every inch of me.

"You're so fucking beautiful." He gently squeezed on my ass.

I smiled and arched my back as I anticipated him to enter me from behind. I could hear him put a condom on, and next thing I heard were his moans and an actual growl. I knew he was behind me grinding, but what was he grinding?

"Bounce that ass back." He slapped my ass.

I wanted to yell out, 'what am I bouncing it on?', but then I finally realized he was in. I wanted to run out the room. Was I that loose, or was his dick really a pencil? I instantly became embarrassed. Did two kids do this to me? I knew he was thinking bad thoughts about my pussy, but as he continued to hump away I actually think he was enjoying every bit of it. I wasn't! I felt a little something, but I would never guess it be a dick. Maybe a thumb, and if he had rythum I might actually enjoy his thumb size dick.

Finally, he pulled out and laid back and told me to climb on top. Of course I had to look and see what that was he was trying to poke me with. I actually felt relief when I seen his dick and thanked the Lord it wasn't me. 'So I'm not loose! Yeeesss!' He just had a little one. I gladly hoped up on his 4 inch pencil dick and began grinding my clit on it. I was getting an orgasm somehow. In a few minutes I was starting to erupt and couldn't believe how I squirted all over him. That was actually a first and I was amazed at myself. He was happy for me, but I still had to make him cum. I was ready to get this over with, so I sat on top of it squeezed, and grinded away. There was no way I could bounce up and down on that. It would keep falling out, but the way I was doing it, I could tell he couldn't take much more of this. He finally exploded, and I fell back, out of breath trying to make us both cum. After he threw away the condom, he got back in bed and cuddled with me.

"Anything you need babe, you know I got you." Rakeem said as he pulled me closer into him.

"I know."

"This can continue if you want it to. Rasheed will never have to know."

"Yeah, I know."

My phone rang, and I jumped up to get it. It was still early, 8:30 in the evening and both the girls were asleep. This was all an accident that I didn't know would actually happen. I was horny, and Rakeem was sexy and helping me put the girls to bed. Next thing you know, we kissing, hugging, and he giving me foreplay like I never had before. I thought I was in for a treat, but Rakeem was nothing like his brother.

"Hello?" I answered my phone.

"Hey Mel, what you doing?" It was Quitta.

"Nothing, why what's up?"

"Thought maybe we could go to Uptown's tonight. I haven't been out to a club in so long. Besides, we still need to catch up."

"I'd love to go, but uh…I need to find a babysitter for the girls."

"Girls?"

"Yes, I had another baby girl about four months ago."

"Really? Awww Mel, I missed it. What's her name?"

"Rasheeda Danielle."

"You named her after my daughter?"

"I did."

"Girl, don't make me cry."

I smiled. "I can't wait for you to meet her. But check it, let me ask Rakeem if he'll babysit, and if so then I'll be by to get you in a couple hours. Just text me your address."

"Okay."

I hung up and looked back at Rakeem who was licking his sexy lips. "So, I'm babysitting now?"

I gave him a sad face. "Please."

"So you going to give me that little whack sad face." He laughed.

84

I crawled over to him and kissed his lips, slowly working my tongue in his mouth. We slobbered all over each other's face for nearly a whole two minutes before Rakeem pulled away.

"Damn!"

I jumped off of him and began moving around looking for clothes. "I haven't seen Quitta in a year. I'll be back."

"So does this mean I'm staying over?"

I looked over at a smiling Rakeem and slightly shook my head. Why this sexy ass man gotta have a little dick. He would've been so perfect!

"Yeah, I guess that does mean you're staying."

"Damn your pussy good babe. Let's do round two before you go, and when you come back wake me and we can do round three."

I slowly walked seductively to the bed and got on top of him. "I got you babe."

I was ready and cute a couple hours later. I was so cute that Rakeem said I look too good to leave. I can't believe how fast I got this man hooked on me. I left after promising him the world when I came back. With no job, no man to help me pay my bills, I was going to use Rakeem to my advantage. It seemed as if he had more money than Rasheed anyway.

Quitta was ready and waiting. She was really pretty and I almost didn't recognize her in her expensive designer dress. Damn, her and Bones gotta be more than friends. Although I was glad to see my friend do well, I felt a bit jealous that she was back. Quitta always had that natural beauty, and now she had that plus a glow, and a baller on the side. When she got in the car I hugged her and told her how beautiful she was.

It was a Thursday night, and surprisingly Uptown's was packed. I was never able to go out to the clubs with Quitta because she was usually out tricking and then it was crack. Now that I'm over twenty-three, this time around it was going to be fun. We settled at the bar and ordered our drinks.

"So what's up with you and Bryson?" I got straight to the point.

She looked at me as if I was crazy. "Oh no! He's my boss and my friend. I'm thankful that he had a heart and helped me through my struggles. I didn't know him well back then, he was my daughter's Bianca's friend. Besides, he wants you. He told me today that you and him were going on a date soon."

"I thought about it, but Rasheed and I are still together."

"Then why'd you accept the date? Oh, and congrats on your baby girl again. I can't wait to meet her."

"You will love her."

The bartender set our drinks in front of us and I took a sip of my cranberry and vodka.

"It's a lot that has happened Quitta."

"Like what?"

I sighed. "Rasheed got eight years in prison."

"Are you serious?" She leaned in and whispered loudly, but not loud enough for the others to hear. "Drugs?"

"Murder."

"Oh no! Who?"

I took in a deep breath a couple of times. "Tip."

Quitta set her drink down. "What?"

"Tip robbed Rasheed, and he retaliated. He did it in the public while he was high off some crazy shit. He wasn't himself when he shot Tip. I'm sorry Quitta."

"And you're still with the bastard who killed Natisha's father?"

"He's Rasheeda's father."

"So, he can't help her from prison." I watched as she wiped away a tear. "How's my mom?"

"She's okay. I'm always there for her. I will never leave her side."

"Fuck that Mel! Rasheed committed a murder. You need to leave him! He can't do shit for you while locked up."

"Trust me Quitta, I think about it. That bitch De was messing with him. She put shit in his head and started telling him that my baby was Tip's."

"That bitch!"

"I haven't run into her yet, but when I do I'm fucking her up for real."

"I hope I'm with you."

Quitta grabs her drink and takes a couple of sips. I watch her as her eyes continue to water up and I knew she was sad for Tip. I reach over and hug her and she hugs me back. Next thing you know, she quickly pulls away and grabs her drink and purse. She pulls out a twenty and gives it to the bartender.

"We can't be hugging up in the club, I'm tryna get a man girl. They might think we lesbians."

"You might get one faster if they did think we were lesbians." I laughed.

She grabbed my hand. "In that case, come on bitch!"

I grabbed my drink and followed Quitta to the dance floor. We probably danced about five songs straight. We then got tired and decided to go to the ladies room to freshen up. Soon as we got in there we seen two girls doing coke in front of the mirror. They tried to put it away thinking we were someone else. I grabbed Quitta by the arm and ready to drag her out. I knew Bones be mad that I brought her here.

"Nah girl, I'm good." She said through clenched teeth.

She really wasn't. Her eyes were glued onto them two girls all the way out the door until they were gone. I knew that look.

"I'm here for you Quitta. I'll never leave your side again."

"Thanks Mel. I'm glad you came out with me tonight. I really needed this. Being stuck in that apartment had me going crazy. Bones really don't understand how hard all this is. He thinks keeping me away was helping. I just need to get stronger Mel so I can go see my mom. She will be so proud of me. I need to be there with her while she grieving over Tip."

"Just promise me that you will call me first if you ever had that urge."

"I will call you Mel. Only if you give Bones a chance. He really is a good man. He's actually the most decent man I've ever met. He's very single and will do anything for you."

As she said those words I could actually see her eyes sparkle.

"I just don't get why aren't you two dating?"

And just like that, the sparkle went away. "We're friends. He's handsome and all but I see him as a brother. He helped me as a very caring family friend guy. He's too much of a pretty boy and you know what I like."

"Actually, I don't. Back then, you took anything with bills."

We both laughed and she playfully push me. She then walked away and into one of the stalls. I looked in the mirror and vision myself with Bones. Then I thought of Quitta. It would be so hard to be in the presence of Bones all the time and not have a crush. I actually wasn't buying it, but I dropped it. What was Rasheed really going to do for me from prison, and Rakeem was a definite NO! I couldn't live off of his sex forever.

Chapter Sixteen

Bryson and I have been on a few dates already and I was stricken by his charm. He was so good to me and still understood how I stayed by Rasheed's side. I liked him a lot and really wanted to get rid of Rakeem, but it was hard. Rakeem was a charmer too and my built-in babysitter. He had my girls all the time and spoiled them rotten. Rakeem and I were a secret, in public and he played his roll well and never took me out on dates. Every night, he was at my house, and we sexed it on a regular basis. He was getting better, and actually knew how to work that little dick of his after all. It was the foreplay that got me every time. He was excellent with his mouth and he knew it. I never complained about any of it. Rakeem was a good friend and a great uncle to my kids. I still never told him that I been dating Bryson on the side. First of all, they hate each other. I still have no idea why, but I dared not to speak each other's name in one's presence. Maybe one day I'll ask Bryson. I might get an answer unlike Rakeem.

When Rakeem was busy, Queen would take both my girls. She loved Rasheeda and didn't care that she wasn't Tip's. Queen wasn't that type of person. Lately, I been dropping them off there more often just so I could go hang out with Bryson or party with Quitta and Tia. It seemed as if the only time I had the girls was when Rakeem came around. Bryson wanted more out of our relationship and so did I, but we haven't had sex yet. I was thinking of ways to break it to Rakeem.

"Hey baby, you here?" I could hear Rakeem's voice enter my house.

I just got out the shower and was trying to get ready for a night out with Quitta and Tia of course. I never expected Rakeem to drop by. So that caught me by surprise.

"I'm in the room." I yelled out.

I just finished snapping on my bra when he walked in smelling like expensive cologne and looking fine as usual.

"You going out?" He asked as he looked on my bed at the black dress.

"Yelp."

"Are the girls still at Tip's mama house?"

"Yelp."

I watched as Rakeem slowly shook his head at me, and then sat on my bed.

"You need to go get your kids!" He demanded.

I looked dead into Rakeem's eyes and rolled mine at him. I ignored him as I walked to my closet to find my red crop top with the low cut front. Next thing I know, I'm being yanked out the closet and thrown on my bed. Rakeem got on top of me pinning me down and I actually couldn't move.

"You acting like a real fucking hoe Mel! Go get your fucking kids, a job and be a mom! Stay your ass out the clubs. I'm done paying all yo' bills and giving you money. You not even trying!"

He let me go, and stood up over me. That's when I got up and began to jump on him. I started hitting on him, scratching and yelling like a mad woman. In reality, I was being reminded of the abuse Tip use to give me.

"Don't you ever put your hands on me! Are you crazy! I will fuck you up, and don't ever talk about what I do with my life. You're not my man!"

Rakeem easily picked me up and pinned me back on the bed with my hands over my head. His body was on top of mine, and I swore he was going to yell and slap me silly. He was very calm.

"Mel, quit being so naïve. You fucking up your life! I use to want a girl just like you, but now you ain't shit!"

"You love me!" I yelled to him. "I'm the shit and you're not! Now get the fuck off of me and stay away from me and my kids.

Rakeem stared down at me for a minute, still had me pinned down. He finally got up.

"Your ass turning into a gold digging' bitch anyway! Pussy good as gold, but attitude going south and I'm not with that. I'll keep taking care of them girls but we done, and get those kids the fuck outta Queen's house."

I wanted to curse Rakeem out and chase him out the door. I wanted to yell out, 'who cares about your little ass dick'. I couldn't do nothing but lay there and cry. I had so much guilt in my heart and I knew I was letting a good man get away, even if he was Rasheed's brother. He was right, I have been pawning off my kids at Queen's house so I could go out and have a little fun every now and then. Rakeem gave me enough money to pay the rent, bills, buy food and still have money for myself and the kids. I didn't want to lose him, cause welfare gave me little cash, and food stamps only lasted a couple of weeks. I haven't had a job since way before Tip, so that was the last thing I was thinking about. Did I just mess up my only income? After laying there contemplating whether or not I was going to get up, I suddenly jumped up and threw on my robe. I ran outside catching him before he got into his car.

"Wait, Rakeem." I begged.

He turned to me and I swear his face looked annoyed as hell.

"Baby, I'm sorry. I didn't mean to go crazy on you. It's just that it reminded me of Tip."

His face softened up. "I figured."

"And, I'm not ignoring my kids. I just wanted to have fun. I missed Quitta, and it's been fun going out with her. I just wanted to be there for her. I'll spend more time with the kids. I'm sorry, just…please baby, don't leave."

"You really want me to stay?"

"Yes. I like you a lot and you're good with me and the girls."

He put his head down and I stared into his perfect waves. When he looked back up at me, his face was sincere. "Well, I don't like you! I love you! I hate that I fell in love with you like an idiot. I know you not my girl but I really want to be with you."

Just before I could say anything a black Mercedes Benz pulls up along the curb behind Rakeem's car. I knew who car it was and I was instantly afraid of what would happen next. I slightly backed away from Rakeem as Bryson got out the car dressed casual but nice. I slightly grinned because he was just too damn sexy. Rakeem notice me pulling away and I think he noticed the chemistry that I couldn't hide.

"Look at the most beautiful woman of the night." Bryson sang out.

He walked up to me and gave me a hug. I hugged him back but it was pretty uncomfortable with Rakeem standing right there.

"You been seeing this fool?" Rakeem barked.

I looked over at Rakeem who wore a big vein in the middle of his forehead.

"We been on a few dates, but nothing more." I tried to defend the situation.

"But I want us to be more." Bryson interrupted. "I wanted to see if you'd go to Vegas with me next week to see the fight."

"Next week?" I repeated.

Bryson grabs my hand. "Hopefully Uncle Rakeem can babysit."

I looked over at Rakeem and seen the hurt in his face. I could tell he wanted to hide it and stay strong in front of Bryson. I had told Bryson that Rakeem has been a very supportive uncle and stayed around to help me out. Rakeem was around so much that Bryson actually asked if we were seeing each other. Of course, I couldn't admit that. I was really trying to be with Bryson if he'd take me. Bryson had it all, money and the great looks. We haven't had sex yet, but he looked as if he was hung. I didn't want to lose my chance with Bryson over Rakeem's feelings.

"You better ask Queen, I gotta go." Rakeem said as he got into his car.

Just like that, he might've been gone forever and we may not have the friendship we once started with. My eyes followed him and before he pulled off we made eye contact. I did feel bad, but that was only until Bryson pulled me into his arms.

"You okay?" He asked me.

"Oh yeah, I was just thinking of calling Queen to see if she can keep the girls while we go to Vegas."

He smiled. "So you going with me?"

"Yes."

"Damn, you just made my night girl."

Bryson slightly picked me up off the ground and kissed me. We kissed plenty of times and he was a damn good kisser. Matter fact, he kissed just as well as Rakeem.

Chapter Seventeen

Three years later

"Mommy, why are you crying?" Natisha walked into my room.

I quickly wiped away the tears I let fall and threw the pregnancy test in the trash. Five year old Natisha stood at the bathroom entrance staring up at me. I turned and looked in the mirror and began to wipe my finger gently under my eyes, trying to keep my make-up looking decent. I then waved my hand in front of my eyes so it wouldn't look like I been crying. I took a deep breath and walked over to my oldest daughter Natisha.

"Cici needs a bottle mommy." She told me. "She's crying."

"Well, I don't hear her crying."

"She bout to, I said."

I slightly laughed. "You better not be messing with her. I told you and Sheeda to play in the playroom."

"But Cici wants to cry. She is hungry and moving around in her crib."

I grabbed Natisha by the hand and we walked together over to the girl's room where there were two princess beds and a crib. I just had my baby girl Ciara two months ago, and I'm pregnant again. Of course I was tired of getting pregnant and I couldn't believe it has happened again. I was on the pill when I got pregnant with Cici, and my doctor told me to wait until I got better and he'd give me the depo shot this time around. I had got ammonia right after I delivered Cici and was in the hospital a week longer. I was still a little weak and I told Bryson not to touch me until I got better, but he was all on that 'your not soupose to deny your man' crap. One time, and his super sperm got me pregnant. I really don't know what to do at this point. I love my kids, but hate my life. I am twenty-six years old and about to have four kids. Bryson was a good dad but a terrible boyfriend. He used to be my dream man. He treated me like a queen, took me out, and bought me gifts. Somewhere down the line things changed. He still did all that, but controlling came over him. He wanted to mold me into this woman that didn't exist in this body. Not only was he controlling, but jealous hearted, so of course I couldn't have any guy friends. I haven't seen Rasheed in two years and he forbids me or the kids to have any kind of relationship with Rakeem. Last I seen Rakeem was almost three years ago. I was practically banned from the world. Bryson wasn't physically abusive, but mentally and verbally. I hated him on many occasions but at the same time he was the love of my life. This was so bad that I was yet, pregnant again. I feel as if he did it on purpose to keep me in the house. His career was taking off with the real estate business, but he was more and more into the street business. He was falling more and more in love with that side of life. He used to be careful and undetected, but lately he's been careless and wreckful. He got a few police officers on his payroll and now he thinks he own the city. He's flashier with his appearance, always out buying cars and showboating. I'm always worried that the FEDS were going to come soon enough. At first I was in love with all this money and love being taking care of. I was practically rich, but I hated that we had to look over our shoulder. I never felt comfortable.

I entered the girl's room with Natisha by my side. I looked into the crib to see my beautiful Cici wide awoke just looking up at the pink and zebra printed teddies on the mobile. She was a good baby and hardly cried. Natisha pushed over her small pink chair up to the crib and looked in.

"See mommy, Cici woke and she going to cry."

"No baby, Cici is okay. She might just be a little hungry."

"Oh." Natisha smiled. "She so cute mommy."

"Yes she is, just like her big sissy." I said as I gently squeezed on her cheek. She giggled out loud. "Now go on back into the playroom with Sheeda. I'll be in there."

"Okay mommy."

Natisha jumped down and ran out of the room. I picked up Cici and kissed on her soft little cheeks. Her bright grey eyes were wide open. She was the splitting image of Bryson. Of course she was, I hated his ass throughout my whole pregnancy. I carried Cici into the playroom where Rasheeda was playing at her kitchen set making fake food, and Natisha sitting Indian style holding onto a Barbie and Ken doll. Soon as they both seen me walk in, they got up and ran over to me. They really wanted to play with Cici. They were so happy that they had a new baby sister. I swear they thought Cici was a doll, always wanting to feed and change her. I sat in the rocking chair and told the girls to go back and play while I feed Cici. They pouted but obeyed. I whipped out my breast and began to feed Cici as I rocked and watched the girls play.

"How's my favorite ladies in the world?" Bryson walked into the room.

"Daddy!" Both girls yelled and ran over to Bryson.

Cici was startled as the girls ran over to Bryson who had many gifts in his hands. He dropped them to hug the girls. He's been gone all week on business so we haven't seen him since. He was always bringing us back gifts. After giving the girls hugs and kisses he shoved all the gifts in their face and walked over to me with the biggest bag of all. He leaned down to kiss me and then looked down into my face.

"You look like shit." He spoke. "I thought you were feeling better."

I really wanted to cry. I had no make-up on, but I thought I looked decent. I had that natural beauty, so for Bryson to tell me I look like shit hurt my feelings. This was nothing new. Bryson wanted me to look my best at all times. I was to never leave the house without my hair and makeup done, which I never had but he had standards. I always had to wear the best. He said I reflected him and I could never look bad.

"I thought I looked fine." I said trying my best to be strong.

Bryson looked down at Cici feeding off my breast and then he sighed.

"Give me the baby." He held his arms out. "Go pump a couple bottles and call up your girls. You need to go to the spa and salon. When you get back tonight, I'll take you out."

"Really?"

"Yeah, and call Queen up to see if she can watch the girls for a couple of days. Maybe we'll go see that new boxer Ronnie James."

"Ronnie James from Ohio? He's a boxer?"

"Yeah, you act like you know him or something. He famous, you don't know him."

I raised my right eyebrow and sucked my teeth. He don't know who I know, and I bet that was the Ronnie James I grew up with. He's a celebrity?

"Do you have a flyer?" I asked him.

"Baby, he not some low class boxer. He the champ." Bryson opened his suit and pulled a small flyer out the inside pocket. He handed it over to me and I looked it over. Ronnie James vs Allen Garcia. I smiled as I looked over his picture. He really made it big, and my stupid ass aborted his baby.

"What you smiling for?" Bryson asked.

"He was my friend. Ronnie's from Ohio like me. We grew up together."

"Oh really? So you know Ronnie?"

"Yeah….he dated my best friend." I lied. I knew how jealous and crazy Bryson could get so I couldn't tell him that I REALLY knew Ronnie. Very well.

I stood up and handed Bryson Cici. I put my breast away and kissed her and then kissed Bryson. I was happy that Bryson came back in a good mood. I was ready to get cute for the night and to go see Ronnie James. Before I left out the room, Bryson called my name.

"Yes babe." I turned to him.

"I take that back, we'll just go to Miami. Ronnie James not really all that any way."

I stared into Bryson's pretty eyes for a moment and he smirked at me letting me know that he knew the real deal. Did I give off that vibe that I was lying about Ronnie?

"Did you forget babe?" He spoke. "You shared your life with me when we first met. I remember you telling me about the boy that broke your virginity and got you pregnant. You said he had a good talent and that was boxing. Well, I don't forget. Did you think you were going to meet up with this man or what?"

"It was his friend that I use to talk to." I continued the lie. "They both were boxers."

"More lies. You're not a good liar baby."

"Well, you're not a good boyfriend!" I blurted out of anger.

"What the hell you mean I'm not a good boyfriend. I do every fucking thing for your lazy ass. I made you! You were nothing until you met me. I take care of your kids! I am the best you ever had and don't you ever forget that! Now get the hell out before I change my mind and leave yo' ass in this house."

I quickly walked away before he went any crazier than he already was.

Bryson had called the spa and made Quitta, Tia, and myself an appointment. I was already there waiting on the girls. I had just finished getting my facial and now I was getting a pedicure. Just as I was about to call them Tia walked in with Quitta behind her.

"I swear you two are late for everything." I snapped at them.

"Yeah, and your boogee ass was probably here 15 minutes early."

"And I was."

Since I been with Bryson Tia been calling me boogee. Bryson couldn't stand a woman to curse, act out, and be loud. Sophistication was all he wanted. I do admit, that Bryson changed me and I was his formal woman.

We all laughed as the two of them got settled on each side of me to receive their pedicures.

"So how are my girls?" Tia asked.

"Spoiled!" I responded.

"You gone have them hands full when they are teenagers." Quitta told me.

"Trust me, I know."

"So, are you feeling better?" Tia asked. "You look real good."

"According to Bryson, I look like shit."

"What!" Tia yelled out.

"He said that?" Quitta asked.

"Yes, I mean I just had a baby. The bad part about it all was that I actually thought I was looking good."

"You do! For having three kids, you look a helluva lot better than women who's had none."

"Thanks Tia."

"I'm only speaking the truth."

"Did you guys know Ronnie James?" I changed the subject.

"The boxer?" Tia knew.

"Yeah, well did you know that he was my first? We grew up together."

"What!" Both women gasped.

"Bryson was being nice and we were going to see the fight. That was until he put two and two together and figured I slept with Ronnie before."

"How do he know?" Quitta asked.

"My dumb ass told him when we first got together who my first was, and that he was a boxer. Then when he told me we were going to see the fight, I didn't know that Ronnie was a boxer. When I told Bryson I knew him, he assumed it was him, and I don't know how to lie. I tried to, but he caught me. Now we not going."

"I swear your man has issues!" Tia spoke. "He never let you go anywhere. He so jealous!"

Tia and I go way back. I met her through Denise and we weren't that close back then. We'd just chill together because of De. Within the last year, Tia's been there for me and Quitta. She was a good friend and I was glad she never gave up on me. Even when Bryson was keeping me on lock down, Tia would come to the house to see me and hang out. Quitta was my best friend. I love that girl to death. I forgot to mention she was seven month pregnant. Tia and I was so happy when we found out. Quitta lost all her kids in that fire, and although this baby will not replace her children, but bring her happiness back that she lost. None of us met the baby father. Some guy name Jose who lives in Washington. She says we'll meet him one day. Bryson and I help her out a lot, so she hasn't been going through this pregnancy alone. If I wasn't there because of the kids, Bryson would be there for her. Thinking about her pregnancy made me think about this new baby growing inside me. Three kids was enough. I did not want two babies in diapers.

"You sure you not carrying twins over there." I joked with Quitta.

"I ask the doctor that every time. I feel like an elephant."

"You're beautiful Quitta. You look good."

She carried that baby everywhere. Especially her face. Quitta was still a gorgeous woman, just fat in all the places fat can go. After she had this baby she will have to go on a serious diet.

"So, how was your visit with José?" I asked.

She smiled and blushed at the same time. "I love that man so much. We spent every second together, and it felt so good."

"I still don't understand why he couldn't come here, and your very pregnant ass had to go there." Tia added.

"I had to get away so I don't mind."

"Well, we still need to meet the man that stole your heart. Better yet, did you guys take any pictures? We want to see what your baby going to look like."

"I told you before Tia, that José hates getting his pictures taken."

"Girl, if you weren't pregnant, I'd think you'd be lying about José."

"Me too." I agreed. "But your belly tells us otherwise. Is there something about José that you're not telling us?"

"Yeah, and what's his last name and family history?"

"Damn you guys; I feel insulted. Why are you guys doing me like this? If I don't want you to meet him, then respect what I want. When the time is right, both of you will get to meet my man."

I looked over to Tia and shook my head no. We were going to drop it for now, but I knew something wasn't right.

"Anyway," Tia started. "Just give me a list of your guests that you want to come to your baby shower."

Quitta looked at me. "Help Tia out with my guest list. You know that I have no friends."

"Okay. Tia, I'll handle the guest list, and you handle the decorations. Bryson says he was going to have it catered, so just give him the menu."

"Oh, that's cool." Tia said. "So, what about the cake?"

"Queen wants to make it."

Quitta smiled. "My mom makes the best cakes ever. Everyone will be there if you tell them that Queen made the cake."

"Girl, everyonegg will be there for you regardless." Tia added. "We are so happy for you."

Quitta's eyes started to tear up.

"I am so blessed to have best friends like you two. When I was down, you guys never left my side or talked shit about me." She then looked at me. "And I know I did you so wrong Mel, and you still never left me. Even when that evil bitch De tried to turn you against me. You two are my rock. And of course Bryson." She then sighed. "He's my rock king. He rescued me from the streets and showed me a better life. He's amazing."

Tia and I looked at each other at the same time. We were both thinking the same thing. I knew love when I see it, and something told me that Quitta had love in her eyes as she spoke my man's name. But they were like brother and sister, so of course Quitta loved him. I quickly got rid of that thought of Quitta and Bryson falling in love with each other. He didn't like fat women anyway and Quitta was fat. I must be going crazy. I decided to end the awkwardness silence with my news.

"So, I'm pregnant again?" I announced.

"What!?" They both said in unison.

"By who?" Quitta asked.

Tia and I looked at her as if she was crazy.

"Who else fool?" I snapped.

"I didn't mean it like that." She corrected herself. "I'm just shocked because you been real sick."

"We still have sex."

"But you just had a baby Mel!"

I bit my tongue and I had to do it hard. This heffa done had five kids back to back and she had the nerve to talk about me.

"I was sick when I went to my checkup. The doctor wouldn't put me on birth control until I got better. Bryson don't know how to take no for an answer. You gotta satisfy your man so he don't go looking for other pussy."

"I hear that, but damn Mel…." Tia frowned. "He should've pulled out or wore a condom.

"He did pull out, but not quick enough. I haven't told him yet. I was really debating on…." I hesitated. "On getting an abortion."

"You never got over your first abortion, so why go through it again." Tia reminded me.

"I think you should go ahead and get the abortion." Quitta said. "You already stressing. Four kids? I know how it feel to have two in diapers and three driving you crazy." Quitta then sighs. "But I give anything to have them back right now."

"There you go!" Tia exclaimed. "Quitta just said in so many words that you shouldn't go with having an abortion."

"Well…I guess." Quitta said sounding like the world was coming to an end.

"What do you mean you guess? First you think I should, then you practically make me feel bad."

"I didn't mean to make you feel that way. It's your body, my opinion don't mean shit."

"No, but you guys are my only friends. I just want you to know that I'm considering, so don't judge me."

"We will not judge you." Tia said as she leaned over to give me a hug.

For the next couple of hours at the spa, we sat around and got pampered. It was fun catching up with them. Even if Quitta was being a hater today. I just excused her for being fat, miserable and pregnant.

Next, we pulled up to the mall, so I could find something cute when Bryson and I go out. The girls rode with me in my brand new Yukon. Soon as I pulled into a parking spot, a red Taurus parked behind me, blocking me in.

"What the hell they doing?" Tia asked looking back.

"I have no idea. Who is it?"

Tia, being the more aggressive one of us all quickly hopped out. I then opened the door and got out as well. Soon as I seen who it was, I tapped the back window and mouthed to Quitta, 'stay in the car.' I knew shit was going to pop off.

De quickly jumped out the car like she gone do something. Right behind her, two other chicken heads got out trying to look tough. One of them looked familiar and I realized it was Taisha. De's two-faced ass done became best friends with Tip's other baby mama. I had no idea who the other woman was, but she can get it too.

"I knew that was your ass pulling up into the mall." De spat. "Still a gold digger I see."

"What got yo' ass so brave? I never did shit to you. You the one tripping and falling in love with my baby daddy and then telling him lies about me."

"Rasheed a good man Mel, and yo' hoe ass fucked that up. Now you trapping the next big thang in the city. You think you all high and mighty now cause you done moved out the hood."

"Bitch, get back in that car and drive off before I slice yo' face up." Tia stepped up. "Rasheed wouldn't want your visit then."

"This not yo' fight Tia, but I'm not scared of your ass neither."

"Mel, get back in the car." Tia told me.

De laughed along with the two other girls. "Aww Mel, you got you a guardian angel now?" She then got loud and serious. "But fuck both of you. Mel, you took everything from Rasheed. You go and fuck with his brother! You trifling as hell bitch. You don't deserve to be happy. I'm a really fuck your life up. I just wanted to warn your gold diggin' ass."

She caught me by surprise when she said I fucked with Rasheed's brother. How the hell she know? No one knows and I couldn't understand how this nosey bitch found out. She the last person I ever would want to know. She was pissing me off and I definitely don't like her calling me out like that. Anger took over me and I blasted her ass in the jaw. She held it for a second but then reacted by pushing me so hard, I fell flat on the ground. That's when Quitta opened the door to help me up. By the time Quitta helped me, Tia was already pounding the shit out of De. I was just about to jump in and help cause them other two bitches was trying to hit at Tia. Right when I yanked Taisha all the way back, screams could be heard and they were horrid. All of us looked over to Tia who was on top of De. Blood was everywhere and De's other so-called friend quickly backed up. I ran over and pulled Tia off. She had a small blade that I never knew she had.

"Tia! What did you do?" I then looked at Quitta. "Call 911! Now!"

Tia stood back and dropped the blade. Her face looked shocked as if she couldn't believe what she just did.

"Mel, I just wanted to slice her face. That's all. I didn't want to hurt her." Tia was spooked. "I think she was moving around too much and…. Is she going to be okay?"

I looked down at De's bloody face. She was barely holding on. Taisha came back over and gave me a shirt to stop the bleeding on her neck. Tia had went crazy with the blade, and it left a very deep cut in her neck. A crowd started to form. De was struggling and tried to speak, but nothing could come out. I hated Denise for so long and couldn't wait to see her so I could kick her ass. I never meant for anything to happen to her. I had love for her no matter what horrible things she said about me. De was once my friend and I didn't want her to die.

Chapter Eighteen

Two Months later

9 cried into Bryson's chest as they walked Tia out of the courtroom. She didn't even look herself and I was going to miss her. It was my beef with De and Tia stepped in to protect me. De died on the way to the hospital and Tia was just sentenced to fifteen years. The jury made Tia look awful and my heart really ached for her. She didn't deserve any of this, and I was to blame. All Tia wanted to do was protect me. Tia never blamed or hated me for being in this situation. Bryson paid for all her lawyer fees, and we made sure she was going to be taken care of while in prison.

Quitta couldn't be here because she went into labor early this morning. She was my only friend besides Tia, and I knew this was going to be a long fifteen years.

"You go ahead and pick up the girls." Bryson told me. "I'll meet you back at the house."

"Oh no! We have to go see Quitta. She probably had the baby already. I know she's terrified without anyone there with her."

"She's okay baby, Cal's at the hospital with her and he said she only dilated four centimeters. She not even close."

"It's okay babe, my sister don't mind keeping the girls this long. I'm going to go sit with Quitta. She needs me. I bet that baby daddy of hers didn't make it yet."

"Mel, he's on his way. I flew him out here. Don't worry babe. You can go later. Right now, you can at least rest for a while. You had a long day."

I sighed, finally giving up on trying to go see Quitta. "I guess. I do feel a little sick, but I'm not picking up the girls until later. I rather take a nap in peace."

Bryson put his hand on my small protruding three month along belly. "You better rest up. My boy needs his rest."

I smiled at Bryson. "I hope this one is a boy, cause this our last baby."

"We going to keep trying until I get my boy."

I slightly rolled my eyes knowing that he was the one that was wrong. I was making sure that this was my last baby. Four kids was enough, and there was nothing stopping me on getting the shot after this baby.

We had drove separately since Bryson had business before court and I had Tia with me. I knew Tia was going to get some time but I didn't know they would take her from me right then and there.

Soon as I got into my truck, I reapplied my makeup since I knew I looked a bit beat. I had been crying my eyes out in there and I wanted to refresh myself. When I started the truck, I remembered that I had needed gas earlier so I thought I get it now. I drove to the nearest gas station from the courthouse and got out. I walked inside to pay for my gas, but before then I went to the cooler to grab me something to drink. I stood in the cooler scanning all the waters and flavored waters, and couldn't decide on which one to get. Finally I looked towards the PowerAde and grabbed a red one. I turned around and seen Rakeem and a very attractive light-skinned woman who wore a cute asymmetric bob. I almost wanted to frown feeling a little salty that he went and found a woman who looked better than me. I was about to turn around and go down another aisle but he laid eyes on me.

"Mel?" He said as he walked towards me.

"Oh, hey Rakeem." I pretended to be very surprise.

I notice Rakeem look me up and down and I could see that same attractive smile I missed. He missed me too. "You look good."

"Thanks, uhhh….." I glanced over at the female who didn't even smile at me, but then I thought who cares. "You look good too."

Rakeem finally pulled the woman into the conversation.

"Mel, this is my girl Jada."

"Hey." I spoke.

"Mel, is my brother Rasheed's ex. She still family though."

"Oh, okay. Hello Mel, nice to meet you."

She stepped forward and extended her hand to mine. I shook it and gave her a small smile.

"So, how's my girl's?" He asked.

"Good, getting big."

"I bet. It really would be nice to see them."

"Maybe soon. I had another baby girl. Ciara."

"Recently?"

"She's about six months old."

"Oh, I was afraid to ask if you were pregnant. You put on a little weight but definitely in the right places."

I could hear Jada clear her throat, but I didn't care. Rakeem was just admiring his old fling.

"Well, I'm pregnant again." I announced.

I could hear the bitch clear her throat a second time. This time I looked over at her and rolled my eyes. I wanted it to be known that I didn't care for her. Rakeem then got the hint when he pulled her to the side and away from me. Whatever he said to her, she didn't like it one bit and gave him a small attitude. Her ass then walked away; probably to wait in the car. Soon as she was clear out the store, he immediately hugged me. I hugged him back tighter than I was soupose to, inhaling his fresh scent that he always had.

"Do you love him?" He asked me.

"What kind of question is that?"

"A very easy one. Do you?"

"Yes! I'm still with him, aren't I?"

"That don't mean shit Mel."

"I do love him. Are you still mad that I picked him over you?"

Rakeem slightly shook his head. I hit a nerve and it showed.

"What I got to be mad for?" He started in. "I do care about you and love you as a friend, but you could never be my woman. You're heartless, selfish, and you don't have shit going for yourself. That woman out there." He points towards the door. "My woman Jada has a teaching degree. She teaches first graders and I loved her enough to get off these streets. I'm not at my goal yet, but I'm doing big thangs Mel. I'm trying to be a legit man and live life without looking over my fucking shoulder every five minutes and dealing with this street drama. You need to straighten yourself up and quit letting that man keep my nieces away from me. That's all I want from you. I love them girls and you let him take them away just because of the hatred he has towards me."

"You really don't know shit Rakeem."

"No, you the one loving a man whose been sleeping with your best friend."

I hesitated as I looked at Rakeem suspiciously. "What are you talking about?"

"Don't tell me you don't know the obvious."

"Wait! Wait..." I shook my head. "What are you saying?"

"People laughing at your ass because you still with him. Quitta's been sharing your man for a couple of years now. As a matter of fact she had him first. I would've told you sooner except, you banded me from your life."

I felt like Rakeem was laughing at me and thinking a whole bunch of 'I told you so's', but he wasn't. I was just stupid and been played this whole time. Bryson had emotionally hurt me day in and day out, and I took every threat and name calling that he threw at me. I looked into Rakeem's eyes and seen the sympathy he had for me. I was humiliated and I wondered if Tia ever knew of this.

"He told me to go home." I wiped my tears away. "I wanted to be with Quitta. She's in labor right now and he told me to go home and rest."

"Quitta's pregnant?"

"We never seen or heard from the baby's daddy. You think its Bryson's baby?"

"It's only one way to find out. Go to the hospital."

I took in a deep breath. "I am!"

I was about to walk away from Rakeem, but then he grabbed me by the arm and pulled me back to him.

"I'm sorry I was so blunt with you. I do think you're better than what you persuade yourself to be. This is not you and I want to see you do better. You want us to roll with you to the hospital?"

"No, I better do this on my own. Thanks Rakeem."

I reached up and gave him a hug and a kiss on the cheek. When I pulled away I looked into his eyes and felt bad that I let a good man go. He did have a little dick but he got better and was working it later on. I could've dealt with that. He didn't make money like Bryson, but he did take care of me and my kids. I could've definitely dealt with that.

"Are you ever going to tell me about you and Bryson's differences? He really hates you and when I asked him about it, he gets real defensive."

"That's because he's...." Rakeem then shook his head. "It's difficult. I don't ever want to talk about it. Be careful Mel. I'm only a phone call away."

Rakeem pulled out a card and handed it over to me. I looked down at the card.

"You work at a cellular store?"

"It's a start for right now. I'm working on getting my own restaurant, but until then you should come by and let me hook you up with one them new cell phones."

"Thanks Rakeem, but I'll be fine."

I walked away with tears refilling my eyes. I even threw the bottle of PowerAde on the shelf and left out the store. I see Rakeem's girl Jada in the car staring at me. I walked to the car not even caring that my tears finally fell down my cheek. She faced me with her window down as if she was ready to get shit started, but I wasn't coming for that.

"It was nice meeting you Jada. Please take care of my friend. He speaks very highly of you. Rakeem deserves the best."

Her face softened. "I will make sure I treat him good. It was nice meeting you as well. You okay?"

"I will be when I confront my boyfriend."

"If you need anything, call us. Any friend of Rakeem's is a friend of mine. Sorry for any disrespect earlier. I thought you guys were on a different level."

"I'm sorry too. Take care."

"You too."

I took a deep breath and headed off to the hospital.

Chapter Nineteen

S oon as the nurse told me Quitta's room number and that she had a girl, I hauled ass to her room. I really couldn't believe Bryson lied to me. That only made me think the worse. He told me to go home and that only had to mean, his ass was here. If Bryson was in that room with her I was going to kill him.

As I got closer to the room, I could see that the door was open. I slowly crept up to the door and stood there. I closed my eyes for a quick second and opened them back up hoping that wasn't my man sitting at her bed side. The man that I thought I loved was interacting with my best friend. The baby lay in the glass bassinet not even getting any attention from neither of them. Whatever they were talking about had them in their own world. They didn't even see me. I quietly exhaled and put on my fake grin.

"A girl?" I walked in towards the bassinet.

Bryson thought he seen a ghost walk in and he jumped up off the edge of the hospital bed. Quitta just wore a pitiful look on her face. She was my best friend, but at that moment looking like a fat cow that I wanted to choke. This baby really made her look hideous. How could Bryson be with her when he had me?

"Mel! Shit! He slightly stuttered. "I thought you went home."

"I got the driving home and was thinking, why the hell would I be resting when my best friend was in labor. I couldn't do Quitta like that. But....hold up, I thought she was still in labor?"

Bryson looked somewhat relieved. "I got the call right after you left. Baby came out fast. I was just about to call you."

"Yeah Mel." Quitta chimed in. "I was just asking Bones about you. I'm so glad you're here."

I slightly rolled my eyes as I looked over at the beautiful bundle of joy laying in the bassinet. She was big but I couldn't tell who she looked like. She sure as hell was pretty light-skinned and Quitta was nowhere near that."

"Her name is Evelyn Marie." Quitta spoke.

"Evelyn?"

"Yes, like my godmother. You don't know her. She lives in Florida."

"Oh, what's her last name?" I smiled all fake and politely.

I notice Quitta kind of look at Bryson, but he looked away. Both they stupid asses never notice that I look on the ID card above the baby's head. Baby O'Neil. How convenient? Bryson O'Neil has the same last name.

"Oh, uh....I wasn't sure yet if I should give my baby mine or his." Quitta continued with the lie.

"And what is his?"

"Smith."

"José Smith? Humph....I thought he was Mexican."

The bitch continued lying to my face and I really wanted to choke the mess out of her and Bryson.

I got closer to the bassinet and picked up the baby. "Aww, she is so precious."

"She is." Quitta sighs. "I love her so much Mel."

I wanted to bite my tongue, but I really couldn't. This was such a terrible situation, and after Tip; I vowed to never play that stupid girl again. I knew Tip had another child outside of Natisha and I just played dumb. He ruined my life with all the cheating with multiple women, and I was not going to be another man's fool. NOMORE!

"Evelyn Marie O'Neil." I looked from Quitta to Bryson. "That's the baby name. I can see her fucking bracelet."

I watched as Quitta looked at Bryson, and Bryson slowly backs into the corner looking like he was trying to figure out his next move. He was busted, and although I wanted to leave and never run back into his arms, I knew I wasn't. Deep down, I knew I was going to be his fool. Why was I even confronting this? Bryson was my income and I needed him.

I kissed little Evelyn and put her back in her bassinet. Next, I punched Quitta in the face so hard, that I knew she was going to have a real bad black eye. I didn't want to have to do that with her baby there, but I hate her. I quickly left out the room as that bitch started screaming like I shot her in the face. I wasn't finish with her ass yet. I will hurt that girl so bad, and make sure she was out of me and Bryson's life.

Soon as I got close to my truck, I could hear Bryson call my name. I stopped and took in a deep breath before turning around. I wanted to punch him next, but I was afraid he'd punch me back. Bryson never laid a hand on me, but I was still afraid of him. His bark was tougher than his bite!

"Baby, that was a mistake." He explained.

I sighed and put my hand on my hip. I was ready to go crazy on him, but my emotions took over and I actually fell to the ground and began to cry with all my might. He got down with me and held me in his arms. I suddenly pushed him off.

"How the hell you get my best friend pregnant by mistake? She hooked us up and I specifically asked her if she was interested in you. If I knew she was, I would've never talked to you. Quitta urged me to get with you. Were you fucking her first?"

Bryson sighed. "No, not at first."

"What do you mean, not at first?"

"I was never interested in Quitta. I only wanted to help her, but when I started dating you, she came onto me one night at the office and I fell for it, but we told each other it would never happen again. About a year ago, she offered to put in more work for me. I needed a runner to run my shit to Miami. She was that person, and she was good. She was like a little ol' me. So, I put Quitta in charge of my spots in Miami. Money was good; it was like she knew my business better than I knew. We did a lot together with traveling and one thing led to another. We were always together Mel, and it just started to happen."

"So you love her? You love her because she do all the shit I could never do? She makes you money, and you sleep with her?"

He hesitates. "I love you Mel, and I mean that. I love you more than I love Quitta."

"But you do love that bitch? You all up in her face with ya'll new baby. You take her on vacations, and you leave me at home with all these kids. You is nasty! I don't even want you anymore. Quitta was a crack head and she sold her pussy. More men than I could ever count been up in her. She had kids by men who paid for her pussy. Then you go up in her raw? Then come back to me" I cry out loud. "I'll kill both of you if I have anything!"

I got up and opened my car door. Bryson was up and right there trying to stop me. He then suddenly grabbed me and turned me around facing him.

"I'm tired of playing this 'I'm sorry' role, and your stupid ass not getting it. Now you going to take yo ass home, take a fucking bath and chill out, go to sleep and when you wake up, all will be well. I will pick up the girls later and we will not bother you. I fucked up and got Quitta pregnant, but that is my daughter and she is here. YOU are going to deal with it. You're not leaving me!"

"You shoulda thought of all this before. I'm not sticking around. Fuck you and fuck your crack whore!"

I tried pulling away from him again, but he was stronger and he just pulled me back. I then slapped him hard in the face so he would let me go. That only added fuel, and he just pinned me up against the truck real hard. Bryson was everything bad except a woman beater. He will hurt me with words and never realize that hurt just as bad as a hit. Just that very moment, I swear he really wanted to knock my ass out. I stared him dead in the eyes daring him. He just don't know, I was use to this. After ten long seconds of stare down he finally backed off me and the mean scrawl on his face softened. I swear he was bipolar.

"I'm sorry Mel! I love you and you know I would never do anything to hurt you. I never been with any other woman. I don't go out fucking around because I really love you. Quitta was honestly a mistake that I kept falling for. She always initiated it, and baby I'm a man. Shit happens. I don't want her like that. You are all I need and you can't leave me. I love you too much, and you love me. We have a family."

I sighed as I shook my head at him. No words were needed as tears fell down my face. Stupid me got played! I let good men go thinking about money, but in the end I'm a dumb ass.

Bryson slowly backed away as I got into my truck and drove off.

Chapter Twenty

ardheaded and gullible was all I was. Time and time again I make these stupid choices. What the hell is wrong with me? A small tear fell down my flawless made up face as I sat in my truck with the police behind me. Why they pull me over anyway? I was going the speed limit, and Bryson checked my truck before I got on the road. Why me? Why fucking me when I had two bricks in my trunk?

So I stayed with Bryson after he got my best friend pregnant. So I made him keep her at a distance. She was no longer working at the real estate business, and he couldn't fire her from the drug business because she knew way too much. He had to keep that fat bitch around and play nice to her. I wanted her far away as possible so I was the stupid one who volunteered to make a few runs just to keep her away. Bryson didn't like the idea and actually said no at first, but then said my pregnant appearance would make me look innocent and they would never suspect me carrying anything. He was wrong, because they pulled me over for nothing. I have been doing this the past few months and it was actually easy. I never had to face anyone, but just drop it off at a certain location and in return there was to be money there. It felt like old times, back when I started this with Queen.

This was not soupose to happen. The police shouldn't have pulled over a beautiful very pregnant woman, but today they did. I really had no business running this shit when I was three weeks away from my due date. I quickly wiped the tears from my face as the officer approached my truck. Maybe he mistakenly pulled me over, I had hoped. All that went out the window when three more cruisers pulled up behind us. They knew something wasn't right. The first officer approached the window and had this shock look on his face when he looked at me. He seem to slightly hesitate.

"I'm sorry ma'am but I'm going to ask you to get out of your vehicle very slowly." He said to me.

"May I ask why you pull me over?"

"We have reason to believe that this vehicle transports drugs. Two weeks ma'am you have been watched, but they didn't say that you were pregnant."

"Are you serious? Why would you believe what you hear? I'm pregnant and do I look like I have drugs?"

"I'm sorry ma'am but this is just what I was called to do. They are about to search your vehicle and you will come over to my car and wait. Pregnant or not, you won't believe what kind of people they have transporting drugs just to throw us off."

I wanted to cry. I really did, but I couldn't. I had to stay strong and I had to get out of this. This officer was young and inexperienced, and I was scared shitless. How would they know all my business? Were they following me all this time? I swear I was being careful. Then a crazy thought entered my head. Quitta did this. She set me up so she can get rid of me. I know she did this. I tried to block that thought out my mind so I could get out of this jam. I let the scary face go and was ready to try and con this inexperienced officer with my charm.

"Please officer, I'm nine months pregnant. I would never have drugs around me. Did someone tell you these lies? Whoever is lying on me, should be checked out."

"Ma'am please. I'm only doing my job. You uhhh…Okay, maybe…."

Just as he was getting soft, two more officers finally got out of their cars and officer weak link finally got his balls back and got me out of my truck.

I was arrested after they found the two bricks of coke and $12,000 in the truck. Of course, I couldn't even look at officer weak link. I was nine months pregnant with drugs in my car. I was questioned like crazy but refused to say a word. Bryson didn't come when I called and that only angered me more. Then one of the detectives broke the ice when they called me the side bitch, and how Shaquitta was the main bitch. I was going to kill Quitta. If this was her way of getting rid of me, I refused to go. She was not going to take my spot and play mommy to my kids. I will kill her ass dead before that ever happens.

Chapter Twenty-One

I had my baby a week later. I finally had my baby boy and I was so proud. Darius James O'Neil was his name. I still haven't heard from Bryson and that hurt me so bad. I had to spend the entire week in jail, and then to go in labor in this hell was horrible. Queen had come to see me and I was surprised that she had my girls and not Bryson. I was glad Queen was still there for me but I didn't want her to have my girls. Quitta was her daughter and I did not want that bitch anywhere near them. I really had no choice because my sister couldn't afford to take them, and my mother was many miles away. None of my brothers were stable except one but he lived way down south. Queen had to take them and now she was going to take Darius. I had to go back to jail tomorrow and that devastated me. I wanted to breastfeed Darius, but if I had to go back, I was not pumping milk from a cell. They wanted me to snitch on Bryson and tell everything I know. Quitta's dumb ass set all this up trying to get rid of me, but in the end she was ruining Bryson. The police knew Bryson was the orchestrater of it all, but they needed proof. All week I held my tongue and refused to talk. Even after Bryson never answered my calls or came to see me, I was still loyal to him. My court appointed lawyer told me not to talk, and I wasn't. Something in me changed today. As I lay in this hospital bed with an officer at my door, I actually contemplated it all. Bryson hasn't even reached out to me, didn't even bother to send me a good lawyer. I had his only son and he not once came to see us. I pushed the call button, and my nurse came right away.

"Do you need anything?" She asked me.

"Is Detective Wilson still here?" I asked her back.

"As a matter of fact, he's right at the door asking if you were feeling okay. I think he has questions for you. If you don't want to answer them,

I will tell him that you're resting. They shouldn't be bothering you while you're trying to bond with your son."

"I know, but I need to get this over with. Can you send him in?"

"Sure thing."

I let out a few more tears as the nurse left me, and seconds later Wilson was taking a seat to my left. He's the one that's been questioning and pressuring me all week. He had even spoke with my lawyer about plea deals before I even went to court.

"You have a beautiful son." The detective spoke. "I saw him out in the nursery."

"Thanks."

"You uh…thought about what we talked about?"

"Only two years?" More tears fell as I thought of doing time.

"Yes."

"Is there any way I can get house arrest? I have four children and I need to be with them."

"I understand, but what you had is a life sentence. We all know they weren't yours but you still had them in your possession. Two years is better than twenty. I can get you out today if you do talk. You be out for a good two months. Maybe more before they sentence you. It will be your boyfriend that will be going down. He will get the real punishment. With good behavior you may serve less than two years."

"Uuggghh, I don't want to do this."

"Where is he? Has he even seen that beautiful baby? As we speak, he could be far away somewhere with this other woman. You were going to take the fall."

"She has to go down too. She's his partner."

"No problem. We'll get shit on her too."

"You promise me that I only get the minimum amount of time. I have to be there for my kids."

Detective Wilson pulled out his recorder. "You'll get the best deal. Now tell me everything you know about Bryson O'Neil aka 'Bones'."

Chapter Twenty-Two

Three months later

The trial was finally over. It was long and stressful, and I promised God I'd never go down that path again. Bryson hates me. When I see him in the courtroom I keep my head down. I could never look him in the eye. His face was angered and I felt bad that I had to put him away. They have been investigating Bryson for a while; way before I was helping him. They actually tricked me and turned him against me. All they wanted from me was my testimony to really stick it to him. They had already had an inside snitch who knew everything including our personal lives. I even told all I knew about Quitta but they couldn't hold anything against her. They had no evidence that she was ever involved. Everything was a lie, even they told me that Quitta set me up. Here I am looking like the stupid snitch that I am. He hates me and he loves her. If only I could talk to him and tell him how Quitta started this all. She set me up to get me out the picture, except it all backfired and put the man we both love away. He was sentence to 20 years for all that they had on him. My testimony locked it in and I'm sure Bryson wants to kill me now. I was able to spend all my time with my family and my kids throughout this whole trial. It just sucks that I have to turn myself in Monday which is in four days. They end up giving me 18 months and I should be grateful, but I wasn't. I didn't want to leave. All I cared about was watching my kids grow up. I was going to miss them.

Today, me and my kids were at Chucky Cheese waiting on Rakeem and Jada, Throughout the whole trial and my sentencing they both were good supporters. I was glad to have friends on the side besides my family who I expected to be there. Rakeem and Jada agreed to have temporary custody of my kids while I was gone. My mom agreed at first, but I really didn't want them that far away from me. I was surprised when Rakeem volunteered. He loved my kids and I trusted him and Jada to take care of them.

As I took little Darius out the car seat Rakeem and Jada walks in. I watched as Tisha and Rasheeda run up to them. Little Cici was at my feet as always. She was spoiled and didn't like anyone else in her face. I had to get her out of that since I was going to be gone. Jada instantly came over and scooped her up. She didn't cry, just wiggling around trying to get out of Jada's arms.

"Oh....not today little girl!" Jada spoke to Cici. "You going to play with me."

Jada sat in the booth across from me and Rakeem moved in next to her with Tisha and Rasheeda all over him.

"How's it going Mel?" He asked me.

"I'm scared." I sighed.

"I know. Rasheed asked about you."

"Was he laughing at me when he asked?" I sarcastically asked.

"Nah Mel, my brother really has love for you. I know you don't want to believe that but he does. He's just upset."

"I know he hates me. You don't have to lie."

"Girl, quit being so down. You really lucky yo' ass only received eighteen months."

"He's right Mel." Jada chimed in. "Lots of women who been in your shoes be serving five to twenty-five years."

"I'm just glad you away from that..." Rakeem then stopped and looked at the kids. "I need to tell you. I should've told you long ago."

"Tell me what?"

"It's deep," He then looked at Jada. "Baby, can you take the girls to play."

"Sure."

Rakeem got up to let Jada out and she took the kids away to play. Rakeem sat back down and looked me in the eyes.

"Bryson is my half-brother." He admitted.

My heart sunk to my stomach and my jaw dropped.

"You and Bryson didn't want me to know this? And why? You should've told me Rakeem. I wouldn't have dared mess around with him. It was bad enough that I was with two brothers, but three?"

Rakeem lowered his brow and I looked away for a moment. My eyes were glued to Jada playing with the girls. I like Jada and she has no idea that Rakeem and I were together, and I hope to keep it that way. It was not her business to know.

"I just wish you told me." I said as I looked back at him.

"Rasheed and I have the same parents. Bryson just shares our father. He was raised by him, we wasn't."

"But, I don't understand why you hate Bryson so much. Bryson hates you, but why not Rasheed?"

"I am the oldest, Rasheed, then Bryson. They are only three months apart. Our father was always in the drug game and although he didn't live with Rasheed and I, he was there grooming us both to be just like him. Especially me. He would always tell us that Bryson was different. He was in the books and he wanted him to succeed out in the world. There was nothing wrong with that and I agreed with him. I kept Bryson away from the streets, even when he tried hanging with Rasheed, I would put a stop to that instantly. We all grew up and Bryson was in college; but while he was away, he was very envious of our relationship with our father. He wanted what Rasheed and I had, but Bryson never understood that he had it better than us. My father was murdered a few years back. I started taking care of everything in the streets. Rasheed was my right hand man, and Bryson was just building his real estate business. I thought all was good. My father had Bryson set with that business, and a month after his passing some phony ass will pops up. What drug dealer has a will? Come to find out, my father had land, houses, and stocks that I never knew about. We all met in the lawyer's office and this phony will says that my father left me and Rasheed nothing, while Bryson got it all. I was angry but I left thinking I had his streets. The connect cut me off, and was only dealing with Bryson. Bryson never sold drugs a day in his life and all of a sudden he stole the 'from me. So, at the end of the day me and Rasheed was left with nothing and started all over. As I investigated that snake, I found out more than I ever wanted to know. Bryson was greedy and wanted it all. He had our father killed and took control of my father's lifestyle, and forged all his documents to go to him. Rasheed don't know any of this and it would hurt to tell him. Bryson knows that I know the truth, and there are times I want to choke the shit out of him, but I don't. I just keep my distance. I never trusted him and didn't want you around him, but who was I to tell you who to date."

"You let me be with someone like that. If I knew who he really was, I wouldn't have been with him."

"Really? I doubt that."

I slightly sighed knowing that Rakeem was still angry over how I picked Bryson over him. Rakeem had really loved me for me but I was greedy and choose money over him.

"I'm sorry Rakeem." I apologized.

"No need Mel. I'm sorry for not telling you. Just keep your head up and let Bryson go. He won't hurt you, and his soldiers are not loyal to him, so he can't get anyone to hurt you."

"Thanks." I smiled feeling somewhat better. "So, you and Jada keep the girls for a few hours while I take Darius to his doctor appointment?"

"Of course."

"Okay." I started to put Darius back in his car seat. "I think I'm going to leave now. Are you guys staying here a little longer?"

"Oh yeah, as a matter of fact we might be here when you finish the appointment."

"I bet you will. You love playing these little kiddie ass games."

"I do."

We both shared a laugh, and I stood up getting ready to leave. I looked down at Rakeem and for a moment we locked eyes and I almost wanted to cry. I really messed up my life, and Jada had the best thing that could've happened to me. I quickly looked away and picked up Darius car seat. Jada and the girls made it back over by then.

"Before I forget." Jada started. "I thought it be a good idea to throw Cici her first birthday party Saturday. That way you can be there. I know you didn't have a chance since the trial and all."

"I love the idea. Just let me get the cake and help decorate. I had a few ideas before all this hell started."

"Great, we can go shopping later on today."

"I be back right after Darius doctor appointment. We can go then."

"Alright."

Jada leaned down to the car seatl and smothered my baby boy with kisses. The girls copied and wanted to do the same. I finished bundling Darius, and grabbed my purse and diaper bag. I kissed each of my girls and of course Jada had to peel Cici off me. I was about to take her too, but two babies in a doctor office was too much. I really felt bad as she cried when I left out of Chucky Cheese. I knew this was really going to be hard leaving my kids on Monday.

Darius fell asleep soon as I got on the road. I turned up Mary J Blige and began singing as I drove a few more miles. I was feeling good and in my own world as I pulled up to a red light. I continued vibeing to the beat until a black car with tinted windows pulled up beside me like they was crazy. The window rolled down and it was Quitta.

"Fucking snitch ass bitch!" She yelled out the window. "This is for my man Bones!"

It was so quick, but soon as I seen her automatic rifle, my foot hit the gas. I felt the burning sensation, but before I could react my truck took a bad crash, and everything around me went black.

Chapter Twenty-Three

When I awoke, all I felt was pain. It felt as if I was hit by a semi-truck, and every slight movement killed me. I tried blinking my eyes a couple of times to come into focus, and look around my surroundings. After a few minutes I finally realized that I was in a hospital with tubes and IV's stuck all in me. My neck was stiff, and I then realized it was held in a brace. I could feel my left arm in a cast, and there were bandages wrapped throughout my body. Something was wrong and it took me a while to finally realize the last place I was before I woke up in this hospital. Soon as I realized that my truck had been shot up and crashed I began to panic. I quickly tried locating the call button, but I was in so much pain trying to reach it. I was mad they had a nurse call button out of reach. When I tried to speak it was barely above a whisper. My throat was beyond dry and it hurt. Tears formed in my eyes as I thought of the worse. Where was Darius? He was in the truck with me.

Finally after fifteen minutes of trying to speak out, my sister Debbie walked in with my brother Jerome. Debbie instantly ran to my bedside seeing that I was woke. My brother left out and I could hear him yelling 'She's up!'

"Where's Darius?" Was the first thing I asked my sister.

Just as Debbie was about to speak Jerome came back in with a nurse.

"Well good morning dear." She started checking my vitals and blood pressure. "A lot of people will be happy to see that your awake. You've had many visitors."

The nurse looked over at Debbie and Jerome who was close to my bedside. "Just let me finish checking her out and then I'll leave to call Dr. Abrams.

I watched as Debbie and Jerome backed up, and instantly Debbie let out a cry. She tried to hide it, but it was too late. I see her cry and it was hard. Jerome pulled her into his arms and I felt bad for getting hurt.

"I'm okay you guys." I tried soothing them. "Stop crying. Where's my kids?"

I slightly smiled knowing that they were in good hands.

"We thought you'd never wake up." Debbie explained.

Yeah, mom went down to the chapel to pray on a daily basis." My brother added. "We thought we had lost you."

"How long was I out for?"

Debbie and Jerome looked at each other. I then looked at the nurse for answers.

"Four weeks exactly." The nurse confirmed.

"Are you serious? But how? Was it that bad, and where's Darius? Did he get hurt? He was in the car with me. Quitta did this! She tried to kill me!"

The nurse finished up and gave me a very uncomfortable smile. I then notice her look over at my brother and sister.

"I need to call Dr. Abraham. I'll be back shortly."

Soon as the nurse left, Jerome walked over and poured me some water.

"Drink." He held it to my mouth. "You feeling alright though?"

I took one last swallow and looked up at Jerome. He didn't look himself. I could tell that outgoing crazy brother of mine was going through hell these past few weeks. His eyes told a story of pain and hurt, and I was the one that put it there. Quitta will pay for trying to kill me.

"Jerome." I spoke. "Please talk to me. Where is Darius?"

"Darius…." My brother squeezed my hand and I see a tear slip out. I never seen Jerome cry. Not even at my daddy's funeral. "Darius didn't make it."

"Noooooo!" I screamed.

"One of the bullets hit the baby Mel. He died instantly."

Soon as I was finish screaming, I bit down on my bottom lip real hard. I could taste the blood that I drew from my lip. My heart was broken, and there was no way I could take the loss of my baby boy. Debbie stood on the other side of me trying to soothe me. Jerome continued holding onto my hand.

"Where is she?" I said through clenched teeth.

"They caught her Mel." Jerome spoke. "She's going to pay for what she did."

"I hope that bitch dies a slow painful death!"

"She will get what's coming to her. Don't think about her right now. We're happy you made it through."

"They let Bryson out to see you." Debbie changed the subject "He sat by your bedside for a little."

"They let him out to see me? He actually wanted to see me?"

"He was out for Darius funeral. They then let him come see you. He was sad Mel. He didn't have anything to do with Quitta trying to take you out. I could tell. He was very hurt."

I sat silently trying to take in the death of my baby boy. Fuck Bryson! He didn't come see Darius when he was born. I could care less about his ass. How was I going to move on? I lost my son, and there was no pain greater than the loss of your child.

Chapter Twenty-Four

Two Weeks later

I recovered pretty well. My arm was in a cast, but other than that I was out of the hospital. Tomorrow I start my sentencing but today I was allowed to have a visit with Bryson. I needed to see him, and wanted to hear from his mouth that he had nothing to do with Shaquitta's shootout.

I was nervous as I sat in the waiting room. Looking around at the other inmates had me on edge. Tomorrow about this time, I'll be where he is. I was not looking forward to that, but I had to hurry and get these 18 months over with. He finally walked in, looking everywhere else but my way. When he finally laid eyes on me, I watched his face frown with pity. He sat across from me and rubbed his hands together. I knew he hated me. I would hate me. He was doing twenty years because of me. Why was I here?

"You alright?" He asked me.

"NO." I rolled my eyes. "I hurt real bad, and I needed closure."

"Closure? How the fuck am I going to give you closure?"

"Did you send Quitta after me?" I went right in.

"I had nothing to do with Quitta's stupid ass. She killed my son Mel, and although your snitch ass did me wrong, I still love the hell out of you. I would never wish death upon you. I just wish you had my back like I had yours. I'm locked up with fucking Rasheed. He up in here talking shit about you, and I'm defending you like you should've defended me."

"I did have your back." I cried to him. "I always stood by you. They just backed me in the corner. I had to for my kids."

"Our kids!" He corrected me. "I may be on the inside, but I will always be a part of our kid's life. I can still take care of them from here. They my heart Mel and although you betrayed me, you my heart too."

I sighed. "So, you really had nothing to do with that?"

"I said NO!" He slightly yelled. "I wasn't talking to Quitta anyway. It's her fault we got into this; and while you were too busy snitching on me, she was stealing. She slipped back and started up again."

"She need to rot in prison, and where is Evelyn?"

"Queen took the baby."

I shook my head.

"Do you hate me?" I asked after a long pause.

"Of course I fucking hate you!" Spit flew out his mouth as anger rose back up again.

"You do understand that they was going to lock you up anyway. You were being watched. You were reckless, greedy and careless. That shit wasn't cut out for you Bryson. It was probably karma from stealing the throne from Rakeem."

He looked at me with devil eyes. I knew I hit a soft spot and if these guards weren't around his hands probably would've been around my neck. He breathed heavily for a minute and I could tell he was finding the right words to say to me. Then out of nowhere he looked away. When he looked back at me, he took a deep breath and I could tell he had calmed down.

"Shut the fuck up about that?" He whispered harshly.

"It's true, isn't it?"

"Quit talking to his buster ass."

"Is he your brother? Him and Rasheed."

"Yes, now shut your ass up about that shit. You shouldn't be talking crazy in these walls anyway."

"Why do you hate your brother so much anyway?"

Bryson smirked. "You really won't shut up?"

"I deserve to know, so answer me."

"Your answer going to hurt!"

"I'm already hurt."

Bryson looked around before moving closer to whisper to me. "$80,000 he stole from me. I let it go, only because I stole it first."

He quickly sat back and shook his head. He seem to feel relieved about it, and I was about to speak until he leaned in again.

"I found out he feel in love with this woman. I pursue the only woman he's ever loved to get back at him. The same woman that he had no business falling in love with because she was already taken. I try to take her, and she takes the bait. I steal her from him. I didn't even care that I was seeing another woman, I wanted what he wanted."

It took me a minute to process what he said, but when I did I wanted to flip out. "You asshole!"

He finally sat back in his chair. "I was really seeing Quitta before you. She knew the deal and all we really was doing was having sexual relations. She was cool because at first she didn't have feelings for me. It was only sex. We were friends with benefits. I did fall in love with you Mel. I left Quitta alone, but then she got pregnant."

"You are a snake."

I stood up and looked down at Bryson. "That's why I gave your big brother custody of the kids."

Bryson jumped up. "What!?"

I was hurt so I had to hurt him back. Bryson did love those kids. All the brothers did. They all had that in common. They were all good fathers. The security calmed Bryson down before he really went crazy. I really didn't leave with closure, just an open heart and to me that was better. I will forever hate Quitta and pray that pain comes to her. Although I wanted Bryson to hurt, I will keep in contact with him. He did me wrong, I did him wrong; but damn he was looking sexy as hell and I still love him. Why do I have for all these bad men in my life?

Chapter Twenty-Five

Three Months Later

I continued filing my nails with the small wooden file while looking around. I rolled my eyes to myself as I listened to Tia's sex noises. Every Thursday at 3:15 pm she met with Tamar in the maintenance shop. I was their look-out girl, but them loud noises she be making going to get us all in trouble. I put on my headphones to drown them out and immediately started bopping my head to some mix CD that Rakeem had made for me. I was so into the CD that I never heard the CO stepping up to me. He snatched the earphones off my head and stood tall over me.

"What the hell you doing back here?" He yelled.

I was scared and didn't know what to say. I been at this prison for three months and never seen this CO before. He was a tall white man that seem to have tattoos all over his body. I could see some peeking out moving up towards his neck, and his sleeves was rolled up showing two full tatted up sleeves. At first glance, I thought he looked like the singer Jon B as fine as he was. I just knew I was in trouble but all I could do was inhale his cologne scent. I couldn't believe they hired this tatted up fine CO. Tamar and this Jon B look alike are two of the finest CO's I have ever encountered. We women be craving for sex, and they throw men like them at us. They wonder why we harass them all. Tia was one of the lucky ones, and that's why her fast ass was in the maintenance shop right now.

"Who you come down here with?" He asked me.

"No one, I just like to come down here to dance."

"Dance?" I watched as his eyes roamed my body but then he looked back up to my face.

"Yes, I'm not doing anything wrong."

"You know the shop is closed on Thursday's."

I wanted to say, 'duh, that's why I'm down here.'

"Yes, and I need peace. I just had to get away from all the madness out there. This is, uh....where I like to hang out"

Just then, the door flew open and Tamar stood there zipping up his pants. Surprisingly, the white boy got happy and almost gave Tamar a hug until he realized what was going on.

"Still being nasty?" White boy stated. "Where Tia at?"

Tia popped from behind Tamar and waved. "Hey Matt. How's the leg?"

"Much better. I see Tamar don't know how to leave the inmates alone."

"Just me!"

"So, why haven't you called me, or tell me you was coming back?" Tamar questioned.

"I didn't know I was coming back. I was trying to quit, but I needed this job so I'm back. I hate to come here and see Celina's crazy ass."

"Yeah, your bitch still causing trouble."

"Celina? The warden?" I was shocked.

Celina was a bitch and we all knew it. She was a pain in everyone's ass including the CO's. She was a very beautiful Latina woman, but her attitude made her look uglier than ugly. I could be nice to that bitch and she'd still find something to hate me for. There was something else about her and it wasn't legit. Celina was involved in something illegal but we could never pin point what she did when she wasn't here. Lately, her ass been on pins and needles about something. Something was scaring her and I hope I find out so I could use it against her.

"Are you close with Celina?" I asked the CO.

He looked at Tamar then back at me. "No."

Tamar and Tia busted out in a laughter

"What?" I was clueless.

"Matt is Celina's favorite so don't let her catch you talking to him." Tia explained.

I looked at Matt and his blushing told it all. No need to explain.

"So, you a newbie?" Matt changed the subject

"She my best friend!" Tia answered for me. "We were best friends before this hell hole."

"Oh." He looked at me weird. "The same best friend you murdered for?"

"You guys talked about me?" I interrupted them.

"I bragged about you." Tia pulled me into a hug.

"So what did you do newbie?" Matt asked me. "Did you miss her that bad, so you had to go murder someone too?"

"No! I only got about a couple years, so it wasn't nothing."

Matt smirked. "You did some stupid shit and don't want me to know, but you know I'm a find out right? Now let's go ladies! Back on top!"

Tia turned to Tamar and through her tongue down his throat, and then we ran back up to our cell rooms. These last three months, time here wasn't easy, and will never be without my kids. On the social side, I couldn't complain. I had my best friend with me and we were a team. I thank God she was with me every day because we did share a cell together. We were both financially taking care of by Rakeem, so we really couldn't complain. Tia had already made a name for herself here, so with me by her side, I was soon respected and loved. Don't get me wrong, I was pretty much tested a few times, but I showed out. I never played around with any bitch and one has never got in my way, so they won't stop me now. When Tia first told me her love for Tamar, I was scared and I didn't like it. I heard too many stories about women getting caught up in that and it never ends well. Then I got to know Tamar and I really ended up liking him. I wished he was there before all of this. Tia would've been so happy.

Matt was a good friend of Tamar's. I found out that Matt started here not too long before I came. Then all of a sudden he hurt his leg and had to take a few months off. Tia never mentioned him before this, but all of a sudden she wants to talk about him, and it's strange. Literally, Tia thinks he's very suspicious. She says he gets hired as a CO, but seems to be in love with Celina, but fronts in front of the inmates and pretends not to like her. So, the next few weeks after that run in, I began to watch Matt very carefully. He was often seen spying on Celina and I thought Tia was probably right. Maybe Matt had this secret obsession with her and didn't want any of us to know because she was evil. Although, I hated that he had his eye on another woman, I actually admired the man. There were times that I found myself lusting over him. Most of the women here did. He was irresistible. Woman usually flirted with Tamar and Matt, but Matt constantly never succeeded in the challenge. Tamar on the other hand only had eyes for Tia, but tried not to show it. Matt and I were the only ones who knew of their secret relationship. These crazy bitches around here would hate and spoil it all. Tamar never gave Tia special treatment, but treated her like he treated us all.

The prison that I was in was pretty minimum. It wasn't as bad as I thought before I got there. Of course we had our strict rules, but I still got to roam the prison as if it was a little town. Tia and I cell was our home and we tried to make it homie as possible. It wasn't the best, but I was at comfort with it. As long as we didn't cause any trouble or break any rules, they didn't bother us. Of course food was horrible and I tried living off of ramen noodles and junk food that Rakeem sends me. He sends me new pics every month of the kids and I cherish them. Now, ShaQuitta was in another prison serving harder time than I thought she would. The bitch killed a child of mine and I was glad she was getting the ultimate punishment. Her time was nowhere near as comfortable as me and Tia's.

I lay on my bed writing in my journal that I never miss a day of. Tia suddenly rushes into our room out of breath and she immediately sits on the edge of my bed.

"Girl, what's wrong with you?" I said as I sat my journal down.

I stared at Tia as she tried catching her breath and gather her thoughts. Then out of the blue, tears began to form in her eyes. I quickly sit up and scoot closer to her.

"What's wrong? Did something happen?"

Just before she could answer, Tamar stood in the entrance of our room.

"Jefferson." He called her by her last name as he does every inmate. "You need to come with me."

He was too formal and I knew something wasn't right.

"What's going on?" I stood up.

"Just Jefferson!" He shouted.

"Everything okay. She's crying."

Tia finally stood and faced me. "I'm okay Mel, don't worry."

"Are you sure? I'll go with you."

"I said just Jefferson!" Tamar yelled a second time. "Let's go!"

Tia left me and I watched them walk out. Other women heard the yelling and started gathering around asking questions. I was just as clueless as they were. Suddenly everyone seem to go back to their rooms as if something spooked them. That's when I looked to the corner and see Celina staring me down. That bitch was waiting for Tia and that wasn't good at all. I was confused as I watched Tamar walk my friend away with Celina following behind.

The next morning, I woke up and looked to Tia's empty bed. I knew something was wrong now. A whole day has gone by and Tia wasn't back. Soon as it was breakfast, I looked around the room for Moe who was also Tia's friend. When I spotted her, I took my breakfast over to her table and sat down. Her and her crew only got along with me because I was down with Tia. Other than that, I knew they didn't like me. I was actually risking my ass trying to speak to them without Tia, but I didn't care. They may be tougher, but I wasn't scared.

"Whass up Moe?" I then looked over at Tammy and Cheryl. "Hey."

"What's going on Mel?" Moe spoke back.

"Lost without cha' girlfriend Tia!" Tammy chimed in and her and Cheryl busted out laughing.

Moe looked at Tammy as if she was going to smack the shit out of her for speaking our friend's name.

"What happened?" I was only talking to Moe. "Tamar and Celina came to get her yesterday, and it had to be serious. Celina don't leave that comfy office for no one. Where's Tia?"

"So, you wasn't with her when it happened? We heard it was you." Moe said.

"What are you talking about?"

I watched as Moe looked to Tammy and Cheryl. Them too bitches started whispering shit, and then Moe looked back at me.

"Well, I guess that tells us why you're not in the hole, and she is. Who the fuck was she with then?"

"Maybe she was alone." Tammy giggled.

"What are you guys talking about?" I got worried. "They put Tia in the hole? What for?"

"Word is….Celina's slick ass went to the mechanic shop looking for her lover boy Matt. He was soupose to have a crew down there working but somehow it was cancelled and Tia was in there butt ass naked. If some other girl was in there, she got away. Tia won't tell anyone who it was. At first we thought it was Matt, but Matt was gone. He tricked Celina into thinking he had a crew in the shop today. So, maybe it was another inmate?"

"Ya'll be diking?" Tammy asked me. "Maybe it was you, and you over there playing dumb. You wrong for letting her take all the blame. Just like you did when she killed that bitch for you."

"Fuck you Tammy! My friend no dike bitch so don't go spreading rumors about her."

"Mel," Moe interrupted. "She going to be in there for like a month, maybe longer until Celina think she can break her. Celina mad she couldn't catch the other woman."

"How do you guys know it's another woman?" I was getting mad they thought that.

"Well duh bitch!" Tammy started up again. "Who else she mucking? Barry and Jim too old and out of her league. Tamar and Matt too conceited and stuck up. They too good to fuck with us. The rest of the CO's are women who are straight and can go home every night to a man. So that only leaves female inmates her choice."

I rolled my eyes knowing the truth, so I had no time to waste listening to their pettiness. Tamar was the one down there and I was mad that he let my girl take the fall by herself. Besides, yesterday was Monday and they knew any day but Thursday at three was risky. What were they thinking?

I left the table leaving my food to Moe like I always did. I went back to my room and waited for Tamar to come in on his shift at 2. On my way, I ran into Matt. We caught each other's glance and I quickly looked away without saying hi. I tried walking past him but he grabbed my arm.

"Can't speak lady?" He said to me.

"I'm sorry, I was in a rush."

"To go where." I notice him smirk.

"My room."

"What's in your room?"

"Nothing."

"Then why you rushing past me?"

I didn't want to smile but he was making me blush. "You do ask a lot of questions."

Matt smiled back, but then an inmate past by and I notice his smile tones down.

"Well, uh….I better go."

"I'm handling Tia. Don't ask me any questions but I'll have her back to you soon. Don't say a word to anyone about this."

"Uh…okay."

He then smiled again. "You know you too beautiful to be in here."

"Thanks." I blushed. "I guess."

"You don't mind me complimenting you do you?"

"No, it's nice to know that I'm still pretty in prison."

"Gorgeous!" He then clears his throat. "See you around."

Matt then walks off leaving me there speechless. I stood there for a moment watching his sexiness walk away.

"Keep them fucking eyes in that dumb ass head of yours." I heard her voice.

I turned around and Celina was there with that hand on her hip.

"I'm just looking." I snapped at her. I wasn't scared of her ass like most women. I hated her and I knew she had the upper power but I was not scared of her.

"Well, that's all you better do." Celina then leans in to whisper in my ear. "That's my dick! Something your pretty little ass won't see for a while."

She then backs away and looks me up and down.

"Let me find out you were in the maintenance shop last night with your girlfriend. I know how tight you two are."

"I would never!"

"So you say."

Celina walked away switching her skinny little ass. Suddenly she stops and looks back.

"You probably enjoying the view of me walking away." She said as she winked at me.

My blood was boiling inside, but I had to stay cool. Bitch ass Celina likes to push us so she can punish us. She was everyone's worse nightmare and I really don't care for her. I bet she was weak and uses this job to get power. I don't know how Matt can even sleep with a woman like her. Celina was far from ugly, and she had that exotic tan, Latina accent and full beautiful lips that mesmerized you when she spoke. That attitude was ugly so that made her unattractive. Matt was always sneaking around and thinking we all don't know he into her, but I will bust them out one day. I don't know what it is about Matt but in a strange sort of way, I was jealous that he wanted Celina.

I spotted Tamar around four o'clock talking with Matt. Matt seem to always be here working a lot of hours. I swear he was up to more than catching up on work. Something was going on with Matt and it was more to it than we all know.

"Hey Tamar, can I talk to you?" I walked up on them two.

Matt stood back and I notice his eyes roam through my body. I tried not to pay attention to him or his sexiness but it was hard. Tamar then grabs me roughly by the arm.

"Not here!" He said. "Come on."

Matt followed me and Tamar to a nearby room where'd we have a little more privacy to talk. For a second I was a bit nervous to be in the same room as my friend's sex partner and sexy Matt who seem to drool over me when I walk by.

Matt closed and locked the door behind himself. He stood near it as if he was guarding. I looked around the small room noticing it was more like a room where they kept inventory of things.

"What's up Mel?" Tamar seem to lick his lips, and I suddenly became very uncomfortable. For a second I thought these two men was going to rape me.

"So, were you with Tia yesterday?" I asked.

"Yeah, but everything is cool. No need to worry. You'll have her back in the morning."

I looked back at Matt and knew he had something to do with this. Celina wouldn't let this go.

"I told you, I got this Mel." He smirked.

I was relieved. "Everyone talking shit thinking my friend was in there with another woman, possibly me. I don't like that."

"Do you want me to get fired and your friend to get transferred?"

"No!"

"Everything's good Mel. They was going to give her 30 days. I looked out for my girl."

Matt cleared his throat.

"Okay, so Matt helped me." Tamar corrected himself.

"And what the hell happened to only Thursday's?" I asked.

"Temptation."

I could hear Matt slightly laugh. I turned around and he shrugged his shoulders. I tried ignoring him and turned my attention back to Tamar.

"I better go, and I better see Tia tomorrow. You guys really need to be more careful."

"Thanks for your concern, now get your ass back out there." He said in his stern CO voice.

I smiled at Tamar and turned away. Matt stood in front of the door and raised his left eyebrow, and he began to bite on his bottom lip in a sexy way. I swear I was going to go crazy tonight dreaming of this man.

"Excuse me." I blushed.

"I bet you had every man wrapped around your finger."

I was about to speak until I realized his voice sounded different. I felt this the first time he spoke but couldn't really tell. Matt was definitely hiding something. He had let an accent sneak out of his vocabulary. He was good hiding it, but I bet he will get weak one day and the true colors will show. Who was this man Matt that I think I had a crush on?

Chapter Twenty-Six

Eight months later

The scene was described horrific and nothing you'd hear about in real life. One of the CO's got ahold of pictures and I actually seen it. She was tortured and beaten really bad. I hated her but I would never want to see anything like that happen. Who would hate Celina that much to torture and kill her? It's been two weeks since her murder and they were nowhere with leads. No one around here moped and cried over her, but we all felt some type of way. It was weird. Not even Matt seemed sad. He was the same Matt that I actually grown to fall in love with. If anyone knew Matt, it was me. Matt was a really good friend of mine. He was sweet to me and actually bought me little gifts that weren't noticeable. We were really careful about our friendship because when we were around each other, you'd know cause we both would glow. Matt was really special to me and made these past few months fly by. He came to work almost every day just to spend time with me and I appreciated every moment. One thing we didn't do was sneak off and have sex. I won't lie, I really wanted to and it wasn't because I was horny. I really wanted to give myself to Matt and make love to him, even if it was in a closet or maintenance shop. I just could never make the first move or express that to Matt. I knew Matt wanted me, but I guess he thought I was too good to sneak around with. At least that's what I was hoping.

"I have a letter for you." I heard his voice.

Tia and I both looked up to see Matt standing in our doorway. I smiled as he walked into our room and sat on the edge of the bed.

"What are you doing?" I panicked knowing he wasn't soupose to get this comfortable with the inmates.

"Just open it." He handed me the letter.

I took the envelope out of his hand and ripped the letter open. I read the first couple of sentences and then looked up at Tia with wide eyes.

"What it say?" Tia jumped off her bed and ran over to mine sitting on the opposite side of me.

She looked at the letter and then looked at me.

"But how?" She asked. "Oh shit Mel, you're getting out."

I smiled. "I know, like tomorrow."

"But how?" She looked over at Matt.

"You're not as easy Tia, but I'll get you out too. Give me a couple a couple months top."

Tia quickly stood up with shock. "What did you say?"

"Sshhhh." Matt looked around. "Don't speak to anyone about this. Just know that you're getting out too. Just give me a little time."

I looked over at Matt and into his pretty blue eyes. "Who are you?"

"Your friend."

"I'm serious Matt. There is something about you, but I can't quite put my finger on it yet. You always seem to have a connection."

Matt grabbed my hand and looked me sincerely in the eyes. "In due time Mel. This will be the last time you will see me for a while. The next time I see you; we will be alone in a beautiful place where I can make love to you. I will find you Mel, so don't worry."

Matt then stood up and smiled at me leaving me speechless. He then looked to Tia.

"Tia, I will see you soon as well. Just be patient."

Matt then walked out leaving us both to wonder who he really was. Soon as he was all the way gone, Tia and I hugged each other and quietly celebrated us going to freedom.

Rakeem was waiting for me and I think our hug lasted an eternity.

"I was so glad to get this call." He whispered in my ear.

"I missed you."

I could never hug Rakeem like this on our visits, and I can now tell how much this man really missed me. When he finally let go of me, I looked up at him and could've sworn there was a tear in his eye.

"I missed you girl!" He looked me over.

I giggled and grabbed his arm. "Let's get out of here."

Rakeem walked me to a brand new Lincoln Navigator SUV. He opened the passenger door for me.

"This you?" I inhaled the brand new car scent.

"Four kids."

"Four?"

For a second, I thought he slipped up and counted my son Darius, but Rakeem's smile wouldn't leave his face.

"Wait!" I exclaimed. "Did you and Jada have a baby and didn't tell me?"

"Nah, I have Evelyn."

I suddenly got quiet. "Quitta's daughter? But….I thought Queen took her."

"Queen's house got raided and Evelyn was placed in foster care. Jada and I went to get her and we became her foster parents. She is my niece and Cici's sister. I didn't want her growing up alone."

"I can't believe you guys did all of this. How is she?"

Rakeem smiles. "Total opposite of Cici. Evelyn is quiet and she don't talk much. She might have a bit of a learning disability. She's two and should know more than she knows. We set up an appointment to get her checked out. She's adorable though, and of course the girls love her. New sister!"

"Wow your amazing Rakeem. I thank you for all that you have done for me while I was locked up."

"Let's roll, I have a surprise for you."

I got settled into the very nice SUV. It was so clean and comfortable. I smiled as Rakeem got into the driver seat and handed me a large yellow envelope.

"What's this?" I stared at the bulky envelope.

"I got you set up real nice Mel. You going to work for me at my restaurant, and these are a few credit cards and your ID is in there but you may have to renew it."

"You never told me that you owned a restaurant."

"When I came to visit you, it was all about you and the kids. I never wanted to boost on what I did."

"So tell me how."

He cleared his throat and smiled. I could tell he was proud of his achievement. "I own a high end restaurant. It's very elegant and we have live bands and shows Thursday through Sunday. I been open for six months and we're in excellent business."

"Where'd you get all the money to open it? I know it wasn't cheap."

"I stole money from Bryson years ago and never touched it. I just finally cashed in and did something positive with it. The crazy shit that happened not too long ago was, he called me and wanted me to come see him."

"Did you go?"

"Of course. That was a few weeks ago."

"What he say?"

"Look in the envelope."

I looked in the envelope to see cards, a wad of money, and a couple keys on a key chain. Of course, I pulled out the wad of money first.

"How much is this Rakeem?" I smelled it, missing the smell of fresh money.

"That's 10g's. It should get you started with all you need. I'll pay you $500 a week. All you do is handle my accounts, bookings, orders and inventory. I trust you."

"Over Jada? She should be doing this."

"Jada has her own job. Besides, yes; over Jada."

I looked away afraid to blush in front of Rakeem. I looked back in the envelope and pulled out the keys.

"I have a car?"

"Actually it's a van. It's real nice and brand new. You'll love it. The other key is for your house."

Oh my gawwd Rakeem!" I wanted to cry happy tears. "You bought me a van and a house?"

I wish I could take the credit for it all Mel. The only thing I gave you was a job. The day I met with Bryson, he told me where he hid some money. He said in a few months you was probably going to get out. I never expected you to call me yesterday and I was glad that house was on market. We bought that for you right after I got the money and the vehicle was bought yesterday. Jada got a crew together and they furnished and decorated your home last night. If you don't like it, you can remodel. That 10 grand is what was left of the money Bryson left you."

I still couldn't get past the fact that Bryson bought anything for me. Why? I betrayed him and he should hate my guts. "Why Rakeem?"

"Why what?"

"Why would he do that for me, and what about when he gets out? How will he survive?"

Rakeem finally started up his SUV and put it in drive.

"He's uh….he done Mel."

"What do you mean?"

"Bro caught him a life sentence."

"What the hell he do?"

A riot went down awhile back. It was right after you got locked up. It was literally that next week. A couple of inmates were killed and two correctional officers. Bryson was the cause of it so they charged him with the murders. He was on hardcore lockdown for six months. He's back in population and that's when he got ahold of me. Besides them adding more time and he'll be damn near dead when he gets out, he needs me. Bryson has no one to support him, so he hooked me up on some money for you and me."

"He trusts you?"

"He has no choice, and yeah he trusts me. I'm all he has."

"Oh wow, that's some big news. So, what did he say about me? Did he say he blames me? I practically ruined his life."

"Nah, I swear he don't blame you. You are not to blame for him being behind bars."

"You're just trying to make me feel better. I am a snitch and everyone knows it. If I didn't testify, he wouldn't be there."

"If you didn't testify, he'd still be in there and you would've got more time than you did. Don't worry yourself, Bryson is good. I'm taking care of both him and Rasheed. Rasheed's doing well by the way. He's with Bryson.

I sighed thinking about my past mistakes. I've really been to hell with my relationships. My life has been nothing but violence, pain, and suffering. First baby daddy dead, second and third both brothers and in prison together. I wonder what people really think of me. I bet all my enemies laughing and calling me all kinds of sluts, whores and bitches.

"So, who's the guy that helped you get out early?" Rakeem snapped me out my thoughts. "Who is this guy, the president or what?"

I smiled a little thinking of Matt. I missed him already, and mad that I had no way of contacting him. I didn't know who he really was. He definitely had some type of connections. I'm out and he was going to get Tia out.

"He was just a friend that worked there. Maybe one day you'll meet him."

Rakeem glanced over at me. "Someone you had a crush on?"

"No," I lied. "He was just a friend."

I notice Rakeem shrug his shoulders and keep on driving.

Soon as Rakeem pulled into the driveway of a nice size two family home, I looked over his way with my mouth wide open.

"So, you upgraded your house?"

"Yelp, I had to get a four bedroom."

He put the car in park, and I immediately got out. I stood in front of the SUV with my hands on my hips. I just looked up at it.

"You're really doing it big Rakeem."

He got out and stood with me and we both looked up at the nice size family house. I admired the neatly manicured lawn, the huge porch with the nice furniture laid out, and the big beautiful tree that sat right there in the front. As I look around, I notice a group of people a couple houses down gathering in their front yard.

"I see another black family lives near you, and they seem to be having a party."

He laughs. "Those black folks that you see down there are partying at my house. That's your welcome home party.

I punched Rakeem in the shoulder. "Are you serious?"

"Yeah, everyone down there! All your brothers, your parents, Debbie, and her family. A couple friends, cousins, aunts, uncles, and all your babies."

I threw my arms around Rakeem ready to drag his ass down the street with me. I then suddenly paused and looked back at the big beautiful house standing before me.

"Okay, then who house is this?"

"Welcome to the neighborhood, neighbor."

I slightly screamed and jumped up and down. Rakeem jumped with me trying to make me laugh.

"My house! Bryson really bought this?" I couldn't believe it.

"Yes, fully furnished. You have no house payments, just utilities. I have you working at the restaurant for me, but that's only temporary. The real estate business is also yours. They didn't take that from Bryson. The business was in his father's name, but he passed away years back. So, it was handed to him as an inheritance. That's why the business is still standing. He wants to go through the paperwork with his lawyer and hand the business to you."

"Bryson really doing all this for me?"

"I told you he didn't hate you."

"But why? He should hate me!"

"You have his children. He loves your kids Mel, and although I had hate in my heart for my brother, he will do for his kids. He did all this for them. So, you take that business and do well with it. Jeremy Miller and Maya Stewart are agents still employed there. They have been running it and until everything is settled, they will continue. When it's yours; you do as you please. Until then, you work for me."

"This is so great!" I said with tears in my eyes as I hugged Rakeem again. "I am so blessed."

"Would you like a tour of your new house?"

"Not yet. Let's go see my kids and family."

I grabbed ahold of Rakeem's arm and together we walked down the street to where the crowd was.

It was so good seeing everyone. It's been a year and I swear it felt like eternity. My kids were so happy to see me. Tisha was six, Rasheeda five, Cici two, and I got to meet Evelyn who was also two. I wanted to take Evelyn home with me for good, but I knew adopting her would take some time. I had a lot of work to do with my life. That night, I did take all four girls home with me to my new house. The house was beautiful and Jada decorated it as if I designed it myself. All the girls had their own room, and in Cici's room there was another daybed which was for Evelyn whenever she stayed over. I was proud of it all and hope all of this wasn't a dream.

Family and friends came and went all week. Every day, my house had someone there. I missed and loved the company, but I was actually glad my mother went back home. Mom was very helpful, but annoying at the same time. She wanted to constantly clean, cook, and tell me how to take care of my girls as if I wasn't a mother before. Then of course, I had to hear about the men I brought into my bed, and all the trouble they caused me. I think I was at peace now with her gone. It's been eight days since I got out, and I've done so much in these last eight days that many people wish they've done in a year. The girls were happy, and even Evelyn finally latched onto me. The first couple of days, she wouldn't stay. Jada would come get her every evening, until a couple days ago she finally cried that she wanted to stay. I think she just didn't want to leave Cici, and I was okay with that. I just wanted all the girls happy. Rakeem told me, after about six months of my job and adjusting at home, then I should go speak with children service about Evelyn. Until then, I was starting parenting classes next week. I knew I didn't need them, but with me just getting out of prison, I thought it be a good look on my background.

Rakeem brought me over a laptop and explained my position. He told me that I could work from home since I had the kids. I love the idea, but I still had a problem. I knew nothing about computers. I definitely didn't want Rakeem to know, afraid he'd take the job from me. I'd probably just call my sister and have her show me. Until then, I jotted down everything he told me on my notes. I was going to show Rakeem that I could really do this job. He was strictly business and soon as he gave me my job description, he was on his way. I enjoyed company and was mad when he had to leave, but I had to remind myself that he was only a friend. That's when I thought of Matt. Damn, I wish I had Matt's number.

Later that night, after bathing the girls I put them to bed and went into the living room with my glass of wine. I turned on the TV hoping to find some good movie on lifetime. Soon as I settled in, my mind drifted to sex with Matt. Where is Matt, and why was he so mysterious? I thought about calling the prison and getting his contact information, but I knew that was a dead end. I knew Matt didn't just ditch me, he got me out early, so why go through all that trouble and then disappear? Who was he? He's been on my mind all week, and the thought of me introducing him to my family came across a lot. I was afraid that they wouldn't like him. Mainly because he was white, but I knew that was ridiculous. A couple of my brothers married white women, but I felt they would turn on me because I was a black woman dating a white man. Matt wasn't the usual man that

I would date, but over the time of me knowing him, I fell in love. Crazy, because we never even made love yet.

Buzz, buzz, buzz!

I felt my cellphone vibrate on the sofa next to me. I picked it up and looked at the strange number that appeared. I just got this phone a few days ago so no one really had my number besides family and close friends.

"Hello." I said into the phone.

"Hey beautiful." A deep voice responded.

I pulled the phone back and looked at the number again. I didn't know it. I put the phone back to my ear.

"Hello?" He spoke.

"Who is this?"

"So you forgot about me already?" He continued to speak.

"Matt?"

"Did you miss me?"

"But how? Who gave you my number?"

"I have my ways."

"This is so crazy. I was literally thinking about you. I can't believe you called me. How Matt?"

"Don't worry about that. I'm just glad you were thinking about me."

"I really was."

"You sound happy."

"I am. Besides hearing your voice, I have my kids back and soon maybe I'll get custody of Shaquitta's baby."

"That's great Mel. You really getting your shit right, huh?"

"Yelp."

"Good. I'm happy for you."

"Thanks."

"So how's everything? Job hunting, getting back into society."

"I'm spoiled Matt." I crossed my legs up on the sofa in Indian style. I was getting a little more comfortable. "My friend Rakeem gave me a job."

"Really? Doing what?"

"He owns this restaurant, and I'm like his assistant or secretary." I laughed out loud a bit thinking of my terrible skills. "I have a stack of notes on my job description and what has to be done, but I'm dumb when it comes to computers. I'm working from home, so I have to do everything on computers."

"You need a computer class?"

"Yeah, you know where I can take one?"

"Me!"

"Really?"

"Yes. I know the ins and outs of Microsoft program. I could help you baby."

I smiled at the sound of him calling me baby. "I'd love that. Can we start tonight?"

I could tell he was smiling. "On my way!"

"Wait Matt…."

"Yes?"

"You know where I live, don't you?"

He sighed. "I'm not stalking you. I like you a lot Melanie, and I just really wanted to know who you were."

I was mad, but tried not to sound it. "Then who are you? It's not fair that you can check my background, and know every little detail of my life, but I still know nothing about you. You show up out of the blue, and then quit when I get out. How did I get out?"

"You trust me babe?"

"I….I think I do."

"Do you trust me?"

"Yes!"

"We'll talk when I get there Mel. I'm on my way."

I hung up with mix feelings. I was truly in love with that man. A man I knew nothing about, so I was confused. I tried to tell myself he was a good man. He was nothing like the men I dealt with in the past. He was far from the woman beater, abuser, and drug dealer. I wanted a man with a very good plan in life. A man who will love and take care of me and my children. I pray Matt was that man, because I really wanted to be with him.

I don't know how fast he'd get here, but I snapped outta my thoughts and ran upstairs to my bedroom. I took a quick shower, did my hair, and splashed on a little natural look of make-up. I wore a sexy lingerie under my new silk robe that I bought yesterday. I bought it especially for Matt. I knew I'd see him soon, but I never guess it would be the next night.

I walked back downstairs and grabbed one of my new bottles of wine and two glasses. I poured the wine in each glass and set them on the coffee table in the living room. Soon after, I heard a small tap on my front door. I closed my eyes and thought to myself, *was I being stupid for not asking questions first?* I just literally put on a lingerie and I knew what I was doing. Even with the idea of him being some type of stalker with power, I trusted him. I grabbed his glass and opened the front door. He stood there staring back at me, stuck on the door mat. My robe was wide open and he got the peek at my sexy almost exposed body in my black lingerie. Damn he was one sexy white boy in his dark denim jeans, plain white t-shirt, and wheat color timbs.

"You just going to stand there and let all my neighbors see all this good shit." I stood sexy and proud trying my damn hardest not to flip out over his sexiness.

"I'm sorry, but I think I have the wrong house."

He then stepped in, and with no hesitation he picked me up off my feet and began kissing my lips. It was wild and intense that I swear I was high off some exotic drug. After his tongue finished attacking the inside of my mouth, he started sucking and kissing all over my neck. His wine was now all over the floor and I was holding onto an empty glass. Matt finally set me on my feet and closed and locked my door. He stood there and looked me over and shook his head. Fine ass white boy!

"I waited just about a year to do all that." He said. "You're gorgeous Mel."

"Thank you, and you are one good kisser."

"My tongue is magic."

"The hell it is!" I laughed.

Matt pulls me towards him and hugs me real tight. "I missed you. I don't ever want to be without you Mel."

"You don't have to. I'm all yours."

Matt kissed me once more before letting me go. He then looks around my new home and shakes his head in amazement.

"This all you?" He asked.

"Yes."

I pulled him by the hand and lead him into my living room. When we got in front of the sofa, I pushed him back. I then walk away around the coffee table and grab the wine bottle and I refilled the empty glass. I then picked mine up and sat down next to him. I handed him his glass and held mine up.

"To new beginnings." I toasted.

Matt licks his lips, then letting a moan escape. "I like new beginnings."

We both drink up and then I grabbed his glass and set them both on the table. I stood in front of him, letting my silk robe fall to the floor. He drooled looking at me in my black low cut, sheer negligee. I then got on my knees in front of him and unbuckled his belt. He smiled the entire time as I helped pull off his jeans. Through his Ralph Lauren boxers I seen the huge imprint and smiled to myself as I pulled out his thick long rod.

"Mmmm, so lickable." I stroked him a few times, loving his length.

"What you going to do with all that?"

"You want me to show you?"

All he had to do was nod his head and I immediately took him into my mouth. I teased his head with a couple of wet licks, then I gave him a deep throat session. I tried to suck him until he came, but he wanted to return the favor.

Matt laid back on my sofa, and I removed my thong. I straddled his face, and he licked and sucked on my clit and made love to my pussy with his tongue. It was the best feeling ever, but I could no longer take orgasm after orgasm. I let go a pool of sweet nectar into his mouth, and he gladly licked and slurped every drop. I moved down onto his thick erection, and with me being so soaking wet, I eased down taking half of what he was working with. It would be too painful to let all of what he had enter me. It's been awhile and I wasn't ready for that yet. We both let out a loud moan as my tightness wrapped around him. Our eyes connected as I sat there for a moment, loving the way he felt inside me.

After a while I was riding him, bouncing up and down on his dick and his big hands dug into my ass pulling me in deeper. I gyrated on him so hard, I could almost tell he was ready to cum. He quickly flipped me over as I lay on my back, legs spread wide for him, and he pushed inside me.

"I love you so much." I moaned out.

"Ya lyublyu tebya." He said out loud in a thick accent that he let slip a few times before.

I could tell he shocked himself as I looked up at his sexy face.

"I'm Russian." He continued to say in his thick accent. "Very Russian. My name is Maceo."

I was silent as he continued to grind slowly inside of me. I loved the feeling, but I was somewhat angry.

"Ty zlish'sya?" He whispered in my ear as he then nibbled and licked. I moaned. "What?!"

"Are you mad?" He repeated himself.

"How do you do that?"

"Do what?"

"You get rid of your accent."

"Practice."

"Who are you?"

Matt's pace sped up and he then lifted my legs over his shoulder and pounded my pussy as if he needed it to survive. He then pulled out and came all over my stomach. That was something I hated, and I was going to have to tell him about that.

"Luchshe vsego kogda-libo kisa." He kissed me on the lips.

"Quit talking that language?"

"I just complimented your pussy, and I can't help it. When I have sex it really comes out."

"Who are you?"

"Call me Maceo. Take my hand, and led us to the shower."

He stood up and extended his hand to me. I looked at it for a brief moment wondering why he keep ignoring the one question I needed an answer to. I sighed anyway and took his hand. Next thing you know, we in the shower in my bedroom doing round two. His sex was even more amazing and his language actually turned me on even more. He said it so sweet and sexy. I didn't even care that I had no idea what he was saying. I fell in love again, but soon as we were in my bed cuddling I was back to being angry.

"Who are you?" I whispered to him.

I was now turned around facing him. It was dark, but I knew we were eye to eye. He kissed my nose, and I tried my hardest not to smile. What the hell, he couldn't see it anyway.

"Don't be afraid of me, Mel. Don't panic, don't run from me, and don't hate me. I am still the same guy you fell in love with. I just....I was doing a job at the prison. I was not soupose to find the love of my life there, and when I did; I couldn't see you suffer any longer, so I went to a higher power and got you out. Tia will be out soon. She's your friend and I like her. Tamar was a man I just met, but he knows nothing about the real me." He pause. "I am Maceo Ankundinov. I am a professional assassin. I was hired to do a job, and I completed it. It took me a year to get some very important information from her, but when I did, I dead her."

"Celina?" I said above a whisper.

"Yes, she was my target."

Silence.

"Are you angry Mel? Do you still love me?"

"I….I do but, you're not what I dreamed of."

"What do you dream of?"

"A man that is good to me, and my children. He has a very good job, and good family. He's important in the world, and he really loves me."

"That is me Mel. I will be good to you, great to your children, and I have a job, and a good family. I am very important, and I will love you more than anything in this world. Be with me Mel, and I promise to never expose you or your children to that life. You will live way better than what you are living. I have power, and money. You will love my family. They protect their own, and you will forever be safe with me. No one or nothing will ever harm you. Didn't you tell me that you trust me?"

"Yes, but that was before."

"There is no before. I'm sorry I wasn't straight up with you, but if you knew I was a Russian assassin, would you have loved me?"

"Probably not, but how can we make this work Matt…I mean Maceo."

"We will work."

"Your parents? Will they like a black woman?"

"My mother would have loved you. She passed away when I was nine. I was raised by five different nannies. My father is Victor Ankundinov, the most notorious Russian boss. He will adore you. He don't see color, just like myself. I see the most amazing woman I've ever laid eyes on, and she will be my wife one day."

A tear slipped out, and I was thankful the lights were out. I hope that Maceo's lifestyle would not affect me and my children. I had prayed to the Lord to send me a good man, and I didn't want to go back to the men

I was used to. In a strange sort of way, I believe he sent Maceo. I kissed him one last time, and fell asleep on his strong chest. His alarm went off at 7am, and I had to rush him out before the girls woke up.

Maceo and I grew to know one another for the next month. He'd come over every night in secret and that was okay with me. He was anxious to meet my family but I wasn't ready. I honestly wanted to know more about him, and make sure we really was going to stay with one another. It was working out so well, and I felt he was my gift from God. He'd come over and help me on the computer, we'd talk, and then we make love. He was skilled in everything he did, and sex was number one. We been recently talking about seeing each other during the day, but I was afraid. I didn't tell him I was afraid, just said okay. I didn't know if I was afraid of his lifestyle, or the fact that he wasn't my race. I didn't know what my family would think and I really cared about it. I had the pleasure of talking to Maceo's father over the phone, and I loved him. He sounded excited to meet me one day and I really hope that was true.

One night, we were snuggled up on the sofa watching a movie. There was a knock at my door and I looked over at Maceo as if to say, *who the hell was at my door knocking at 1am?*

I got up and walked to the door. I could see the silhouette of a man holding onto something or a little someone. I knew exactly who it was, but why was he here? I opened the door and he rushed in, mad as hell. He had Evelyn draped over his shoulders with a blanket covering her. He almost looked as if he was crying but stopped everything when he seen Maceo standing behind me.

"Who the hell are you?" Rakeem shouted out.

"Her man," Maceo replied. "Who are you?"

Rakeem looked at me, then back at Maceo. He then looked at me again. I looked away.

"Mel?" Rakeem was waiting for me to explain.

"Rakeem, this is......" I looked back at Maceo wondering if he wanted me to expose his real name.

Maceo stepped forward, with his hand extended. "Maceo, it's finally nice to meet you. She speaks very highly of you."

It took Rakeem a minute. He just stared back and forth from me to Maceo, but then he finally shakes his hand.

"This your man?" Rakeem asked still surprised.

I stepped up to Maceo and grabbed his hand. I had to be ready to show my friends and family my new boyfriend. I loved Maceo, and didn't want to lose him.

"Yes." I responded. "Maceo is my man."

"Really?" He seemed dazed. "This your man, and this the first time I'm meeting him?"

"Well....yeah. I really didn't want to introduce him yet until the girls met him. They haven't met him yet. I...I wasn't ready. BUT, I'm ready now! So, Maceo, Rakeem. Rakeem...Maceo."

All Rakeem could do was nod his head. Something told me that he really didn't approve. I hope so, because I was going to introduce my man to the family tomorrow. Rakeem will never be satisfied with any man I end up with. He used to love me at one point, and not to sound conceited, but I think he still does.

"I'm a take Evelyn to her room, then we can talk." He explained.

I nodded my head, and watched Rakeem take Evelyn upstairs.

"I don't think he was happy with us." I told Maceo.

Maceo pulled my body close to his and kissed my lips. "He'll survive."

I smiled. "I love you."

"I love you too." He then pulled away.

"I'll be in the kitchen, while you two talk in private."

"Thanks babe."

I watched Maceo walk away, and Rakeem came downstairs a couple minutes later. He stood there looking stressed as he ran his hand across his low faded cut.

"I need a place to stay for a while. Just until I figure some shit out."

"You know you can stay with me anytime. What happened with Jada?"

"Let's just say, I'm glad I trusted you with my business." He then looks toward the living room looking for Maceo. "I'm sorry to bother you two, I'm just.....I'm fucked up!"

"Please Rakeem, don't be sorry. Maceo and I will go upstairs. I'll get you some blankets and pillows."

Before I walked away, he grabbed my arm. "Keep me away from that bitch. I swear, if she comes back, I'll kill her."

"Is it that bad?"

"They took my house this morning. Evelyn and I just got home. I took Evelyn to see my mom, which is a two hour drive. We just got back and there was a note on the door. I can't even get shit out the house. It's all bolted up. After we got the house, she never paid a dime on it. It's in her name, so there isn't shit I can do. I thought she was going to be my wife, so we had joint bank accounts and I had a separate one that she knew of. She cleared them all. She even took my hidden money and the bitch bounced. The restaurant is all I have and I'm glad she didn't have access to that account. I been calling her for the last hour, and her phone goes straight to voicemail. Mel, I swear I want to fuck something up right now."

I touched his arm. "Please don't go getting into trouble."

"I'll be fine. Give me your keys, I need to cool off. I'll be back before the girls wake up."

"Okay, but I'm serious Rakeem. Don't go fucking anyone or anything up. I can't lose you."

"You won't."

I reached up and hugged Rakeem. He kissed me on the cheek and left out the house. I locked the door behind him and went into the kitchen where Maceo was doing a little cleaning. He stopped and walked over to me.

"He left?" Maceo asked.

"Yes, but I think he might do something stupid."

"Do you want me to follow him?"

"No." I grabbed Maceo's hand. "Let's just go to bed."

Chapter Twenty-Seven

$\mathcal{I}$ looked around surprised at the turnout of Rakeem's funeral. It really was a surprise that he actually knew this many people. I knew he was loved by all, but this was a blessing at how many people really cared.

Exactly one week ago, Rakeem left my house. I just knew he was up to something bad, but I trusted what he said when he told me he was okay. Rakeem was looking for revenge. What I didn't know was, that he had gotten a call from someone telling him the location of Jada. She was at a motel 60 miles outside the city. Rakeem found the exact room and busted in on her. Jada wasn't alone, but was with her ex-boyfriend that has been taking money from them for a while. After they took the house, she made her move in clearing all his accounts and being with her ex for good. She had taken all his money. When Rakeem busted in, the ex panicked and pulled out his gun right away sending five shots Rakeem's way. He took all five into his body, and one included his face which instantly killed him. Jada and her ex then packed up their stuff to leave the motel and tried escaping, except the police arrived before they could leave. They both are being charged with murder. I wanted my friend back.

Maceo was there with me, and although it was Rakeem's funeral my nosey family still questioned who Maceo was. The girls have only known him for six days and they were taking a liking to him. Evelyn seemed as if she knew what was going on, and she cried when she seen Rakeem in the casket. I was surprised she noticed who he was, because he looked totally different. I could tell where they shot him at in his face but they made him look unbelievably decent. It just didn't look like HIM. I felt bad for Evelyn because she wanted Rakeem to wake up. So did I. It was very sad for us all, and I felt extremely bad for Rakeem's mom. She had lost both her boys, and I pray Rasheed gets out soon so he could be there for her. Right now, I knew he wouldn't get out until Rasheeda was up in her teens. Natisha, Cici and Evelyn would never grow up to see their father.

After the funeral, they had a nice dinner for Rakeem's friends and family at my home. Everyone seemed to enjoy themselves, happy to see people they haven't seen in years. Rakeem's mother only stayed for an hour before she got on the road to head home. She said she'd be back later on in the week and together we'd go through Rakeem's things. We were able to get the bolts lifted and get into his house. I haven't step foot in there yet, and I knew it was going to be hard.

Most of the family was still at my house later that evening. Poor Maceo had everyone in his face asking millions of questions, but he didn't mind. I actually felt good about my family finally getting to meet him. The only thing I really had on my mind was that Rakeem and Maceo would've really hit it off once they got to know each other.

I was sitting in the kitchen with my sister and a friend of hers. We were just cleaning up a bit, and one of my brothers entered with a look of disapproval on his face. Next thing you know, he steps aside and a middle age white woman walks into the kitchen.

"Hello, I'm looking for Melanie Lewis." She spoke.

I stepped forward. "And you are?"

"Janice Clark. I am Evelyn's social worker. First off, I'm sorry for your loss."

"Okay thank you. I'm glad you come by to offer your condolences. I am Melanie and I was coming to see you in the morning about taking Evelyn into my home."

"Yes, um Rakeem did mention that a while ago, but right now…. The state wouldn't approve of you taking her in. I do understand your situation and that you have custody of your three children; but we do need to go over a few things in order for you to have Evelyn in your custody."

"No, miss. I can't lose her. She has no one but us. I am her stepmother so I should be able to take her in. She needs her family."

She sighed. "I'm sorry. I really would, but my boss wants you to take more classes, show your job history. Your home is beautiful, so I'm sure you won't have a problem there."

"Call your boss right now. Tell them you approve of me. Please ma'am, we are all she has."

"Again, I am sorry. I do recognize that you have visitation until you get everything in order. Please make this easy on both of us. I do have an officer waiting outside."

I rolled my eyes wanting to punch that bitch in her face. Don't she know Evelyn had a bad week? She has been crying all day, and now that she's happy playing with her sisters all afternoon this bitch wants to ruin her again.

I walked passed everyone going upstairs to where Evelyn was actually sleep next to Cici in my king size bed. My brother's wife Danella was just leaving the room.

"I just got those two to sleep." She whispered.

I pouted. "I know, and I feel bad waking Evelyn up but the social worker is here to take her away."

Tears began to flood my eyes, as I said that and Danella reached over to hug me. "You'll get her back. Don't worry yourself."

"I know I will, but I hate what she's going through. She's going to be scared. She shouldn't be going through this shit."

"I went through the same exact thing with my daughter. All I'm saying is, do everything the right way. Do what they ask of you, and your new friend Macao; get rid of him. At least until this custody battle is over."

I sighed again knowing Danella was right. I looked over at them precious girls sleeping and I began to cry again. Evelyn wasn't my daughter, but since I met her she became mine. I love her as my own.

Chapter Twenty-Eight

This is why I love Maceo. He understood my situation and never protested. He knew I loved him too, and if I wanted custody of Evelyn I needed to show social services I was serious about getting MY little girl. We backed away from each other in case someone had eyes on us. Once in a while he'd sneak over in the middle of the night like old times. He did ask if he could fix my situation, but I told him that I wanted to get Evelyn the right way. With Maceo being son of a mafia boss who knew what he was thinking of doing to CPS.

The restaurant was all mines. Surprisingly, Rakeem had a will and insurance. He left his mom and grandma all the insurance money, and me the restaurant. I was fine with that. I was more than fine. I owned a high end restaurant that made half a million dollars this year and this was the year it opened. That alone had me on high, because I was about to do pretty damn good for myself. Then everything had went through with the real estate Agency. The company was mine and I couldn't be any happier.

It's been three months since Rakeem's murder and I have been running the Restaurant pretty well, thanks to Maceo. He showed me the ins and outs of owning a business and I couldn't have done any of this without him. When Rakeem was a young boy he had told me that his grandmother could never say his name right. One day she gave up and started to call him "The R". It was a funny story he use to always tell me, and I took that story and ran with it. Today, the restaurant was renamed "The R".

It was soupose to be a huge renaming event tonight. We had a very popular local band performing and I knew it was going to be a big turnout for "The R". In memory of Rakeem. I was in the restaurant at 9am, bright and early preparing for our opening. I had the same employees that Rakeem had hired and kept them all. They all gotten to know me, and

I couldn't complain about the professional staff. Even the waitresses and waiters were all professionals at what they do. Lisa was our evening hostess, but very smart and always well organized. I needed her as my assistant and that's what I upgraded her to. She was doing my old job. Mainly inventory and party planning. I didn't trust anyone with the accounts, so I did that on my own.

"Good morning Mel."

I looked up from my desk to see Lisa walk in smiling.

"Good morning Sunshine." I smiled back to her.

"Hey, there is a lady outside the restaurant wanting to come in. Are you expecting anyone?"

I got up from my chair. "No."

I walked out front towards the entrance and noticed that it was Evelyn's social walker Janice. I immediately opened the doors and let her in.

"Sorry, were you waiting long?" I ushered her in.

"Oh no, I just arrived." She said as she stepped in looking around. "Wow, it's amazing in here. I see your doing pretty well for yourself."

"Thanks, so what can I do for you?"

"I'll just get right to it. You've done well over the last few months and I am very proud of you. You tried really hard to get custody of Evelyn and I'm proud to say, she's all yours."

"Really?" I almost jumped for joy.

"Yes, and her foster parents can drop her off to you later if you like."

"Can I pick her up?"

"Of course. Just let me call them so they can get her ready."

"Thank you so much. I appreciate your faith in me. I know I have a past, and I'm glad you see change in me. I...."

Just then, I felt a terrible feeling. I felt the urge to vomit. I immediately held one finger up to Janice and quickly ran to the bathroom. I threw up everything I had for breakfast and then some. Soon as I finished, I rinsed my mouth and washed my hands. I looked at myself in the mirror and slowly shook my head.

"Not again...."

Chapter Twenty-Nine

Thirteen years later

*H*is smooth hands massaged every inch of my naked body. I moaned with every touch, and when his hands glided over my ass that tingling feeling aroused even more. I arched my back, giving him access to go a little further. Further was exactly what he did when I felt his warm, wet tongue lick me from front to back. Every part of my pussy to my ass crack got the attention. It felt so good as I grinded all over his face. I bet he was suffocating with all this ass smothering him, but I didn't care. I bounced back hard and came multiple times in the long minutes he was eating me out. Soon as he pulled back, I could hear him unzip his pants. I quickly turned around and sat up on the bed. I stared right at him, daring him.

"You love her?" I pursed my lips.

"No!" Maceo sighed. "It's nothing baby. I told you we didn't have sex."

"But you two had dinner? You like her?"

"Baby....I...."

"Do you want to fuck her?" I cut him off.

"No!"

"You lying! Tell me the truth. Please be truthful. I love you too much and I never lied to you, so please don't lie to me."

Maceo sat on the edge of the bed and looked at me. He tried grabbing my hand, but I pulled away.

"Mel, baby. Don't be like that."

"Who is she? What's her name?"

"It don't matter. I never had sex with her. It was only dinner. We had business to tend to."

"Business don't involve a kiss. I heard you kissed her too. Did you kiss her with passion?"

Maceo shook his head in frustration. "Who told you that shit?"

"Who cares! You did it, didn't you?"

"Okay Mel, it was only a kiss. It meant nothing."

"So, why'd you go after another woman? You have me! What's wrong with me?"

"Baby, nothing is wrong with you. You are perfect in every way. I love you so much. I don't know what happened." He moved in close to me, taking my hand. "Look, you may not understand but I'm going to keep it real with you. Thirteen years we been together and I never been with another woman, and I don't want no other woman. You are all I need; but I'm forty years old. I just needed a little attention from another woman. I was a ladies man back in the day and I wanted that feeling. Don't be mad Mel."

"I'm not."

"You're not?" He sounded surprised. "You understand?"

"I didn't say that!" I snatched my hand outta his. "You want to try new pussy, don't you?"

"What?"

"That's what you really want to say."

"Babe, I didn't say that."

"You don't have to, I just know."

"Baby, I'm not the bad guy. I promise you that little dinner meant shit to me. Why would I want any other woman when I have you? You do it all for me. Sex with you is never a dull moment. I promise you that shit with her was harmless. Just got a little attention from her then I was on my way. I knew it was wrong, but it happened and I'm sorry."

"Where'd you meet this hoe?" I snapped.

"She's not a hoe."

"So you sticking up for this bitch?"

"Nah, but she really not. She just a woman I had dinner with. I met her at the office. She was a potential client."

I shook my head knowing he was lying. I still ran and owned 'The R', but I also had Bryson's reality company. When Maceo and I married, he gave up the life style of being an assassin and tried to become a business man and run the agency. I let him take that over completely while I focused on the restaurant. We were doing pretty well in life and there was nothing I could complain about. Well, except this new woman that I heard he had dinner with. Maceo was nowhere near the men I had in my life. He went far and beyond to please me, and I never had any reason to ever not trust him. Maceo was every woman's dream. He stopped a job that could've cost him his life, and he did it for me. I was grateful for him, and loved him with all my heart. I just wanted to know, why?

"I'm done!" I got up off the bed mad.

Maceo pulled my naked body down on the bed and he got on top of me. He was all in my face, looking like he was ready to attack. Deep down inside, I love this side of him. He was a natural born killer and it turned me on.

"What the hell you mean, you're done?"

"This whole conversation! You leave that bitch alone, and change your fucking number. I'll forgive you after this. Just this one time. If it ever happens again, your ass is out!"

Maceo kissed me, while spreading my legs with his hands. I knew he was trying to make me forget, but I was serious. I was cheated on way too much in the past and it broke me down. I was sure Maceo was different and maybe he was. If my sister Debbie and Tia never seen them and told me about it, then who knows what would've happened. I just hopes he stops this affair instantly.

Chapter Thirty

"Is she pretty?"

"She don't look better than you." My sister Debbie spoke.

"But she was pretty." Tia teased.

"Tia!" I yelled at my best friend. "Who side are you on?"

Tia got out a few months after Maceo and I got together. Soon as she got out, she and Tamar married. They lived a happy life. Tamar worked with Maceo at the Realty business. They were the only ones besides Maceo's family that knew who Maceo really was, and they were great friends as they kept his privacy.

"Yours boo, but the girl was cute." Tia continued on. "Reeaal cute!"

"I swear I will smack you if you say another word about that bitch!"

"I really didn't see her as well as Tia, but I did see the kiss. He was practically blocking her face from my view."

"Both of you really rubbing this in."

"No we're not!" Tia added. "It was nothing Mel. He admitted to it, and he told you it was just dinner and a kiss. I believe him. Besides, that hoe initiated the kiss."

"Do you think he'll leave her alone?"

"You stupid if you believe that shit!" Debbie added.

"Well, he's never cheated before."

"No, he's never gotten caught!"

"Debbie, shut up with the negative shit!"

The door opened to the dressing room, and Tisha walked out in her sixth prom dress.

"Ooooohhh, I love that one!" I cooed.

"Nah, too revealing." Debbie complained.

"I like it." Tia stood up and walked over to Tisha fixing up her hair as if she was actually getting ready today.

"I think this the one." Tisha turned around and showed up the coke bottle figure in the back.

"Too much booty for that dress!" Debbie continued to complain.

Natisha did a slight booty dance and Tia smacked her butt.

"None of that on prom night!" Tia told her.

"You ain't cute!" We heard Rasheeda's voice.

We all turned around to see sixteen year old Rasheeda and my other two girls, fourteen year old Cici and Evelyn. Rasheeda had two dresses in her hand ready to try them on. Cici and Evelyn both squeezed in on the sofa with me and Debbie.

"You know I look good." Tisha smiled and posed.

"Wait until you see me." She held up her dresses. "You like mommy?"

"Black? You can't find any other colors?"

"Black is sexy."

"Why you trying to be sexy?" Debbie asked.

Rasheeda slightly giggled thinking my sister was far from serious, but I knew she was. She always talked about how she didn't want these girls being fast.

"It's prom Aunt Debbie. You soupose to go all out." Raheeda told her.

"Well, it better not fit like Tisha's dress." Debbie then looked at me. "Your girls have too much ass sis."

I agreed as I looked around waiting to see my fifth daughter Desiree pop up somewhere. She is my youngest daughter with Maceo. Dezzie was twelve, and she was my tomboy. You wouldn't ever catch her in a dress.

"Where's Dezzie?"

"In the arcade with Will." Cici spoke.

I slightly shook my head knowing she would be in there. Debbie has three kids. Lisa and Darnell who are both away in college and then Will, whose seventeen. Will played games all day, every day and Dezzie was right there with him. Her long hair stayed in a braid with a baseball cap on. She wore nothing but Jordan's and baggy jeans. She actually reminded me of the singer Aaliyah. Looked and dressed like her.

Rasheeda tried on the first dress, which she fell in love with instantly.

She was far from picky like Tisha who finally found a dress after searching for two weeks.

It was going on seven in the evening and I had to hurry and get back to the restaurant. I kissed Tia and my sister goodbye and then dropped the girls off at home. I then rushed to the restaurant to make my appearance. It was a Friday evening and very crowded as usual. It was date night for most, so the scene was romantic with saxophonist Jeffrey Evans on stage playing his love melodies. I spotted my husband Maceo behind the bar helping out. He was one that you'd see working side by side with the employees. That was something he love to do when he wasn't at the reality office.

"Hey babe, how's everything going?" I approached him.

He smiled as he reached over to kiss me. "Everything's good, and look at you looking all sexy."

"Whatever, I wore this to the mall."

"You was sexy at the mall?"

I rolled my eyes. "Boy please!"

"Anyway, I hear you have a meeting with this director tonight. You never told me that this guy was a director."

I rolled my eyes again at Maceo. He knew I told him a couple weeks back. Matter fact, it was around the time that I confronted him about that woman he had dinner with. He forgot all about me because he was probably thinking of her. It's been two weeks and I try to forget about it, but I can't. I haven't brought it up to him but it really does bother me. Tonight when we both get home, I was really going to talk to him about how much it bothers me.

"Hopefully, he'll shoot his movie here." I told Maceo. "He says he want it to be the main scenery."

"That's good babe. It will all work out. You're really doing well with this club. Rakeem would love what you made of 'The R'."

I slightly smiled at the comment. I always go back to if I choose Rakeem over Bryson then he'd still be alive. Then, I wouldn't have met Maceo, and I wouldn't trade him for the world. He is a good man and a great father.

"Okay. I'm going to run home and change into an impressive outfit."

"You don't need to change. You look good."

"Evelyn will hook me up."

I pecked Maceo on the lips one more time and sashayed out of 'The R'. As I was driving home, I called Evelyn and told her about my important meeting. Evelyn wanted to be a fashion designer and dress celebrities. Ever since I knew of this, I encouraged her, by letting her dress me. She picks out my wardrobe; what I wear on a daily basis down to my shoes and jewelry. I'm constantly complimented and I always give props to my baby girl. I told her that when she turns sixteen, we'll start her a business. ShaQuitta lost all rights to ever contacting Evelyn and I adopted her. Of course, I knew that bitch was mad, but she killed my son and should never get out of prison. Evelyn knows who her real mom is, and she knows who I am, but in the end she choose to call me mommy. Then I had Tisha who was my hair and make-up girl. She starts cosmetology school this fall and she was beyond good. She was perfection. Rasheeda was my basketball star, and Cici was going to be a doctor. Deezie was an athlete in everything. She was good in every sport you put her in, and a daredevil. Only if she wasn't in front of a video game.

Soon as my girls dressed and did me up, I was back out the door. I was known for my style and appearance, so I had to always stay on top of my game.

Mr. Adam Calvert was waiting for me in the VIP area where the more private parties attended. This was a very important meeting, so I made sure it was special. My five star waiter Bernardo escorted me to where Mr. Calvert waited. Bernardo was our waiter for the night, and of course he was the best I had. Before sitting, I looked at Bernardo.

"My husband still around?" I asked him.

"No ma'am, he left a little after you did."

'Then where the hell he go?' I thought. I put on my happy face and introduced myself to Mr. Calvert. The entire meeting I swear I was so unfocused, and when I gave Mr. Calvert a tour I couldn't help but to constantly look at my phone and text a few words.

Where the hell u at
Call me asap
Im a kill u when u get home
R u with her

He never answered any of my texts and I was so angry. I knew he was with that woman.

It was 11:30 when Mr. Calvert finally left, and I went to my office to blow Maceo's phone up. I left message after message and still never got a call back. I finally gave up and left the restaurant a little after midnight. The girls were all in the family room with a couple of friends playing music and acting silly. Cici and Deezie ran to me and gave me a hug.

"How was your meeting mommy?" Cici asked me.

"It was nice. I see you guys have company."

"Sheeda and Tisha's stupid friends. Me and Deezie bought to go upstairs and watch a scary movie."

"Ok baby. Did your father ever come home?"

"No." Both the girls responded at the same time.

"Okay.....well you girls have a good night. I'm going to take a hot bath and then head for bed."

I kissed them both and walked upstairs to my bedroom. Of course I went crazy up there. I called Maceo again and then went through all his stuff looking for answers. Then finally I found something in his suit pocket. It wasn't mine, and it confirmed my suspicions. A red thong!

"Fucking liar!" I said as I threw them across the room.

I wanted to scream and throw things, but I had five girls plus two more roaming the house. I was all the way mad and wanted to confront him now. I tried to calm down by taking a bath with vanilla and lavender scents. Then I drunk a full bottle of wine. I don't even remember getting out, let alone putting pajamas on and falling asleep across my king size bed. Someone shaking me and yelling 'ma', woke me up.

"Ma! Ma! Wake up!"

I finally jumped up and my oldest daughter Natisha stood there with Evelyn and Deezie behind her.

"What!" I looked around the semi dark room. "What are you guys doing?"

"Police are downstairs." Tisha continued. "Rasheeda let them in."

"What!"

I was wide awake now. "What time is it?"

"A little after 4am."

I looked over at Maceo's side of the bed. He was not there. Deezie handed me my robe, and I stood up to put it on. I walked downstairs with my girls following close behind me. Rasheeda, Cici, and their two friends stood in the middle of the foyer with two police officers. My heart dropped when I looked at their faces and I instantly knew something happened to Maceo.

"Yes?" I stood at the bottom of the step.

"I'm very sorry to bother you early this morning ma'am." One officer said.

"What is this about?"

"Maceo Ankundinov, your husband?"

"Yes he is."

"There was an accident near route 7." He began.

"Nooooo!" I yelled out. "It was my husband?"

"I'm so sorry Mrs. Ankundinov. He and another victim was burned to death in the accident. They both didn't survive."

"Another victim?" I sobbed. "A female?"

The one officer looked to the other officer, then to me. "Yes, she was in the passenger side. They both were burned in the car beyond recognition. Your husband's license plate and a few unburned documents verified it was him. As of now, we still don't know the identity of the woman. Do you…"

"No!" I heard Natisha speak up. I couldn't even move.

It seemed after that, my oldest daughter took over. I was no good. It seemed as if the world stopped, but it didn't stop for long because I then heard all my daughters scream. Some even fell to the floor and I notice Deezy run upstairs. The officers patted my back asked if he could call anyone. I told him that we be fine. I wasn't, but I had to be for these girls. Five girls just lost their father. Maceo was Deezie's biological father but for my other four Maceo was all they knew. The best stepdad ever. Evelyn and Cici had contact with Bryson. That was the least I could do for him. I never took his girls from him. I take them along with Rasheeda to see their fathers. When I first started to bring Rasheeda he wanted to see Tisha. We weren't together long, but he did love Tisha. Soon, she found out why he was there, and refused to be a part of his life. Tisha latched onto Maceo more than any of them. This was going to be a very hard struggled for me and my girls. Although I just lost my husband, I very upset that he actually died sneaking around with her.

Chapter Thirty-One

Two weeks later

I pulled into the reality office and stared over at the black Mercedes Benz with tinted windows. I really didn't think anything of it. It could've easily been a client, but Tamar cancelled every client for the next few weeks. He was taking it a little harder than me, which was understandable. Tamar was his only friend and they grew to become brothers.

I got out grabbing my purse and briefcase. I walked up to the building still staring at the Benz. I was mad because the windows were beyond tinted and you couldn't tell who was in that car. Soon as I walked in, I greeted Pam who was the secretary.

"Good morning Pam." I smiled at her.

"Oh, good morning Mrs. A." She called us both that never knowing how to pronounce our Russian name. "You look stunning as usual."

"Thanks." I looked out the window. "Hey, did anyone get out of that black Benz out there?"

Pam pointed. "He's getting out now."

We both looked out the window at the gorgeous black man who looked tall enough to be a basketball player. He was in a very well distinguished grey suit that yelled $3000. He looked around before walking towards the building.

"He was parked there since 9:30." Pam added.

I looked at my phone to see that it was 10:15. "I wonder what he wants."

"I don't know but he can come in here anytime. That man is hot!"

We both laughed at her comment. Looking at Pam, you'd think she was this innocent white woman who does no harm. Wrong! Pam was in her early fifties and she's been with us for the past five years. She was a great woman who did her job right, but outside of work she knew how to have fun and party.

The man walked in, looking around. He then set his eyes on me then smiled. He was a very sexy chocolate man who wore a full grown beard that was neatly trimmed and a nice low hair cut that reminded me of my ex Bryson. Deep sexy waves.

"May I help you?" I walked over to him. He was very tall, and I had to look up at him. Even in my 5 inch Alexandra McQueen's, he still beat me.

"Are you Mrs. Ankundinov?" He asked.

"Yes I am."

The man's smile widened and he lipped the word 'wow'.

"I see he love the sistah's." He tried to mumble.

"Excuse me?"

His mumble wasn't low enough, and I knew what he said loud and clear. He looked at Pam and then back to me.

"Is there a more private spot we can talk?"

I waved my hand towards Maceo's office. "Follow me."

I walked to the office and before I opened up the door, I looked back to see the man staring right at my ass. He quickly looked up and I smiled turning back to the door to open it. We walked in and I closed it behind us.

"Have a seat Mr....."

"Daniels. Please call me Jermaine."

"Okay Jermaine. So what can I do for you?"

Jermaine looked around the office and nodded his head as if he was pleased. I stood there and watched as he looked upon the shelves at the many pictures of our family. He then picked up the one of Maceo and I on our wedding day.

"You have a very beautiful family Mrs. Ankundinov."

"Thank you, but you can call me Melanie. Most people don't pronounce my last name well. You say it as if you know the family."

He act as if he didn't hear me. He just stared at our wedding picture for a very long time. I watched as his hand put more pressure onto the picture and I felt he would break it. His face seem to tense up, but then I think he realized something and calmed himself.

"Ummm, what can I help you with Jermaine?"

He took a deep breath and set the picture back down. He then turned to me and there was a smile. The smile wasn't fooling me, because something definitely wasn't right with this man.

"A couple weeks ago, I was doing a little grocery shopping. My wife went away for a while to see family. That's what she told me. She's a very sweet woman, so I had no reason to not trust her. Anyway, I notice my phone goes dead while I'm shopping, and that's not like me. I was going to run to the car and charge it, but I still had a little shopping to do. I finished maybe….uh….twenty minutes later. I get to my car, and I charge my phone. Soon as I get home, I put the groceries away and even cook me a small dinner. When dinners finished, I sit down and turn my phone back on. I have a voicemail from my wife. The message makes me not hungry and I'm angry."

"What did it say?" I asked as I was curious to what he was getting to.

"She left me a message telling me that she's been lying about who she really is, and that we're both in trouble and that someone is going to hurt us. She said she had a friend that was going to get us somewhere safe. Then she forgets to hang up the phone. I hear a man's laugh and he tells her she's crazy for thinking the Russians are after her."

"Hold up! Russians?"

"Your husband is Macao Ankundinov. My wife was the passenger in the car."

"Your wife? Your wife was the whore my husband died with?"

I walked away and towards the window. I tried to take a couple deep breaths and I soon felt a panic attack come on.

He touched me and I jumped. "Why'd you come here? I didn't want to be reminded."

"Please don't get upset Melanie. I came to talk to you in peace. I need your help, and I need to talk to Maceo's father."

"What the hell do you want with him? Do you have any idea who he is? You don't want to ever fuck with a man like Victor Ankundinov."

"Of course I know, he protected me. I don't know why he didn't kill me until after my wife was gone. She had all the information in a safe."

"How do your wife know Victor?" I wanted to go crazy. "He introduced her to my father-in-law? That son of a bitch!"

"Melanie, please calm down and sit. What you think happened never happened. I've been going crazy trying to piece all this together. I just got back from Sacramento last night and that was the last place I should've ever been. Can I tell you the truth, and you have to believe everything I say. Then you need to take me to Victor and we're going back to do some serious damage in that city."

"What are you talking about?" I was now thinking he was crazy.

"My wife was an assassin hired to kill me three years ago. I never knew of this until their accident. Maceo trained her. She called him for his help because she thought his father was after her for not killing me. Truth is, Maceo was not soupose to kill anymore. He promised you, and his contract says he was to stay away from my wife. Victor made a deal not to come after us as long as we stay under radar. Of course I thought I pulled a fast one and met a nice young woman. I changed my name to Jermaine. She knew everything about me all these years and refused to kill me. We fell in love."

"So, Maceo wasn't cheating on me?"

"No, he was helping my wife. She thought the Russians were going to kill us, but they were no Russians. I heard them on the phone. She never hung up the phone and I heard everything on my voicemail. They were taken to Sacramento and I need your father-in-law's help."

"Wait, are you trying to tell me they didn't die?"

"Their alive and their in Sacramento. I've been researching and I have an inside man. He tells me that Marques and his wife Delia runs an underground prison. We have to go get them."

"Are you sure about this?"

"The burned bodies we cremated was not our spouses. Our spouses are very much alive."

I walked over to the phone and speed dialed the only person I knew who could fix all of this.

"Hello." He spoke into the phone.

"How are you feeling?"

"I'm fine dear, how are you and the girls?"

"We're good. Girls are dealing but they good too."

"What can I do for you?"

"I need you to see someone for me. He has information about Maceo's death."

"Who is this that speaks of MY son?"

I looked up to Jermaine and gave him that look. He knew that look because he instantly replied.

"Tell him, Malcom Jamieson." He said.

I took a deep breath knowing that my father-in-law might not like what I have to say.

"He says his name is Malcom Jamieson."

Underground Prison

Chapter Thirty-Two

Maceo

*M*y father and mother was like Bonnie and Clyde. Mom grew up on a farm in Russia, but when she met my father at the age of sixteen she started smuggling drugs for him on the mules. She then showed my father her loyalty and killed his enemy with no hesitation. My mother was trigger happy. She'd kill first, and never attempt to ask questions. I was then born and you'd think she'd settle down for her child. She was stronger than every man and woman I knew including my father. Mom just had a weakness of thinking the world was against her. Maybe they were, and that's why she stayed ready. Anna was my mother. The most beautiful woman ever. She had ocean blue eyes and her hair was platinum blonde, and she never wore it down. I use to hear her say it attracted too many men. She only had eyes for my father. Loyal and faithful woman. Anna was down for whatever and head of my father's business. She was his number one killer and very proud of her.

I was twelve, and it was our first year in America. Mom had a target and she was teaching me the ropes. Many people would think Anna was a terrible mother for teaching me how to kill, but it only made me love her more. Anna was the best; my everything.

Junior Barros was our target. He owed my father a lot of money. Enough to get his ass killed. I was excited about this one because everyone feared Junior and me and mother were going to be the ones to put his ass to rest. My mom didn't trust me going in with her. She left me behind and told me to stay in the car. She said I was too young to handle danger like him. Unbeknownst to my mother, I was ready. I had a cousin name Irene who was the same age as me and his father had him killing on his own

173

already. I was jealous and wanted to be just like Irene. I was determined to make my father proud, just like Irene did. I followed her and she had no idea, but that was the worst mistake I've ever made. My mother was never careless, but when she spotted me and took her eyes off the target for one second, Junior got to her first. I was her distraction, and caused her to lose her life. Junior shot and killed my mother before she got to him. I didn't have time to cry. I had her other gun and didn't hesitate to blow his head off. Junior Barros killed my mother and I killed Junior Barros.

I knew the day I see my mother again, we'd both be in hell. She was no saint, and I definitely didn't fit that description neither. I was dead and I'm seeing my beautiful mother with her long platinum blonde hair cascading down her back. Her face was as pure and pretty as a porcelain doll. She was the definition of beauty. She had angel wings and innocence floated around her. I was dead and I went to heaven. God knew my heart.

"Maceo." I heard a very familiar voice calling my name. It wasn't my mother. I opened my eyes to reality. I seen Ashley's angelic face staring back at me. First instinct, 'Did we have sex last night?' I quickly sat up to look at my surroundings. I cringe at the sharp pain I felt all over, but that pain seem to fade away when I didn't notice where I was. Four walls, two twin size beds, a couple of dressers, and the room was mildly decorated. Who bedroom was I in? I looked over at Ashley and could now see the bruises on her face. She wore a small bandage on her forehead. Instantly, it all came to me. Memories of a car accident, and then an attack came to me. I remember two men, and then I was gone.

"Where are we?" I asked her.

She seem to look around as if it was her first time taking it all in. "Not sure. I woke up and seen you."

We both looked at the closed door and then back at each other. I got up first and then Ashley followed close behind. I was surprised when the knob turned, and slowly I opened up the door. The smell of bacon and syrup was now stronger. I poked my head out to see a huge live-in area. I finally realized we were in a house, and everything in the house was big. There was a couple of huge sectionals that seem to fit at least seven people each, a huge flat screen television, and a nice size kitchen. There was a very long dinette table that had many chairs around it. This was one huge open area, and then many doors circled around it. It was one big huge circular room. I assume the other doors were rooms like the ones Ashley and I were in since they all lined up together. I focused back on a woman coming out of an open door near the kitchen area. She seem to be the one cooking all the food that I was smelling. I was just bout to step out and approach the woman, but one of the closed doors opened. A man came out in nothing but jogging pants, while he was stretching. He walked over to the woman and slapped her butt. She playfully hit him and then he kissed her on the lips. Ashley and I stood back to observe.

"You know yo' ass can't cook." He told her.

"It's my day to cook, whether you like it or not." She then suddenly got serious. "Oh, I'm still pose to be mad at you. Get out my face."

The man sighed and shook his head before he spoke. "The shit will never work babe. He so untouchable."

"It's you Tay! You do it wrong every time. Now we have to wait another month before he shows his face down here."

"We should wait for Delia to come."

"That fool will never let Delia down here since Arlo came, besides I'm still fucking him so our plan will work. I can seduce that asshole better than anyone."

"You may have Marques wrapped around your finger, but you will never have them big ass body guards he bring with him. Them some serious dudes and they don't mess around."

"You, Tony, Arlo and Santigo could easily take two body guards. I got Marques so don't worry about him. We have to do this Tay. Aren't you tired of being a slave to him. We can't even feel the fresh air. I'm not living like this forever. I don't care how good he take care of us, I cant do this no more."

The man sighed and seem to get a little frustrated, but then seem as if he had an idea.

"Maybe we can do this. That new guy looks pretty strong."

"No, I don't trust him."

"Why? Cause he's white?"

"No! Carmen and Santigo white, so color is not the problem. I've been around Marques more than any of you. Marques talks about some Russian mafia. He works with them, and I know a Russian when I see one. That guy is Russian."

They were now talking about me and I didn't like being talked about. I stepped out the room into the open area.

"I am Russian." I startled them both. "But not with this Marques guy."

They were silent as they stared at me with shock written all over their face. I walked closer into the room and towards them, getting a better view of my surroundings.

"What is this place?" I asked them still looking around.

They both just continued to stare at me. Ashley finally came out and stood by my side.

"We are not the enemy. We were kidnapped and brought here. Were you guys kidnapped too?"

They were still hesitant, but the woman finally came from around the counbter. She was beautiful. She had nice hair, nice skin, and even her long tight fitting sundress was nice. Why was a beautiful, nice looking woman in a place like this where I believe we were all kidnapped. What was this place? Who the hell was Marques and Delia?

"My name is Shannon." The woman extends her hand to Ashley, and they both shake. She looks at me and hesitates before she shakes mine.

"What are you afraid of?" I asked her in my sexiest voice, which held the accent.

She seem to blush. "I....I just know your Russian."

"That offends you? I am married to a beautiful black woman you know."

She looks over to Ashley, and I shake my head no.

"We're just friends. So, tell us about our situation."

She looks back at the man. "That's Tayvion. We were also kidnapped along with others who live here. Those are their rooms."

She pointed to the many doors that surrounded us, and then she looked back at Tayvion.

"Push the button." She told him.

Tayvion goes over to a shelf and he pushes a button. An alarm goes off and seconds later all the doors begin to open. More people come out of the rooms, and I look around and finally counted eight others.

"Sit around the table." Shannon told them. "We have two new ones."

"Can I at least brush my teeth?" Another woman asked with an attitude.

"No! This is imoportant. There is always a reason why Marques brings us here."

"Give us five minutes Shannon. We're all just getting up."

"Uugghh! Fine!" She walked back around the counter. "I'll fix the plates while you guys go freshen up. Five minutes!"

Everything seemed weird as these normal people scattered around this live-in area. Ashley and I stood there thinking that we were in a fantasy world. At least that's what I was thinking.

"Have a seat." Shannon announced. "Breakfast is ready."

Ashley looked over at me and I assume she wanted me to take the lead. I sat at the huge table that seem to probably fit us all. The woman Shannon started to put down big bowls of bacon, grits, eggs, and a stack of pancakes. The man Tayvion set out the plates.

"Is this our home now?" Ashley leaned over to whisper to me.

"No!" I grabbed her hand under the table to assure her. "I promise you that I will find a way."

She slightly smiled and I could tell she was scared. First time ever I seen fear in this woman's eyes. I looked around and seen Tayvion staring at us as if he was listening to our conversation.

"We been trying to find a way for three years." He told me.

"Three years?" I repeated to myself.

I looked back over at Ashley, and she let out a tear that she must've been holding. She quickly wiped them away as everyone came back into the room and sat at the table. Shannon was last to sit as she set two large pitchers of orange juice on the table. For us to be kidnapped, I do admit we were eating well.

"Well." Shannon clapped her hands together as she looked our way. "I'll start this off."

She cleared her throat. "Three years ago, Kizzy and I were kidnapped." She points across the table to another pretty girl that wore a great smile. She was the same girl who had the attitude about brushing her teeth.

"We wake up in a basement with a couple of beds. Later on comes Tayvion, Cassandra, Antonio and Tameka. It was just us six for a year. Well....six survivors. There has been a few in between. Roger comes to get them, and when Roger comes, we know that person isn't coming back. I'm not for sure, but we all assume they kill whoever Roger comes to get. Anyway, then comes Carmen and Santigo. That's when we were all relocated here, and behind those black doors is the lab. Arlo and Cassie came six months ago, and now you two. Now let me break this down. Marques has gone insane and he thinks he is God. I know him more than anyone here because I was married to him."

"Wait." Ashley interrupts. "You were his wife? Why'd he….I don't fucking get it. He has to be really sick to put his wife here."

Shannon rolled her eyes, and flipped her hair as she began the second part of her story. "Marques got ahold of some power and went crazy with it. His father is a killer and his father works for killers. Marques one day came up with the idea of imprisoning people who have done him wrong. At first, he just kept us in a basement. Then he became a genius and made us work. That lab he has, we work eight hours a day making this new drug he introduced to the streets about a year ago. It's called sohoga, better known as 'soso'. It was foundlast year through a drug called whoonga which is used to treat HIV. Whoonga is one of the many ingredients in soso. One of us has been taking many meds to treat the HIV disease."

"Someone here is HIV positive?" Ashley interrupts.

The most gorgeous woman in the room raises her hand. I had my eye on her since she entered. She had exotic features, including these bright pretty greenish hazel eyes. Her body was sexy as ever, but of course no one nowadays look like they have the disease. Ashley's husband sure don't look it.

"Is that a problem?" She politely sassed Ashley.

"No, it's just….mu husband. He has it too."

"I'm sorry. My name is Tameka. If you ever need to talk, I'm here."

"Thanks."

"I was the reason soso was created." Tameka went on. "I had a chemical imbalance once with a few of the drugs I was taken. I wasn't myself and he noticed how happy and crazy it made me. At the same time, I became addicted to that certain pill along with an herb that was brought from Alstralia. He then brought in a guy name Maze and started switching up drugs and feeding it to him. Carmen and Santigo are Marques scientist and help create soso. Maze was overly addicted and it made him crazy. One day Roger came to get him. Soso became real popular real fast and we are the only ones in the world making it. It's amazing what soso can do to you. Anyone who gets hooked on it, it's impossible to get off. Marques is making millions onm this. In return, he lets us live well, and once a month we make a list of what we want, and we always get. We have cable, with a few TV's, but no radio, phones or internet. We get no contact with outside people besides him, and them two body guards or Roger."

I took in a deep breath trying to take it all in. Then I realized everyone in the room did something to hurt Marques. Why were they all here?

"SO, what did you all do to him? Why'd he lock you up?" I asked.

"After we tell you, you two have to tell us everything about yourself." Shannon explained. "A Russian and a black girl together?"

"Go ahead." I replied. "I'll tell you."

Shannon smiled and then looked around at the others. She then clears her throat and got serious. "Like I said; I'm Shannon his ex-wife. He hates me because I left him when he had nothing. That devastated him, and he turned to crack and fell all the way off. That is.....until he found his father Harold. Harold was rich and he works with the Russians which gives them power. I assume you know that, but still have no idea why you are here."

"He Russian?" Tameka asked with a shocked look.

Just then, everyone seem to stop eating and gasp. Some seem afraid, and some were angry. Everyone was just going crazy.

"Please...." I began. "Let me explain myself. I promise I am no threat. Just tell me a little more about yourself. I will tell you about me and Ashley."

"Fine." Tameka started next. "I'm Tameka Bee, and I'm married to Harold. From what my stepson Marques tells me, I'm here because he's saving my life. I cheated on Harold with a man I fell in love with. I accidently gave him HIV and he gave it to his girlfriend, so now Harold wants to kill me. Thanks to Marques, he cant find me. With the Russians behind him, I was for sure he's find me......Are you sure your not the spy looking for me?"

"No, Im not a spy." I assured her.

"Well, unlike everyone else here I'm thankful."

I look over at Ashley, and I notice her tense look. She slightly shakes her head. Tameka was drop dead gorgeous, but I could sense a little cockiness in her. To be HIV and giving it away like it's candy, she seem a little selfish.

"My name Antonio, call me Tony." The skinny kid two seats down from me announced. He looked very young and I'd guess maybe early twenties.

"I uh....i did something bad to a young lady that was very close to Marques wife Delia. I honestly didn't know I hurt her until I seen the video."

"I didn't know until we got here." The man Tayvion interrupts.

"Yeah." Tony agreed. "They say I raped Brooke, which is a friend of Delia."

"I was there too." Tay said. "Brooke went crazy over that shit and my best friend got killed in the process. We regret it and feel bad but we really didn't know. We were college kids and we thought she was having fun with us. There was a few other guys involved but were killed in the process of getting here. They fought back and that Marques quit being Mr. Nice guy after this drug came out."

There was a small silence before a girl with long braids stood up. She was very plain and had the look of innocence. Nerdish but still cute in her own way.

"I'm Cassandra. I'm here because I was the one who set Brooke up. I may be the one at fault because I knew she had a date rape drug, but I was stupid and was trying to have fun. I didn't think she'd be hurt by it."

She quickly sat back down and grabs a piece of bacon as if she just didn't reveal the worse news ever.

"I'm Kizzy. I was Marques lover at one time."

I almost smiled but I knew the blushing was coming out, because this dude Marques had the most beautiful women ever at his feet. Then he traps them here. I wonder what his wife looks like.

Kizzy smiled when she finally realized my blush. "I use to work for him as his personal assistant, and we had sex....a lot." She then rolls her eyes at Shannon. "We still do."

"He uses you like he uses me, so get over yourself."

"Whatever! You need to leave Marques alone because you have Tay. You fucking stole Marques and now Tay. Stay the hell away from my men."

Tay pounded the table. "Chill out Kizzy! We all family now so you two need to get over this thing you have over each other."

Kizzy sighs. "Anyway, I set Marques up to get robbed by my brother. My brother is dead, and I'm here so we failed."

Kizzy then crosses her arms over her chest, and she stares at the woman across from her.

"I guess it's my turn." The woman says. "My name is Cassie, and this is my husband Arlo. Arlo couldn't keep his dick in his pants. He started seeing Delia and got caught by me. I followed the bitch one day and when I confronted her, her husband Marques was there. I didn't hold back and at that moment I didn't care. I guess I did the wrong thing because that night Arlo and I go to sleep in our home but we wake up here. I see our face on the news and our family is worried about us."

Cassie let out a small tear and her husband Arlo pulled her into his arms. Next, the nerdy white guy clears his thorat. I assume he wanted to speak next.

"Santigo, and this is my lab partner Carmen. We are scientist from Ashford laboratories and two of the best. We are both here because Marques had us experimenting, creating soso. I assume we will never see home. I just got married and I know my wife is probably dying right now."

"My family too!" Shannon interrupts. "Marques comes down once a month to pick up the supplies, and most of the time to have sex with me."

"And me!" Kizzy adds.

Shannon rolled her eyes. "That bitch too. But my point is, we've been trying to trap him. When he comes, he brings two big body guards and they stand at the entyrance and never blink an eye. Delia's not allowed to come here because of Arlo. We need a plan to take them down and get the hell out of here."

"Tell us about yourself." Tay interrupts Shannon. "Why Marques got you two?"

I look over to Ashley and she nods her head. I was going to let her take over.

"Don't judge us!" Ashley starts off. "You guys were truthful and we didn't judge you. Now it's our turn. You may not like what you hear and you may even be a little uncomfortable when I tell you this, but we are all in this together so don't turn on us and we wont turn on you."

I watch as a few of them stop eating and was ready for Ashley to speak.

I was even ready. She had me on my heels and I actrually knew what she was going to say.

"Three years ago, I worked for Victor. For those who don't know, he is THE BOSS! Leader of the Russian mafia. He gave me a job an di failed to complete. I fell in love and married the victim I was to kill. Surprisingly, Victor didn't kill me for it. He actually left us alone and told Maceo to stay away from me. I called Maceo a few weeks back. I thought the Russians had went back on their word, and I needed Maceo to helop me. Come to find out, the Russians were not after me. It was Marques and his people. I think the night they took us, they thought they were taking me and my husband Jermaine. They didn't expect Maceo to be with me. I don't think they know they kidnapped a Russian."

"Your balck and you work for the Russins?" Shannon asked. "What you do?"

"I was an assassin. I kill people."

"And I trained her." I announced. "She had skills. Besides, I love black women."

"So, you two are together?" Shannon was confused. "But, I thought both of you were married to other people."

"Ashley is my ex. I am married and have five children. My father is….."

Just before I could speak the big steel door opens. In walks two big men and three average looking men. Two of the men looked familiar. Another man who also seemed pretty strong stepped up. He was dressed in a expensive suit and seem very distinguished. His eyes went directly to me and Ashley.

"Fuck!" He yelled out, and I knew he didn't like seeing me. I was about to be trouble.

Chapter Thirty-Three

Marques

"I cant believe you dumb fucks!" I blurted out. I looked over at Bryce and Leon, my two henchmen. I nodded my head and they pukked out their silencers sending one shot to Roger and Pete. A couple of the women almnost screamed but knew better. Roger and Pete were two of my men who helped put all this together with me. I trusted them and they never gave me a reason not to. That was until I seen who was staring back at me. Everyone in the room seem to silently scream as Bryce and Leon dragged Pete and Roger out the stell doors. Seconds later, they were back standing right behind me but all I could do was stare into the eyes of Victor Ankinudov's only son. I didn't know Maceo, but Victor talked highly of him. He loved his son and would kill for him. He wouldn't care how much money I've made him at Aries, I bet he'd still kill me if he knew I had his son.

So, I betrayed my father and Victor by kidnapping a few people they wanted. They were out to kill and at first I just wanted to keep them prisoners forever. I didn't want to kill anyone. After my first kill, it felt good, and I wanted to do it again, except Delia was in my way. She didn't like that side of me and I promised her I wouldn't kill again. I fonally found the man everyone was looking for. Malcom was a very wanted man and it really surprised me that he married the woman that was soupose to kill him. I was for sure Roger and Pete made me happy by getting both Malcom and Ashley, instead they call me this morning with the news no one would ever want to hear. Now I'm in a fucked up position. I couldn't just let Maceo go now.

"Maceo?" I looked at the Russian.

He stands and my two men steps forward. I hold my hand up letting Bryce and Leon know it was cool. Maceo wasn't that dumb to step to me in my kingdom.

"You the guy Marques?" He asks me.

"That would be me."

"Why am I here?"

"We made a mistake. As you witness, they paid for it. I'm sorry you're here and had to see my secret. I was actually going to finally meet you and thought we'd be good friends. Then I get a call from your father who says you were in a horrible car accident and didn't make it. I'll make sure to send flowers to your father."

"Fuck the flowers." He spat. "Your going to let me and Ashley go, and we can forget any of this happened. If you know my father, then you know me. I would keep all I've seen a secret. You have my word."

I took in a deep breath and looked back at the others. My eyes specifiacally landed on Shannon, my ex-wife. I hate that bitch but could never get enough of her. They way she feels is amazing and I need a pice of that ass every now and then. I shook the thought of Shannon sitting on my face and looked back at Maceo.

"Ashley...no! I need her and I want Malcom. You....hell no! Your father would have my head. He thinks you're dead and we'll keep it that way. I will make sure you are treated good and have the best of everything. You don't have to work in the lab like the others. Whatever you want, I will deliver." I gave me an evil smirk. "Except your freedom."

His face was red, and I knew he was mad. He reacted quick when he charged me and I fell to the floor. I immediately went down and he was now on top of me throwing blow after blow to my face. It felt as if he was beating me for an hour and I wondered when my two most trusted henchmen were going to save me. I thought my life was over when he started choking the shit out of me. This man was strong and I knew why Victor named his only son his number one killer. I amost took my last breath until suddenly he was kicked off me. I tried getting up and catching my breath but it was extremely hard. I didn't want to go down again, so I coughed out all I had to catch my breath so I could quickly get the hell out of here. When I got up, I seen Maceo having Leon in a choke hold, and then we all heard it. He broke Leon's neck. That could've been my neck a minute ago. I then heard a gun being cocked back and I looked towards the door and see Bryce pointing a gun at MAceo. I quickly stood all the way up holding onto my sore neck.

"Noooo!" I yelled to Bryce.

Leon's lifeless body falls out of Maceo's arms as I back up to the steel door. Bryce gets in front of me trying to block me, but still pointing the gun at Maceo. Right when I was almost at the door, Bryce goes down and his gun goes off. I slightly pause trying to figure out what just happened. I looked down at Bryce who was now dead with a knife straight in his neck. I looked up to see aAshley in the kitchen bout ready to throw another knife. Quickly, I exit the doors and push the button on the outside securing it locked. I could hear the knife hit the door. A second time I almost died in the last five minutes.

"What the hell?" I said to myself.

I ran over to the elevator and got on. Soon as it went up and opened to the abandoned gas station, I felt safer. The gas station was my cover up for where I keep my prisoners. No one would ever know there was a drug lab and prisoners underground. I ran over to the limo that waited and I quickly got in. My driver Ken looked through the mirror wondering where they all were.

"Just drive!" I yelled out in frustration.

He pulled off leaving the abandoned gas station

That was practically in the middle of nowhere. There was an old house across the street behind some trees but I checked that out and some old lady who has no clue what's going on live there. I tried catching my breath and for some reason looking out the back window every few seconds as if dude was going to escape. He killed my best body guard with his bare hands, and almost killed me. Then that bitch Ashley killed the other one. I unlocked the safe in the limo and pulled out my special powers. These two combined was unbelievable, and when I go back down to "the clinic", I had to up my powers. Fuck doubling, I'm tripling! I done kidnapped some real killers and if I didn't get my shit right, I was going to be next.

Chapter Thirty-Four

Maceo

"Everyone okay?" I looked around at each and every shocked face in the room. No one said a word. They all seem stuck. I walked over to Ashley, who started walking over to the guy she stuck with the knife. Ashley's always had good game when it comes to throwing knives.

"He's dead!" She then looked at me. "I'm too damn good."

"Shit." Shannon mumbled. "Where the hell you guys learn all tjhat? We almost had Marques. We can actually get out of here with you two."

Ashley looked at Shannon and the others. "I wasn't lying when I said that I was an assainsin. I was hired to kill my husband, but I fell in love with that man. He's my everything."

"Marques mentioned Malcom's name." Tameka spoke up. Malcom Jamieson. You guys know him?"

"He's the man I was hired to kill. The love of my life. He goes by Jermaine now......" Ashley stopped talking and had this confused look on her face, while at the same time taking a step forward toward the group. "Wait, you know him?"

Tameka seem to hesitate. "I....I do. He's uh...."

"Was he the man you gave your disease to?" Ashley shouted out, scaring everyone around her.

"It was an accident."

"Accident my ass! You ruined him."

I seen the kill in Ashley's eyes, and I immediately went to her and stood in her face.

"We're all in this together." I grabbed her shoulders and made her pay attention to me. "She is not the enemy."

Ashley stared into my eyes for a long time, then finally I seen them soften. She let out a small sigh. "She hurt Jermaine."

"And you healed him. You are the love of his life, and need to put your anger toward getting us out of here. We all have to stick together. Look what you did. You protected us. We're going to get out of here."

"How Maceo!" She yells at me. She then pulled away from me and kicked the dead guy in the head a few times. I let her get her frustration out, but Santigo made it his business to go to her. He pulled her away from him and tried calming her down. Surprisingly it worked. He mustve had that gift because Ashley was a feisty one.

"Do you know what you just did?" Shannon said to Ashley. "That was something we been wanting to do since we got here. None of us couldk ever do the shit you and your friend just did. We need you two and we need a plan. That shit was fire."

"You think his punk ass would come back after this shit happened?" Tavion waved at two dead guys.

"Oh, he'll come back." Santigo announced. "We have twenty-eight pounds of pills he forgot to collect while he was here. They will be accumulating and Marques won't forget his money maker."

"Good." I spoke. "First off, what we going to do with these two big ass men?"

"Trash compactor." Antonio mentioned.

All eyes went to Antonio, and I knew everyone was wondering if that was a good idea. I was wondering what it lkook like. It might work.

"Too small." Tayvion said.

"We have chemicals in the lab that could almost melt them. It's as good as acid."

"It will smell horrible." I told them.

"Burn them."

"Still has a smell."

"Let's do it anyway." Tameka got back in on the conversation. "Whatever we do, they going to smell. Their dead! We have to get a move in on this. Marques will be back."

"I thought you don't want to ever leave." Shannon reminded her.

"I don't, but…..Ashley needs her man and I'm willing to help any way I can."

I notice Ashley roll her eyes, but I knew she'd leave Tameka alone. Tameka was willing to sacrifice her life to help us all to get home, then Ashley would keep her distance.

We all hustled together and dragged the men in the bathroom. After stripping them naked, taking all their belongings including the gun, Ashley and I took

Everyone looked his way, wondering if that was a good idea. If I knew what it looked like, it might work.

"Too small." Tayvion said.

"We have chemicals in the lab that can melt human skin, maybe not the bones, but it might be pretty messy."

"And it will smell." I told them.

"Burn them!" Tayvion voiced.

"Still might smell!" I said again.

"Let's do it anyway." Tameka stepped back in on the conversation. She then looked over to Ashley. "I know if I get out of here; I'm a dead woman, but I'm in this with you guys. You need to see Malcom again."

Ashley made a face, but I knew she understood.

"We need to get moving." Tameka continued. "You never know when he'll come back."

We all hustled together and dragged the men in the bathroom after stripping them naked and taking all their belongings including their guns. Ashley and I then took over and started cutting them up. No one else could stomach what we were doing. I hated this part of the job, but someone had to do it.

Chapter Thirty-Five

Ashley

The first time I murdered someone, I remember standing in the shower for a couple hours. I scrubbed my body raw, and still felt his blood all over me. He was my stepfather, and I did him the same way I just did these two men. At first Maceo and I tried chopping them up, but with little to no tools it was pretty much impossible. Then Santigo gave us some type of chemical he had mix together that was toxic, but not hat strong. It just made their bodies really messy and harder to deal with. In the end, we got them pretty much cut, and melted up to fit into trash bags. I haven't killed in three years, so I felt some type of way. This shit wasn't normal, and I vowed not to ever do this again. Meeting Malcom, made me realize that wasn't who I wanted to be.

At first, I loved the power of people fearing me before I killed them; not to mention I did have the skills. I turned my life around when I met Malcom, and started praying with him. He was a good man; not perfect, maybe even a great man! He had issues and problems in life, but still had God. God was never in my life, and my mom didn't raise me to know him. I had a weak mother who thought it was cute for men to beat them black and blue. She never cared about me or my well-being. I even graduated from high school with honors and put my own self through college, and that's when I met Maceo. At first glance, he got your attention. He wasn't your typical white boy. His strong acent use to turn me on, and his tatted up body had me weak every time. Maceo was smart, strong, attractive and aggressive. I loved all that about him, and thought I be with this man forever. I even loved him more when he taught me how to kill, and life couldn't get any better. I fell in love, but as time went on I found a new love and that was murder. I had an addiction to killing and needed it as if it was a drug. Malcom came into my life and cured me. He was my new drug. I needed and missed him.

"Are you okay?"

"Maceo!" I yelled out in shock as I tried covering my naked body with my hands, but this co-ca cola shape was not hiding behind my small hands.

"I'm still in the shower!" I continued yelling.

"I was worried about you. It's been like an hour."

He stood there for a second staring at me from head to toe. My hands were barely covering my breast and my vagina that wasn't so balad anymore. It's been awhile and I felt embarrassed that Maceo seen me this way.

"Stop looking at me that way." I told him.

His eyes finally met with mine and he blushed. "You sure you okay?"

"Pass me a towel please."

He grabbed a towel off the shelf and gave it to me. I turned off the cold shower and wrapped my body with the towel. I stepped out and Maceo leaned against the sink watching me.

"I've seen it all before, so quit being shy." He said as he continued to admire me.

"I'm not being shy. Your married and I'm married."

"I would never cheat on my wife Ashley. Even if we stayed in this place for years, I'd stay celebant."

I shrugged my shoulders. "So will I."

"So why'd you give me your thong, and why'd you kiss me?"

I looked away from Maceo and stared into the mirror. I tightly closed my eyes trying to trap the tears that wanted to fall.

"No, no, no!" He came over to me. "We will not do that!"

Maceo pulled me into his arms and held me tight. I tried my hardest not to let all my feelings out, but the loudest cry just flowed. I cried into his chest and he held me tight while stroking my hair.

"I will get us out of here Ashley. You will see Malcom again, and I will see my family. I know it hurts to be away from him, but we've got to stay strong for. Them people out there are depending on us to help get them out. We our natural born killers and we are going hard to get the fuck out of here. Stop crying!"

I took in a deep breath and tried wiping the tears away. I looked up at Maceo and he looked at me. For a second, I was ready to kiss his lips. I was going to; just as I did before at the restaurant, except this time I was a lot stronger. I quickly pulled back at the same time he did.

"It's getting late. We been doing that shit all day and I know your tired. Dude may come back in the morning and we need a plan. Shannon wants us all to get up early and talk this over."

"Okay."

I tightened my towel around my body and walked out the big bathroom. It was like a dorm bathroom. There were five showers, five stalls and five sinks. There were curtains around each shower and doors on stalls so at least we had a bit of privacy. Actually, Marques had his prisoners living very well, but were all shielded from the outside world and our families. We were even forced to do illegal work. Living here might be nice, but I refused. I couldn't do this another day without Malcom. I lived and breathed him, so this was hurting me more than anything.

Walking out into the living area in front of the others felt odd. They all watched me walk into my room and I felt like a piece of meat in the lion's den. I knew they probaky thought crazy thibgs about me since I just literally chopped up some people. I tried not to care, but lately I did. I didn't want ti kill again, and I truly felt disgust all over me.

Soon as I got into my room, I shut the door and stared off into space. I use to love that feeling, but I didn't like that they seem to be scared of me. I mean, I did just chop and deteriate two body guards.

Chapter Thirty-Six

Delia

"Ms. Delia, your sister-in-law is here." I heard my maid Patty's voice.

I looked up at the time and shook my head to myself. It was 8:15 in the evening and Marques was still not back. Corrine has been calling me all day asking for him and telling me he's nmot answering his phone. I was hoping she didn't just show up, and definetly not this time when the limo driver Ken just called and explained that he was dropping off a very high Marques. Ken said it wasn't his usual high neither. He was going crazy, and very unlike the Marques I had gotten use to.

Over the past year and a half Marques had became addicted to snorting cocaine and shooting steroids. The stress of power had really gotten to him, and he feels he has to be high 75% of the day. I've grown tired of it, and keeping it a secret from his family. When he does it, he feels like superman. I hate that he does coke because I'm afraid he'll dip into his own creation soso, and once he does that shit; it's over! A soso addict is compared to an heroin addict, and he was once there before. I hate for my husband to go backwards. We've worked so hard to build our empire, making Aries millions of dollars and undercover drug Lords whom also gotten rich with our new drug Soso. Having them prisoners was a good idea at first, and then I started feeling bad. Instead of freeing them, we decided to give them a good home, good food, and the best of everything. They live good, and I still feel bad and I know Marques do too. Ever since he lost Angel, he's gotten worse. SHe was the first and only prisoner he kidnapped and had no idea how she escaped. Angel was a murderer and hada psycho problems, so she was making him nervous.

I couldn't take it all. All this madness had led me into having an affair with this sexy CEO name Arlo. I really fell hard for him and his stupid wife found out and told my crazy husband. Now both, Arlo and his wife are locked away underground thirty miles out. I'm angry that we let it get this far, and now Marques has gone crazy over it. We have one son and I do want more children, but not like this. Sometimes I feel I don't want anymore with him.

I am nmot allowed at the clinic without Marques. The Clinic is code word for the prison, and that's what we been using these past couple years. There has to be a way I could go there alone, because Marques has changed all the alarms and codes. I've been once without him, because our most trustworthy body guard had helped me see Arlo. We were able to talk, but I couldn't touch him. Definetly nmot with his wife starng back at me. I really think I love Arlo, and I feel he loves me back. I did get to tell him that I will fix all this. I just hope I can keep my word.

"Is she comning back here?" I asked Patty.

"Yes ma'am." Patty admitted. "She's yelling throughout the house. She seems very angry Ms. Delia."

"Uuughhh!" I slightly yelled. "Okay, thanks."

Soon as Patty left me, I could hear Corrine heading my way."

"What the hell's going on Delia, and you better not lie to me!" Corrine yelled at me from a distance as she headed my way.

I sat there, waiting for her to reach me. I knew she'd go crazy when she finally came around. Of course she would! She hasn't been able to talk to her brother lately. She's been assuming he has fallen off. She was right, but I couldn't tell her that. He was wasy worse than before, because it's affecting his personality to a very dangerous person.

"Delia!" She was finally in my face. "I know you heard me calling you! What are you not telling me? Marques hasn't been answering my phone calls, and he missed the meeting with Mr. Kim Tou. That wasn't like him to miss that. He has been anticipating this meeting since last week. My father is extremely mad cause Marques been fucking up. Not to mention the missing 3.5 million that's still unaccounted for."

I heard her, but I didn't know how to answer her. What do I say? Marques would be pissed if I told her the whole truth. Delia was my friend, more like my sister and I hated the lies that have been flowing out my mouth to her.

"Earth to fucking Delia!" SHe stood there tapping her foot, waiting for me to respond.

I finally looked up at her. I was ready to have my breakdown and she was about to witness. My eyes were cloudy and fuzzy with tears, but I was still speechless.

"Oh no!" She sat right down beside me. "What's wrong Delia? You can tell me. Is it Marques? Is he on that shit again? I knew something wasn't right."

"Everything is fine babygirl!"

We both turned around to see Marques standing there with shades on. Hi voice was cool, amd his appearance seem to be alright, but I noticed the tremor in his left hand. Lately that was something he couldn't control due to the coke and steroids. It wasn't noticeable to others because he tried hiding it, but I knew. Today it was actually worse than any other time and I was surprised Corrine didn't catch that. She quickly left my side and ran over to Marques. She snatched the shades off of his face and threw them at him.

"I knew it!" She yelled out. "What the hell is wrong with you? Why'd you go back? Daddy has done so much for us, and you go back to being a junkie! Why Marques?"

Corrine then walked back over to me and slapped me across the face. I didn't know how to react because that took me by total shock. I held my cheek with a look of shock across my face. I thought I was the victim.

"It's probably your fault!" She yelled at me. "You got him back on it, didn't you? I knew something was up. You two been very distant."

Then out of nowhere Marques comes over and grabs Corrine by her neck, practically throwing her back. She landed hard on the patio almost hitting her head by the stoned sidewalk. I quickly jump on Marques to get off of her.

"Marques! What are you doing? Stop it!" I yelled as he stood back to watch me help Corrine. "You okay?"

"Get the fuck away from me!" She yelled out with tears comning down her face.

Corrine then screamed out as she tried to get up. I coukd tell that fall really hurt and she was in pain.

"Let me help you!" I tried helping again.

"NO!" She continued to yell. "I'm so fucking done here! I'm telling daddy your back on that shit and you fucked up the deal with Mr. Tou."

I looked up at Marques to see something in his eye. It was something I seen before but this was worse. He immediately walked away leaving me and Corrine.

"Corrine please go. You have to hurry and get out of here. Your brother has really gone crazy, and he's sick! I didn't get him started on any drug, but he does coke and shots steroids. It's made him crazy and he thinks he's untouchable. He hurts people now and I don't like it. He did take all that money from Aries and invested it in his prison he has created. He also made this new street drug and wont replace the money to Aries. He keeps hiring all these bodyguards and kidnapping people. I think he's trying to put you there. You have to get out of here now before he comes back."

"What?!" She seemed confused. "My brother does what?"

I tried helping her up. "Come on, I'll tell you later."

I finally got Corrine on her feet, and helped her off the patio. We ran out through te backyard and to the left side of the house. WE went all the way around the house, and when we seen the driveway with her car there, I just knew she was going to be safe. Suddenly, Marwues appears out of nowhere like a mad man.

"I love you Corrine, but you're going to ruin everything I've built." He said.

"Nooooo!" I yelled as I tried to push Marques away from her.

He quickly swung his arm and I went flying into the bush. I look up to see he had caught Corrine and stuck that needle into her shoulder. She instantly was out. I quickly got up and started hitting him. I couldn't believe he would di his sister that way. He back handed me in the face, and it felt as if he hit me with a brick. I had fell back again, but this time I didn't get up. I just laid there sobbing as he picked his sister up and threw her over his shoulder like it was nothing.

Chapter -Maceo

I stood outside the bedroom door waiting on Ashley to get herself together. It's been awhile and I wanted to go in there, but knew she needed time. I stared off into the live-in area at Shannon and Tayvion who were cuddled on the sofa talking small talk. I assume them two were a couple just like Arlo and Cassie, except Arlo and Cassie were more distant. They also sat on the sofa staring at some sitcom I knew nothing about. Tameka entered the room in a silk robe wrapped tightlky around her curvy body. Her long hair was down her back and she was rubbing lotion in her hands. She walked staright over to me and stood in my face. I slightly inhaled without her noticing me sniff up her vanilla and coconut scent.

"You should go get some rest." She said. "It's getting pretty late and I know your tired."

"I wish I could but Ashley need a little time alone."

"She hates me, don't she?"

"She'll be okay."

"I fell in love with him." She admitted. "There was no man that showed me love the way Malcom did. It really was an accident."

I nodded my head, feeling somewhat sorry for this beautiful woman. Such beauty, and she was living with HIV.

"May I ask you; how'd you contract this disease?"

She sighed. "I long time ago I fell in love with my mother's boyfriend."

I raised my eyebrow and made a slight face.

"Don't judge me!"

"I'm not. It's okay, we all go through some type of crazy shit in life."

I could see a grin sneak up on her face. "Well...I loved him. Then I cheated on him and got pregnant. He couldn't have kids, so he knew my child wasn't his. I was afraid so I ran away to be with the father of my child. Come to find out, he didn't care for me and started to treat me like a whore. He made me have sex with different men, so I killed him."

"You killed him?" I was surprised, because Tameka looked like a very sweet woman.

"I did."

Tameka leaned against the wall with me and she folded her arms over her chest.

"One of them men gave me that disease, and my ex took me back and we got married. We were always careful and he never caught it. I really don't know how Malcom got it. He shouldn't have caught it. Now my husband wants to really kill me. Not only did I cheat on my husband for the second time, but his daughter was Malcom's girlfriend. She got the disease too.

Before I could respond, the steel doors opened and everyone jumped up on guard. It was too late, because everyone was so relaxed and we reacted slow. Marques had a plan. The entire room was filled with smoke and coughing could be heard. Next thing I know, I was out.

I opened my eyes and the first person I seen was Tameka. She was on the floor laid out sleep just as I was a minute ago. I sat up slightly dazed as I looked around the room. Everyone was laid out on the sofa or floors. I stood up trying to shake the headache that was pounding in my head.

"What happened?" I heard a voice.

I turned around to see Tony coming out of his room looking like how I felt.

"Did we all just get drugged?" I asked him.

"I was on my headphones, next thing I see was smoke before I went out. I don't know what the hell happened. It's about one in the afternoon. We all had to be out at least thirteen hours."

Kizzy then came out her room looking all frantic. "Someone's here!"

Her loud voice stirred everyone else, and it seem to take them a second to get up but soon realized they were all drugged.

"What do you mean Kizzy?" I asked her.

"There's a woman in my room. I think I know her. She looks real familiar. She's in the other bed. I think Marques brought her in here last night. That's why he drugged us all."

I rushed to Kizzy's room with practically everyone following me. Soon as we all entered, the beautiful indian looking woman started to scream and I could tell we were scaring her. Tameka entered the room, and she stopped yelling and looked around.

"He really does this?" She stood up, looking at us all.

"Corrine?" Tameka walked up to her. "He brought you here?"

"Apperhently he did!"

She then looked at everyone and then back to Tameka. It took us all by surprise when the woman punched Tameka dead in the eye. Tameka fell back into Tayvion and Arlo quickly grabbed the feisty woman that looked as if she wasn't finish with Tameka.

"Bitch!" She yelled. "I been trying to find you for three years so I could fuck you up!"

Tameka didn't say anything back, but instead her eyes began to water. The woman puled away from Arlo. Tameka looked back at him.

"I'm fine." She said as she looked around again. Her eyes scanned the bedroom, and all of us. It was quiet for a minute. "Delia told me that my brother had prisoners. Are you guys them?"

"Yes." Shannon spoke up.

The woman sees Shannon and I see a smile appear on her face. "Shannon.....I was wondering what ever happened to you. Damn, this is bad."

I watch as she looks over to Kizzy. "I know you too!"

"I was his assistant." Kizzy said.

"Yeah, you were. My brother has gone crazy."

She continued looking round in disbelief, but when her eyes landed on me she began to walk closer. "You look very familiar.....I don't know where I know you from."

"Maybe I look like my father, Victor Ankuinov."

The woman cupped her mouth with her hands and eyes slightly got big. "Marques put you here? But why?"

"He thought I was Ashley's husband Jermaine...I mean Malcom."

"Malcom?"

Her face seemed confused and she looked around the room again. I looked around with her and that's when I noticed Ashley was nowhere to be found. Then it came to me; earlier I waited by the door nearly an hour for her to come out. Marques drugged us all before she ever came out. I never went back in to check on her.

"Hey, who is Ashley?" The woman asked me.

"Fuck!" I yelled out.

Something wasn't right, and I knew it. I pushed past everyone and made my way to the bedroom I left her in. I never checked on her. The door was closed, but I knew we all were drugged. I opened the door and seen Ashley naked laying on the bed. Blood was filled around both her wrist area. I yelled out, running to her side and I countinuously called her name. Nothing. There was no pulse, no heartbeat. She was slightly warm, but I knew she past on hours ago. I looked up to see Shannon and Tameka crying, looking back at me. Everyone else sort of stood back.

"How'd she get a knife in here without us noticing?" Shannon asked.

I looked back at Ashley, and her wrist which were sliced open. I then noticed there was no kinife or blade any where around her.

"How'd she cut herself?" I continued looking around.

"With a knife." Tayvion walked into the room with the answer that we all knew. But, what knife?

"I had a gun." He said. "I took it from the bodyguard, and I nticed all the knives and blades are gone. I think he took everything that can harm them out of here, including the knife she slashed her wrist with. There are no sharp objects in this place."

"That mutherfucker took everything!" Arlo shouted out.

I put my head down, and let out a small cry. I was heartbroken and sad that Ashley would do this top herself. She lost faith in me.

"What happen to her?" The new woman walked closer to us.

I stood up and faced the woman. "She couldn't take this! I told her I was going to get us out of here, and she didn't believe in me. I could get us out."

"Damn, I thought she was cool." Tayvion added. "She had skills killing that dude!"

I looked over at Tayvion and squeezed back a few tears. "I think that's what led her to kill herself. She didn't want to kill anymore. After falling in love with Malcom, she became a different woman. Better!"

"She married Malcom?" The woman was shocked. "My Malcom?"

Everyone looked at her, including me.

"That's Corrine." Tayvion tole me. "She' sthe woman I was telling you about. Malcom's girl. That's why she slapped Tameka."

"Well, Ashley was his wife, and now we have to figure out what we do with her. We cant do her like them men."

"I can come up with a formula that will cremate her." Santigo said. "I would hate to do her wrong. This may take me time, and skills but I will do anything for Ashley. She helped us out by killing that guy."

"She did that?" Corrine was shocked again.

"She was an assassin." I spoke. "Just like I am. She was hired to kill Malcom but she fell in love. She was good at what she do."

I took the sheet and pulled it over her body.

"Let's go Carmen, we have work to do." Santigo said as him and Carmen left the room.

I sat back down on the bed and stared at her body covered by the sheet. I was hoping the sheet would move and she'd breath again, instead blood instantly seped through. Cassie stepped forward and said a prayer. I was grateful for her. I looked around and seen everyone with there head bowed, even Corrine. After Cassie said her deep an dthoughtful prayer, every one said amen. Cassie then gave me a hug and I hugged her back. I appreciated it. I lost my friend, and now I was more than ready to get this guy Marques.

Chapter Thirty-Seven

My phone rung again, I knew I should've been pushing her away, but I couldn't. Her sex was addicting and I couldn't get enough of her.

"Wait babe." I tried getting up another time. "I need to get this."

"Mmmm, Get it then." She said in her most sexiest voice.

She then bounced her ass on my dick harder as if her life depended on this sexual ride. She finally slowed down and all I seen was her big beautiful ass gyrating slowly and I tried my hardest not to cum. I reached over on the nightstand and was finally able to grab my phone. It was Malcom, and I knew I had to take this.

"Babe, stop." I finally demanded as I pushed the talk button. "Yeah?"

"Everything in place?" He asked. "I'm coming back this weekend and I got someone with me."

"Who, you know I don't trust no one." I pushed Angel up off me and tried sitting up. "I don't think we should be getting anybody else involved."

"It's Victor's daughter-in-law. Victor only has our back if Melanie's with us."

I was all ears at the mention of Victor. "So you did speak to him?"

"Yes. It was all with the help of Melanie. I told her my story and she brought me to Victor. It wasn't easy, because I was the enemy telling him that I think his son is alive. He grilled me and grilled me until he felt he trusted my word. That was the hardest thing I ever had to do. I thought I was going to die. He actually sat back and had a drink with me. He told me he believed something is up with Harold and his family and he didn't trust them. Shit's not good and I can only speak to you in person. Melanie and I are going to stay with you."

I frowned my face at the phone and knew I didn't want Malcom at my house. I use to hate him and dispise his ass. Now we've been working together to bring down Marques and we do work well together. I looked back at Angel's sexy ass and knew it was now or never. I was in love with his ex-wife, and when all this was done and over with I wanted to marry her. I had to tell him and he was going to have to deal with it. Besides, he should understand because he was now a married man. He moved on and so did I. We both moved on from Farrah.

"That's cool, but your not going to like what's going on in my life. We can't have any issues or drama. Your going to have to deal with who I'm with."

"Are you serious? I don't care who your with. We both know it's not Farrah. She's the only person I would have a problem with if you two got back together."

"Are you sure?"

"You know what….she's your wife, so I really don't care."

"Good to know, but it's not Farrah. Farrah actually took me off her visitor list. I'm pretty sure she'll be happy to see you."

"Yeah, I probably should. With Dame gone, she don't have much family."

"Corrine sees her, and I hear Harold does too. She also has her aunt."

I could hear the sigh coming through the phone. "Anyway, You ever figure out who the other person was that was taken in that gas station?"

"No, I'm working on it."

"Alright, we'll call you when we get into town. It'll be a long drive, so maybe tomorrow evening."

"Cool."

I hung up and looked at the very sexy Angel. She was sitting on the bed massaging her breast. I knew she was teasing me. That's something she love to do.

"Malcom?"

"Yes, and he's going to stay here with us. Don't get any ideas!"

"Ewww, are you serious?" Angel made a face. "I would never! He's HIV positive."

Indeed he was, and so was Corrine. A little over three years ago, I hit rock bottom. I had turned to alcohol and it was no occasional thing for me. I was down and out, and ready to give up. I was out by the lake in the woods near a cabin I bought for Farrah and I. It was a place we hid most of the time when we wanted to get away from the city. Especially when we took Kiara and moved to New York. I had went back to the cabin to kill myself. I was that down and out and I didn't care anymore. I just wanted to end my life. It seemed as if I had no one. My father kept me from the family, so after he died; all I knew were the nanny. When I grew up, I left her and never looked back. I met Farrah and she was all that mattered. It hurts that she didn't like me anymore.

That day I wanted to kill myself, I entered the cabin and noticed that it was being lived in. I immediately took out my gun and quietly searched the house. When I went upstairs to one of the bedrooms, I noticed a male body on the queen size bed. He had a fan going on his naked body in only boxers. I put the steel gun to his head and ordered him not to make any moves or his brains would be all over the pillow. I then ordered him to slowly get up, and when I seen who he was; I felt everything fall to my stomach. Just a week back, I heard the rumors of him getting HIV from Tameka and then giving it to Corrine. Corrine had came back to New York to accuse that one dude she use to se. It was a shocker when she told me it wasn't him. I was highly angry that Malcom came to hide in my cabin and I wanted to dead him for Corrine. All that changed when Malcom told me that Farrah was the one that told him to hide here. I was all ears after hearing my wife name. I loved her dearly and I wanted her to acceot me. At first, I went back and forth in my head about killing him. I had the upper hand, but I wanted to hear more about his visit with Farrah.

Malcom actually saved me. For the next five months, I let him stay there. I'd go run errands and go into the city to get things he needed. He kept in touch with Farrah while she was in prison, and because of him she finally agreed to see me. That's when I moved all the way to Sacramento. She was being held there and I wanted to be closer to her and I brought Malcom along. Along the way, we changed his identity to Jermaine and he grew his beard out and cut his hair balad. Then he met Ashley and they became an item. Malcom and her developed a relationship and I was finally in a great place in life. I was seeing Farrah every week, and I even bought a house far out in the country outside Sacramento. Malcom and I became good friends and I was glad.

Living out here with no neighbors was great but nothing exciting to see. I decided to by a telescope and there was actually nothing to see except for an old abandon gas station. Not much of a scenery so I never paid it no mind. Every day, I still look out that telescope but one day seen activity. There was a limo that pulled up and a few men got out and went into the station. I was curious on why they went in there, so when they left, I got into my car and went there. I found nothing and like I thought, it was abandoned. On another day, same thing. The limo would come and men would get out and go in. Sometimes carrying loads of boxes in and coming out with sacks. I was getting mad when I'd go back over there and find nothing. It was pissing me off, and finally I got smart and put up a small unnoticeable surveillance camera. After a week of nothing, I finally started to see lots of commotion. Them same strong guys would bring lots of boxes, big and small into the station. I even notice the guys carrying a couple people in that looked dead and they didnt bring them back out. When they all leave, I go over there and still find nothing. Not even the two people I seen them bring into this place. I then put in a hidden audio camera. I had to hear what they were saying inside the station. Everything I heard had me in shock, and that's when I knew I had to call Malcom. By the time, I called Malcom, it was all too late because they kidnapped his wife, and the guy name Maceo whom later I find out was Victor's son. We had to come up with a plan and fast. I had no idea how to get into this secret prison. It had to be a fingerprint or some voice code. I couldn't even find a secret door in there. I just knew we had to do this with no mistakes so I was careful.

There was a day I had went back over there to install a few more cameras at different angles, and when I came out I notice a woman lying on the side of the road. It was right out side the station, and I wonder why I didn't notice her there before. She looked tired and dehydrated. I put her in my car and drove her back to my home. I nursed her back to life and found out she was kidnapped by them and escaped somehow but ended up close by the station. She said she only came out by the side of the road because she seen my car stop and knew I wasn't them. She said she was hiding for days. The woman was Angel Jamieson and that was a few weeks ago. I'm already in love and she wasn't going anywhere.

Angel stood in front of me and leaned down to kiss my lips.

"I'm going to take a shower babe." She told me as she kissed my lips a second time.

"I'll be in there to join you."

"Don't keep this ass waiting."

"I slapped her ass real good and she jumped. "Oh, I won't."

I watched Angel's volumptous ass walk away. It was nice and round, but still jiggled with every step she took. I was mesmerized.

I look at Malcom's name again on the phone, debating if I should shoot him a text with Angel's name. I wanted him to know and I wanted him to be okay with it. I let out a big breath as I quickly dismissed that thought and joined Angel in the shower.

Chapter Thirty-Eight

Marques

"Please tell me you know something!" Harold yelled.

I sat in the chair, in front of my father's huge desk. I let out a sigh, hoping he'd quickly let this shit pass.

"I'm sorry dad," I shrugged my shoulders. "Still nothing."

My father pounded the desk and then leaned back in his chair. The look on his face was pitiful. This past month he's been through hell and act as if he didn't know what to do without Corrine. I was his only son, and running his damn company. I felt as if he forgot about me and Corrine was all that matters. I really wanted to choke the shit out of him, but I had to contain myself. At least until I know he signed everything over to me. These past few weeks, murdering him was all I wanted to do. I use to dispise murder and that's why I created my prison. Then coke and steroids became apart of my diet and murdering started to become heavy on my mind.

Over the past three years, I've encountered twenty-eight victims. Today, only thirteen of them live in my prison which means I killed fifteen. At first, a few died while experimenting my drug on them, but then my soul turned black and I started not to care. Arlo should've been on my hit list, but I promised Delia I wouldn't harm the ass hole. Sometimes I feel like doing it behind her back, but afraid she'd find out. I love Delia, but was more in love with myself. I started to feel selfish and felt like no one else mattered. I needed Delia, because of the kids. My son, and Malcom's kids were my life. They were the only reason, I stay with Delia. I keep cameras in the prison outside and in, to watch her sneaky ass try to visit.

Of course, she tried and I caught it all on camera. Onky I had the access og getting in, and you had to be with me to get in.

Lately, since that Russian came, I haven't been there. I did a couple times but had to bomb the place and put everyone to sleep. We went in and took every sharp object, and the guns my bodyguards had left. I wanted to make sure they never tried coming at me or my team again. He and that Ashley were some slick killers and I noticed what he had up his sleeves. Too bad the bitch killed herself, cause I had a plan for her ass too. I upped my security and was in the process of training more. I also added another dose of my steroid shots and I was beyond feeling good. Mixing that with coke only added fuel, but none of it was good enough. I needed Carmen and Santigo to go into the lab and make my shit stronger. I needed strength and stamina cause shits getting too real. I needed to up my game.

"What the fuck are your guards doing about my daughter?" My father took over my thoughts. "I thought you hired more!"

Anger roared through my father's voice and I slightly closed my eyes trying to keep cool. If only he knew how bad I wanted to snap his neck.

"There on it dad. What about Victor?"

He quickly looked up at me as if I told him the worse news ever.

"No! No Russians! Victor's been on my ass lately and word is, his son was kidnapped. I feel he's trying to blame me. He wants to meet with me and look me in the eye, but I been avoiding him. I have nothing to hide, but I fear that man. He's mad and I don't want any part of him right now. He lost his son, but I also lost my daughter."

Inside I smiled. I wanted Victor to think my father had something to do with it all. Maybe Victor will get rid of him for me. I need my father to sign everything to me in his will and then killed instantly. If all goes well, then I'd actually be true owner of Aries and all my father's millions.

In the beginning when he made me owner, I thought it was all mine. In actuality, I was "acting" as owner and only managed Aries. I made this company so much money while my father sat around and did shit. I was tired of him getting all the credit and I wasn't getting paid like I wanted. My prison and all it took to keep it going was started from me stealing from his company. That's also how I started soso. My drug business was doing good but I knew it wouldn't last long. I was running low on a chemical that I had no way of getting the natural product. Carmen was my source, but

I made the mistake of kidnapping her and making her work here. Now I needed another. I knew I was getting greedier and things almost fell apart for me. Having the Russian in my prison almost fucked everything over, and then my sister trying to turn on me almost got shit spilled too. Soon as I calmed Victor down, I'd sleep much better at night. I had a plan that will bring everything together at the end. The one person I finally wanted will be in my touch real soon. Malcom Jamison will not be able to keep running from me. He just don't know how close I really have him.

Chapter Thirty-Nine

Malcom

I closed my bible and stared straight ahead at the beautiful woman sleeping peacefully in the bed. The bibles been the only book I've been reading lately, and it somewhat brings a little peace to me. Sometimes I think when I was once a minister and actually loved it. Maybe in the beginning I became a minister for the wrong reason, but it the end I loved it and it became real to me. It's just that, somewhere down the line, I slipped and fell completely off. It made me think of Farrah and how madly in love I was in with her. We had a son together and although I didn't get to raise him, we bonded soon as I met him. Then loosing him, hurt more than anything. I miss Dame and I miss Farrah. When I found Angel, I thought she could replace that hurt that Farrah left me. Angel was gorgeous and at first glance a goddess. She was nowhere near that, and only made the hurt, hurt more. Jasmine somewhat helped. My two children she gave me completed my world, and although AJ wasn't biologically mine, I love him as my own. Jasmine had grew on me throughout the years. She wasn't the woman I wanted to love at first, but as time went on, she changed and my heart had changed for her. I started to have strong love for that woman. Corrine was the topping on my cake, and I was the stupid fool to mess that up. She was going to be my next wife and we were going to have a baby. The pain fron loosing Dame had got in the way and of course me sleeping witeh Tameka killed it all. Now I live with HIV and even had passed it on to her. Wherever Corrine may be, I still love her. I didn't even know if she had my child, or if she adopted AJ and Blessing. Ashley was my savior. At first, she may have been hired to kill me; but she risked her life to be with me. Even knowing I was HIV positive, Ashley looked passed that. I knew she was the one I'd spend eternity wife. I couldn't wait to rescue her, so I could finally tell her that I knew all along who she really was. I want us to forever stay honest with eachother and move on. I couldn't wait to tell her that and hold her in my arms again.

Looking back at the bed at Melanie really had me tempted. These past couple of weeks I got to know her and the time we spent together only made me love who she really was. I was married and she was married. We both knew that and always kept ourselves at a friendship level. We were becoming good friends while rescuing our loved ones.

We shared a hotel room last night. Melanie didn't want to be alone while we were here in Sacramento. Yesterday, I paid for two rooms and we parted ways. In the middle of the night she was knocking on my door wanting to come in. At first I was confused, thinking she was trying to make a move on me, btu then she explained that she wasn't comfortable alone. I understood and didn't mind. I was practically sleeping on this chair anyway.

Melanie finally stirred around in bed and I watched as she felt the other side of the bed for me. She then popped her head up and looked around. I smiled at the thought of her actually thinking I slept next to her last night. When her eyes finally hit me, she sat all the way up in bed.

"What time is it?" She stretched her arms out.

"A little past noon."

She jumped up out the bed as if she was late for something.

"You let me sleep that long? I never oversleep."

"I guess you were tired."

Melanie walked over to the dresser where she had sat her cellphione. She then came back over to the bed and sat back down. I watched as she scrolled through her phone and I even seen a smile appear. She must've gotten a message from one of her girls. She then looked over at me. Her eyes went straight to the bible in my hand.

"You read the bible?" She asked me.

"Yeah. I know the bible from front to back."

I notice Melanie purse her lips as if she didn't believe me.

"I use to be a minister." I adnmitted.

She slightly laughed. "Noooo. Impossible."

"A pediatrian and a minister. I had my own clinic and almo st a church."

She hesitates. "Your serious."

"Yes."

"Why are you just now telling me this?"

"We're always too busy talking about Ashley and Maceo. Neither one of us know eachother personally. I mean….I know enough about you and your girls and same goes for me. What I don't know is…your past. What kind of person are you?"

"An assasins wife." She smirks. "You want to know how I met my husband?"

"Yes, tell me."

"I was in prison. He was an undercover CO. On an assassin job."

My left eyebrowrose from the shock of hearing this beautiful, sophisticated woman did any time in a cell.

"My girls are by four different men." She began. "I adopted Evelyn. I fell in love with an abusive drunk, a drug dealer who was killed the abusive drunk, then kingpin dealer who got my best friend pregnant. I then snitched on him, but still had to do time in prison. Oh, and don't forget the man that stood by my side and loved me regardless of who I was but I had no children by him. He was murdered by some thieving girl he was seeing. Three of my ex's are brother's. Then I meet the love of my life….. the Russian assaiaain who was kidnapped."

She gave me a small smile but was serious. Melanie was a tough woman. She's been through a lot and survived it all.

"Yeah….I got around. I had a heart that fell in love with any man that gave me attention. So, what's your story?"

I slightly hesitate. "It's not all that great."

She laughs at me while walking over to where I sat in the chair. She sat on the edge of the bed near me. "Come on…I told you my story. I'm pretty sure you have more drama than me. I mean, you do have HIV. An ex-minister with HIV."

I sigh. "You ready?"

"Run it down."

She spoke so seductively that almost stuttered trying to get my sentence out.

"Farrah was the first girl I ever loved; I was responsible for her mother's death. I got her pregnant and didn't know until my son was sixteen. I felt bad for participating in her mother's murder so I became a minister. I had a gay best friend who fell in love with Farrah, but then I stole her back from him. She then left me when she learned the truth about her mother. I had to settle with Jasmine who lied about getting rape, but in reality my gay best friend was having sex with her and got her pregnant. Then I met Angel who was an escort. I married her, and that psycho bitch was having sex with my son. She was a murderer. She killed people and didn't know she was doing it. Somewhere in there, I go back to Jasmine and get her pregnant. Angel kills her and steals my kids. Then after finding my kids, I meet Corrine who was a detective. She found her very rich daddy and we all move to Sacremento into his mansion. Corrine's brother Markus has a girlfriend name Delia and Delia brings in her friend Brooke to live with all of us in the mansion. Brooke claims my son and his friends gang raped her and she kills my son. I fall into deep depression and also fall into the arms of Corrine's father's wife Tameka. I didn't know she was infected with HIV until my girl finds out she's pregnant and carryiong the disease."

I took a deep breath and stared into Melanie's face. Her mouth was wide open but no words were able to come out. I stared at her; she stared at me.

"A lot of people died and your life, and how the hell your gay best friend go around and fuck your women?"

"He never admitted he was gay until the day his lover killed him."

Her eyes got even bigger. "Why aren't you dead?"

"Trust me, I ask that question every day. I rather it be me than Dame, and everyone else who died in my life."

"You've had so many deaths around you. Maybe you're still here for a reason."

"I just want to rescue Ashley and move out the country."

"What about the other kids?"

A spark flared through my heart at the mention of them. I miss AJ and Blessing and may even have another baby out there by Corrine. If I had to, I'd risk my life just to see them one last time. That's all it be. One last time! Harold wanted to kill me, and he wouldn't hesitate when he finally lay eyes on me. I wouldn't even have a chance to kiss my children.

Besides, I was the one that abandoned them to get away from Harold, so they probably forgot about me.

"Their better off with Corrine." I finally admitted. "I know their loved and well taken care of."

The sound of Melanie's phone interrupted us and she looked at it. She immediately jumped up as she answered the phone.

"Good afternoon Victor….."

The sound of his name took my attention from staring at her firm, curvious body in her tight t-shirt. She smilied and giggled in the phone so I knew all was well.

"Yes sir, would you like to speak with him?" She asked, but was looking at me. "Yes……are you sure……I don't think Malcom will be comfortable going there……Okay."

She handed me the phone and sat back on the bed. I was silent as she stared at me awaiting to speak to her father-in-law. I cleared my throat."

"Good afternoon sir."

"Hello Malcom." He spoke to me. "I hope all is well because I'm ready for you to go visit Harold."

"Oh no, I can't do that sir."

"You'll be fine. No one will touch you. You'll have back-up."

Victor then hung up and I looked at Melanie.

"He just wants his son, and I want my husband. You have to."

I didn't want to do this, and I didn't want to blow what Eswaldo and I were building. We wasn't finish investigating this gas station that we believe he was holding people including our loved ones. Soon as I knew what was really going on, I was going to break the news to Melanie. I didn't expect to do it now.

"I been talking to someone." I admitted.

She cocked her head and raised her left eyebrow. She wanted me to explain.

"It's someone that use to be on the force; a detective."

"You brought police into this!" Melanie jumped up. "No Malcom! Victor will kill you."

"No, he's not on the force anymore. He was kicked off. He was also married to my ex and now he's my friend. When I was on the run, he helped me and I helped him. He found where Maceo and Ashley are being held."

"What?!"

I could see anxious all over her face and her eyes began to water.

"Where? When? Why didn't you tell Victor?"

"Calm down. We need to investigate first. That's why I don't need to meet up with Harold, but I will to satisfy Victor. Besides, we need to investigate before we take action."

Melanie stood up and began pacing the room. Finally she stopped and looked over my way. The tears in her eyes were heavy.

"Just get my husband back please. Your friend better do us some good."

"And he will."

Chapter Forty

Malcom

I can't believe I missed this place. Driving into the gates of Harold's mansion brought back many memories and of course Corrine and my children were those memories. I didn't think it was a good idea for Eswaldo or Melanie to tag along. Especially not Melanie. I didn't want to put her in any danger, but she wasn't staying behind. She didn't care what anyone said, including Victor. She wanted part in rescuing her husband and helping to keep me safe from Harold.

Eswaldo got out the car first and looked around. After surveilling the area, he opened the door back up.

"I expected guards. There are none." He said.

"Well, don't trust what you don't see."

Melanie and I then got out, and all three of us stood looking up at the mansion. I thought of all my memories here, good and bad. My son was murdered here and that alone sent a small chill down my spine. Melanie must've notice because I felt her hand on my arm.

"You okay?" She asked.

"Yeah, let's go."

I lead them to the front door. On the outside, I acted tough and didn't want anyone to see my real fear. Of course I was afraid. I slept with Harold's wife and infected his only daughter. If I was him, I'd kill on first demand. I just pray he don't kill me right away.

The door opened before I could knock and there stood a woman I never seen before. She looked as if she was the housekeeper. Maybe her late fifties and a tad but on the heavy side. She smilied as she opened the door.

"May I help you?" She asked with a caribien accent.

215

"I'm here to see Harold." I spoke. "Is he available?"

"Let them in Celina." I heard his voice boom from behind her. She opened the door wider, and there stood Harold leaning on a cane. When did he get a cane? As I stepped in, I seen them. Two men from each side came out as if they were ready to kill me right there. They looked as if they were loaded, and I knew those two were his bodyguards. Eswaldo stood beside me as I walked in, and Melanie behind us.

"Finally, you face me." He spoke. "It's a pleasure to see you."

"Is it?"

"Very much." He slowly walked toward me limping on that cane of his. When he finally reached me he took his hand and grabbed my arm, pulling me into his embrace. I couldn't believe this was happening. A hug? I was afraid he'd stab me somewhere.

"What happened?" I nodded toward his leg.

"Bad knee. Nothing I can't handle….." He then nodded his head toward Eswaldo and Melanie. "Who are your guest?"

I wasn't sure how to introduce Melanie. I didn't want to say who she really was.

"This is Eswaldo. I'm pretty sure you've heard of him. He married Farrah."

Harold raised his eyebrow and looked from him to me, and then Melanie.

"Your friends with Farrah's husband?" He asked.

"Yes. I moved on."

"With this beautiful woman?" He stepped forward and grabbed her hand. He kissed it and she didn't look flattered one bit.

"She's only a friend, and she's married."

Harold smirked. "Then why are you with her?"

"Like I said, she's a friend." I cleared my throat and looked around. "Can I see my kids?"

Harold became serious and turned away from us. He limped away on his cane leaving us wondering if we should follow.

He got to the entrance of the next room and turned around to us. "Well….."

I looked back at Eswaldo and Melanie and shrugged my shoulders.

We were following Harold. Maybe he was showing me to my children or maybe even Corrine.

The house looked totally different. It was as if they remodeled everything. I almost forgot where I was going in this huge house. He led us into a huge living room that sat the biggest sectional ever. The same sectional that was there when I first met Harold in this house. We all sat on this sectional watching my ex-wife go through her crazy moments. Harold sat down and nodded for us to do the same. I then noticed the two guys enter the room. I guess they follow him everywhere.

"I have a problem Malcom, and your all I have." He started. "You ruined my marriage, and I don't know if my wife is dead or alive, but what I do know and I will never forgive myself if something happened to her..... but Corrine's gone missing."

I looked over at Eswaldo and he shook his head confirming what I thought. Harold had nothing to do whith what Markus was doing. I doubt he knew since he put his own sister there.

"Do you know anything about my daughter disappearance?" Harold slightly raised his voice to Eswaldo. He must've read his face.

"Do you know your son?" Eswaldo replied.

"What's that soupose to mean?"

"Lately, how has your son been acting?"

Harold squinted his eyes and gave Eswaldo that look. "Tell me what you know."

"Where are my children?" I interrupted. "You want info, then tell me where my kids are."

Melanie grabbed my arm, and I seen her shake her head no. I didn't understand so she got up and pulled me with her to the corner.

"You're going to tell this man what you know?" She harshly whispered. "No the fuck you will not! Don't risk my husband life. He will destroy our chance at rescuing them."

I sighed. I didn't believe that, but I had to respect what Melanie was saying. She wanted all this to stay between us, but I knew Harold now was thinking something isn't right between us all.

"Okay." I finally said. "But I need to see my kids. What if he dont let me see them."

"Then he's an asshole!" Melanie then walked away from me and sat back in her original seat. Soon as I turned around Harold was burning a hole through me.

"You and you girl finish making secrets over there?" He said.

"We weren't making secrets." I walked back over to the sofa and sat next to Melanie. "Now, can I see my kids?"

"I want my daughter back. Can you guarantee me my baby girl?"

I looked from Eswaldo and then Melanie. They both assured me and when I looked back at Harold he just stared.

"And I want the scoop on my son."

"I will do my best to find Corrine. As for your son, don't trust him."

Harold nodded and then looked over to one of his men. "Tell Celina to bring the kids down."

"Yes sir." The man replied and then disappeared.

Harold'e eyes went back to me but he just stared. He stared so hard that I began to get extremely uncomfortable. I knew he hated me, so what was I to say.

"I'm sorry." That was the only thing I could think of. I never appoigixed and I hope he accepts.

"I don't care about your apology. All I care about is Corrine. If you don't bring her back to me by the end of the week, your ass will be sorry."

I looked away not knowing what to say. I just hope Corrine was in the same place Maceo and Ashley were in.

It was quiet for the next five minutes that we waited, then suddenly the cutest little girl ran into the room followed by another cute little girl chasing her. They looked similar except the second one had longer hair that flowed down her back. I couldn't tell if one of them were mine. I don't know what Blessing would've looked like. A young boy then walked in who looked about eight or nine. He was the splitting image of my best friend. I knew this had to be AJ., I stood walkeding twards them. The boy stared at me back, while the two young girls ran to Harold yelling 'papa'.

"AJ?" I called to him.

"Hey."

"DO you know who I am?" I asked.

"My dad."

A tear then welled up in my eye at the sound of those words. I was happy that he didn't forget about me. How did he recognize me with the beard?

"Yes…..you're so big now." A tear fell as I took a couple steps forward.

"Mom shows me pictures all the time." He spoke. I kneeled down to him and opened my arms, hoping he'd hug me back. He hesitated but he did and I felt so good.

"She does." I heard Harold speak. I let go of AJ and looked back at Harold who was holding both girls.

"I don't know why that woman still loves you but she does." Harold said. "You will bring their mother back. If not for me, for them."

"I will."

"Charity." Harold kissed the one little girl with the long hair. "This one here is your youngest." He then kissed the other child who was an inch or two taller and just as cute. "And you remember Blessing."

I couldn't contain my emotions as I let out more teats than I ever had. I opened my arms to the gurls and they didn't hesitate to jump out of Harolds lap and into my arms. I kissed them both and hugged them tight. I was complete. I had my three kids and soon my wife. I couldn't imagine taking them away from Corrine since she did such a good job raising them. I then thought of the problem that I learned to live with. I had HIV, and Corrine had it to. Did I pass this along to my babygirl? My eyes made contact with Harold and I finally seen a little sympathy in his eyes. I was glad this was getting to his heart. Maybe after I bring Corrine home, he wont kill me. I finbally let the girls go, and began rambling with questions on who I was. After telling them I was daddy, they were happy and pulling and falling all over me. I enjoyed tyhis moment and never wanted it to end.

"She's fine Malcom. She was tested six times. Every time she is negative." Harold slowly stood up on his cane. "Now, down to business."

I was happy to hear the news but mad Harold was rushing my moment.

"Can I spend the day with them?" I asked.

"Spend the day finding my daughter. When I get my daughter, you can spend all the time in the world with my grandchildren."

I kissed each of them and promised them their mother. AJ was so big and cool as he said his goodbyes to me and then ushered the girls out the room. I stood up ready to get everyone home safe so I could see my kids again.

"Give me the week and I'll bring her home." I told Harold.

"And I want the scoop on my son." He demanded. "Why shouldn't I trust him?"

"Just don't." I replied.

"Does he have anything to do with my daughter's dissappearence, because if he does you need to tell me. I want Delia and her son safe."

"Markus wouldn't hurt them, and he didn't hurt his sister."

Harold sighed as I seen the frustration written all over his face. I wish I could say more, but I couldn't.

"Just don't trust him…like Eswaldo says. I really think Markus may be out to get you."

Harold nodded as we all began to leave his presence. I then turned around to face him one last time.

"I'm sorry." I said.

He didn't say a word back but I could tell he accepted.

Chapter Forty-One

Malcom

Eswaldo took us back to his place and said we were going to make our move tonight after midnight. We had dropped Melanie back off at the hotel because I honestly didn't trust that everything was going to be okay. I gave her the address in case she didn't hear from us in 24 hours. I just felt uneasy with everything and didn't want to put Victor's daughter-in-law in harms way.

The house was nice and I was impressed that Eswaldo kept was doing pretty good. He was a great friend and I never thought I be in a situation with him where we were actually good friends. I followed him up to the porch and before he opened the door he looked back at me.

"Don't be mad when you see who I have in my house." He said.

"Dammit! I'm so tired of surprises. Who is it?"

"Just tell me that we still cool."

"We always going to be cool." I then started to think. "Wait, is Farrah here?"

"No! Nothing like that. Farrah's still doing her time, and not getting out anytime soon."

"Then open the door. Who cares."

Soon as he opened the door, I looked around searching for his surprise guest. The house was nice and I smelled fresh pine. Whoever he had in here knew how to keep a clean place.

"Babe?" He yelled out.

"Who's your babe?"

"You'll see."

Just as I began to walk to the center of the living room three guys came out of nowhere. One of them was Markus and I had to question Eswaldo's loyalty. I looked over to him and he gave me the same look I was thinking. 'where the fuck he come from?'

"Woooowwwww." Markus walked a little closer to me with a smirk on his face. "Malcom in the flesh. Good to see you bro."

"Do you have my wife?" I anxiously asked. I was face to face with the man I knew kidnapped Ashley and Maceo.

He laughed a deep, evil laugh. Markus wasn't the same. He didn't look or act like the cool ass Markus who rescued and took care of my kids. I didn't not know this man. He seem dangerous and I didn't want him around me. That deep evil laugh was up to something.

"I like the beard on you." He complimented. He then looked over at Eswaldo. "And I thank you."

"For what!" Eswaldo spat out. "Where's Angel?"

"Angel?" I was lost.

Markus laughed his evil laugh again, and he got closer to me. He threw his arm around me and pulled me in as if I was his best buddy.

"You see…..everyone is not your friend. That mutherfucker right there been sleeping with your ex-wife. Matter fact, that was two ex-wives he slept with. He didn't tell you?"

"Angel? But how did you find her?" I asked Eswaldo.

"Not important." Markus backed away from me and nodded his head to his men. "This is what's going to happen. You two sit."

"No." I yelled out. "Not until you tell me that my wife is safe."

"Really Malcom? You're going to make my life so difficult right now."

"You're the one not answering easy questions."

He smirks. "You want to know?"

"Yeah, and you're going to tell me."

"Okay…." He then looks at his men. "Shoot em'."

Next thing I see was both men pulling out a riffle and immediately shooting a dart at us. One went in my neck and I felt the sting, but soon seen darkness.

Chapter Forty-Two

Angel

I took two pills and chased them down with the red wine I was sipping on.

"You shouldn't mix your medication with alcohol." He said.

"Who cares." I rolled my eyes and took another gulp.

"Your too beautiful to act the way you do. Change the attitude. Everything's cool now."

"I want the kids." I pouted.

"It's going to take time. You just chill the fuck out and in the end you'll get everything you want."

"So....did you take her there yet?"

"Yeah. Right before I came here."

I jumped up from my seat and ran over to where Markus was. I kissed him all over and hugged him tight. I was waiting for the day he finally got rid of Delia. I wanted her dead, and long gone but he wouldn't do it. I was tired of sharing men, and finally got Markus to myself.

Yelp, I been through hell and back. I was in and out of psychiatric hospital but I survuived. Everyone abandoned me and it stirred hatred for the entire family. I wanted to kill them all and I probably would've if Markus didn't come visit me from time to time. He paid them off to release me and he took me in. I love him so much for that, and he loves me te way I am. I do relize I grew up with this problem and now I'm on plenty of meds to control the killing sprees I go on.

Markus said he needed me to trap Malcom. He said it was hard to get him and he wanted him on his prison. Now we got Malcom through Eswaldo and playing them all was fun. I don't regret any of it one bit and actually couldn't wait till Markus lets me see this prison of his. I waned Delia to see me on her husband's arm. I wanted her and Corrine to see me taking care of their kids. I finally got a man who loves me and children that I could never have.

"DO you love me?" I asked him.

"Yes babe, I do."

"Good, cause I love you too much!"

"I know you do, now get your ass back over there and eat this good food."

I kissed him one last time before sitting back in my seat.

Chapter Forty-Three

Melanie

I walked into the restaurant not trying to remove my shades. I looked around for Victor and spotted him in a VIP corner. I walked over his way and discreetly sat down in the booth across from him.

"Good to see you." He said.

"I'm glad you flew in."

"Why the hell you guys didn't tell me you knew about the location? I have trained men ready to attack."

"Malcom wanted to make sure before he brought you in."

Victor shook his head. "Now they're all gone. Markus has gotten way over his gattdamn head. I'm calling my nephew Irene. Irene is my last resort because he's bipolar and crazy."

"What do you mean?"

"Irene's dad was my brother. He was in the same business as me. It was him who started and pulled me into it. My brother Borya was attracted to a woman name Althea. She was a black woman who everyone wanted to sleep with, including me. I never did because Borya was worse than I was. He'd kill me with no hesitation. Well, Althea and my brother got married after only knowing each other for a month. She was pregnant right away and after that she became a different woman. Her moods were crazy and was later diagnosed as bipolar. He tried to handle her until he couldn't handle her no more. After Alethea gave birth to Irene he sent her away and she was never seen again. Sometimes I feel he killed her, but we'll never know. Borya raised Irene as his own and raised him to be tough. Borya never realized he had that crazy streak in him like his mother. He is a well-mannered respectable boy but crazy. He was sixteen when he called me and said his father was dead. He killed him and I helped cover it up. I tried to raise Irene with Maceo but that didn't work. I loved Irene but he was afraid he'd hurt someone he loved, so he asked me if he could leave. I gave Irene $100,000 and told him to go far away and make a life of himself. I thought he'd fuck the $100,000 up and come back begging for more, but Irene has money. Lots of it, and he gets it by killing. He is also an assassin all the way in Baltimore. Killing is more of his life than it is ours. He strives and feeds off it. He tortures and it makes him high. I talk to Irene maybe once or twice a year to see how he's doing. He's actually doing well right now. He says he found a woman and wants to marry her but I'm honestly afraid for her. If you can murder your father and not shed a tear, then you'd murder anyone. Irene is good for the job. He will kill Markus and all his men with his bare hands. He's a real live serial killer."

Printed in the United States
By Bookmasters